Lost Wolf

ALSO BY MAX BRAND

Lost Wolf

Max Brand, 1892-1944

DODD, MEAD & COMPANY
New York

Originally published in *Western Story Magazine* in 1925 under the title *The Squaw Boy*, written under the pseudonym of Peter Henry Morland, and first published in book form by Macy-Masius Company in 1928 under the title *Lost Wolf*.

Published by Dodd, Mead, & Company, Inc.
79 Madison Avenue, New York, N.Y. 10016
Distributed in Canada by
McClelland and Stewart Limited, Toronto
Manufactured in the United States of America

First Edition

1 2 3 4 5 6 7 8 9 10

Library of Congress Cataloging-in Publication Data

Brand, Max, 1892–1944.
  Lost wolf.

  (A Silver star western)
  "Originally published in Western story magazine in
1925 under the title The squaw boy, written under the
pseudonym of Peter Henry Morland"—T.p. verso.
  I. Title. II. Series.
PS3511.A87L67 1986   813'.52   86-6182
ISBN 0-396-08829-5

Lost Wolf

1

This narrative has very little to do with Thomas Tucker, because he dies in the first chapter, but he is important partly because he was the father of the hero and partly because he was himself. And from the time that he was given a name out of Mother Goose at the baptismal font, everyone agreed that Tommy Tucker was worthy of a great deal of attention.

A great deal of attention he got, too; a great deal more than was good for him, because he had smiling green eyes and a handsome face and a winning way. Partly, also, because that name of Tommy Tucker fitted him ridiculously well. He was patted and petted and loved by men and women until, in his twenty-eighth year, there was nothing left to Tommy Tucker except the following items:

First: Rose, his wife, who still loved Tommy as much as ever though she had long ago stopped respecting him.

Second: A five-year-old son who looked more like his wife than himself. "And a rare good thing he does!" said the family friends. This little boy had his mother's black hair and eyes, but he had not her beauty and never would have it. He was rather grandly named: Glanvil Tucker!

Third: A great host of friends who still would lend Tommy a *little* money but would never employ him in their businesses.

Fourth: A whole table covered, from week to week, with invitations to weddings, and wine-parties, and driving and yachting trips.

These were all of Tommy Tucker's possessions, and one day he told his wife about it. She said pleasantly: "Then I suppose that we'll have to stop being children and start out to do something for ourselves. Don't you think so too?"

Tommy Tucker was frightfully hurt. He went out into the dark of the night and sat solemnly and sullenly smoking his strongest pipe—so that Rose could trace him by the scent of it when she began to miss him and worry about him. But Rose did not come; and finally he heard her in the upper part of the house singing to little Glanvil, who had wakened out of a bad dream.

When he heard the lovely voice of his wife singing, the heart of Tommy Tucker stopped, and then swelled until it almost broke before it beat again. He stood up and said something not worth remembering; then he went to see a friend. The friend was very glad to see Tommy but terribly sorry that bad luck in business—don't you know how luck runs?—had quite cleaned him out. However, if fifty dollars helped at all—

Tommy went from one friend to another and came home haggard in the small hours of the morning. Rose was reading in bed and she met him with a smile and with eyes that were full of love—and no respect. For the first time Tommy saw it, and a nail was driven through his heart. He said: "Dearest girl, I have enough money to keep you and sonny for a year; and I have enough besides to take me to California and tear a whole fortune out of the ground—"

She stopped smiling.

"Would you do that, Tommy?" said she.

"I will do it!" cried Tommy Tucker, and he threw back his shoulders, which were thick and very broad and cushioned with muscle, not fat.

"Then I shall go with you, Tommy," said his wife. "It takes a long time to cross the plains. But I think that it doesn't cost a great deal. I shall go with you. Besides, what would Glanny and I do without you? We would break our hearts, of course!"

And so, exactly six weeks later, they were part of a train of horse- and ox- and mule-drawn wagons which toiled and moiled across the plains, left the belt of trees, reached the treeless prairies and moved on and on until the land became like the sea, a dead vast thing with a blue horizon ringed around it and the caravan bobbing slowly up and down in the middle of the ring, never getting forward and never sliding back.

So it seemed to Tommy Tucker, but since that night when he had seen a certain quiver in the smile of Rose, he no longer mentioned his own feelings but lived, as you may say, with his head turned towards his wife, hunting for *her* thoughts and reading them eagerly, tenderly, sadly, gaily, just as he found them. He discovered that though this was an oppressive journey to him, it was delightful to his wife. She could hardly content herself in the wagon. She had to be out on the back of one of their two saddle ponies riding as far from the side of the caravan as her husband's voice would let her; riding sometimes so perilously far that her singing would float to Tommy like a song out of fairyland.

Then one day an ox in the team became a little lame, and the wagon of Tommy Tucker, which carried in it his wife and his son and the other things which were all that the hands and heart of Tommy held in this world, began to drift back through the train of the other wagons one by one. One by one they turned out and passed him, laughing and waving to him and leaning and craning their necks for a sight of Rose, which she always made sure they got. For, though she was a modest girl, she understood a little of the hunger that was in them for the voice and face of a woman after they had been embarked for so many weeks on that land-sea. In the end, however, Tommy Tucker's wagon was the very last one in the whole list; in front of him were the latest joiners of the caravan—men with fine wagons drawn by fine, long-legged mules.

Nevertheless, Tommy was just as content to be at the end

of the caravan as at the head of it, for he was that way. The ox-team lagged more and more. He was very busy with the goad. And still they lagged. For the leaders of the caravan were pushing hard to so stretch that day's march that they might come to a certain tiny stream of water. In the meantime a little gap opened up; only fifty yards between Tommy's oxen and the little three-month colt which trotted at the tail of the wagon just ahead.

Fifty yards of daylight is not a great deal. On a nice open road it is better—it is pleasant. But when the dusk comes over the prairie, then fifty yards may mean—oh, Tommy Tucker, hurry on, press on! Do not spare the oxen. Do not mutter so sympathetically as you watch that poor beast on the right of the yoke stumble and strain and grunt in pain. Push on, mercilessly.

But how could Tommy be merciless? And how could he be in a hurry? Not even for his wife and his baby boy, and all that he held dear in this dust world!

"Why does Glanvil make so much noise?" said he.

"The little scoundrel!" said Rose. "I have taken off his clothes—all except a shirt—and put him to bed. Because I think that we'll be marching into the starlight for an hour at the least. He doesn't want to go to bed, of course—poor Ganny!"

"I don't think you ought to call him that. It's a baby name, you know."

"Heavens, Tommy! At five isn't he a baby still?"

She scrambled off the tall seat and went back.

"Tommy, will you believe it? This bad boy had taken off his shirt and crawled out of his bed, and he's as naked as the day he was born!"

"Spank him, then, and put him back!"

"Tommy, he's beating *me* with the stick!"

How they laughed at that. And then Tommy canted his ear and listened to the foolish, crooning sounds which Rose made as she tucked little Glanvil back into the bed, until at last, she stole back to him.

4

"He's asleep, so soon! Oh, he'll be a soldier!"

"He *does* seem to have courage, Rose. I—oh God, I hope that he has courage!"

"Why do you say it that way?"

"Rose—because I don't know—I mean—"

"Thomas!" cried his wife.

A dreadful silence fell between them, and it was a full five minutes before she moved closer to him on the seat.

"Tommy dear—just because you have never proved yourself—"

Now, just at this moment a wild voice cried out far, far ahead, where the dark, snaky body of the caravan was winding through the dusk and where the lanterns were beginning to be lighted—lanterns turned white and dim behind the smoke which the wheels were rolling ceaselessly into the air. The cry ran forward in the caravan; and it ran back, like wildfire spreading both ways, a shout thickened with the deep voices of men and edged with the screams of women and children.

"Indians!"

The caravan began to curl up like a caterpillar that is wounded in the belly. The head turned to the side and then back, the middle bulged swiftly to the right, the rearmost wagons hurtled ahead and to the left to meet those backward-rolling wagons of the van. A frightfully important maneuver, for if a circle were made, the Indians would have a care about pressing up to such a natural fortress. But on the other hand, if the circle failed of completion by the time the charging redskins could slide in an arm of their force—ah, then, the poor caterpillar would be stricken head and foot, and heart as well, and would soon lie helpless, while red devils rushed from scalp to scalp!

I said that the rearmost wagons of this caravan lurched rapidly up to join the leading wagons as the latter turned back. But I was mistaken. The rearmost wagon of all did not hurry. Alas, it could not hurry. For as Tommy, now in

5

haste too late, thrust the goad deep into the lame ox, that poor creature stumbled and went down on his knees and there he remained and refused to get up for a moment.

Only a moment—but a long line, a shrieking nightmare line of shadows now dipped up over the horizon and strode suddenly huge upon the eye of the caravaners. Brandished arms, thrilling screams like death cries; and ponies stretched out in level flight . . .

Tommy looked and looked again to the caravan wagons which, just ahead of him, widened the gap from a hundred to two hundred yards. He stared at this and knew that the time had come when he was to leave these tired, sweating oxen, and this creaking, complaining wagon, and the little sleeping boy in the bed, and his wife, his dear wife. He knew that he was about to die and that she was about to die also. So he took her in his arms and held her against his breast.

"Tommy!" she screamed at him. "What are you doing? When—"

"Don't you see?" said Tommy gently. "My sweetest and dearest girl, it is too late to do anything, for you and I are about to die! I have never told you what happens to the white women the Indians capture. But—no, I cannot tell you now. This is the better way."

He gave her an old pistol.

"My grandfather used to own it. It's terribly old but it still shoots straight. Put it beneath your left breast, and when the time comes, pull the trigger. But don't do that until I—will you promise, Rose?"

She did not faint. She only looked wildly about her for something—an ax, a club—to defend her baby. But all she had was this foolish old pistol which Tommy had brought along for sentimental reasons. And then she remembered having read somewhere—or had it been told to her?—that there was one chance in three for little children when the Indians attacked—and conquered. If they were not too old to be conformed to Indian ways, and if they were not so

6

small as to be helpless, then they might be adopted into the tribe unless there was a particular lust for blood—

She saw the caravan formed into a solid loop, and from every joint of that loop the fire flashing. She saw the long and resistless line of charging braves split away in two parts: towards the head of the caravan and past it, towards the foot of the caravan and straight at that solitary wagon. And out there beyond the oxen stood Tommy Tucker with his head high and a rifle at his shoulder, dropped from the back of a pony. Then a crash of revengeful voices, a little ripple of fire, a splattering thunder of old muskets and new rifles, and Tommy Tucker tossed his hands to heaven and fell.

Rose was rather a Puritan in her upbringing. She raised her head also, and she said to the stars: "Here are two lives. Gentle God, do not ask for three!"

Then she drew the trigger of the pistol.

2

When that wave of shrieking warriors reached the prairie schooner, the blast of their yelling blew the little white boy out of his bed. He tumbled out of the tail of the wagon and, seeing a whirl of dark bodies of men and stamping horses drive towards the front of the wagon, he crawled busily away through the grass.

There was just enough instinct in him to keep him quiet, as the young antelope lies still when danger is near it. So it was with the white boy. He wriggled away through the

7

grass, which was fortunately tall here. And, when it grew short, he was at a sufficient distance to get up and run unseen, for the dark was closing fast. Half a dozen times, as he crawled, the feet of an Indian pony battered the ground near his head, but he made no outcry, merely flattening himself against the ground on every such occasion. And so the fear passed, for that wave of charging Indians had paused only long enough to slaughter the oxen, scalp the dead, and loot the wagon—an instant's work to a hundred snatching hands. Then the horsemen whirled away in another charge towards the main body of the caravan. Like hounds which have been blooded, they were merely keener for the kill.

The son of Tommy Tucker wrapped himself in his small arms and stared down on the scene. The dark and serpentlike body of the caravan was outlined by the spurting fires from the mouths of many rifles, and around this core of the battle the shadowy lines of the Indians curled and swept with such an accompaniment of curdling shrieks that Glanvil Tucker opened his mouth and his eyes and forgot to be afraid. Only he frowned as he saw red flames begin where the wagon that was home to him stood. He saw those flames rise and crawl up the sides and then in a sudden flicker and flare sweep across the canopy; he saw the naked ribs outlined with creeping streaks of red. And after that the whole body of the wagon was belching fire.

Glanvil Tucker had been loved and spoiled too much to have very much affection for anything—even his parents. He took them for granted. They were the only world he knew. Now they were taken from him and Glanvil Tucker felt—well, not exactly grief, but emptiness. He did not cry, however. I am ashamed to say that that naked little boy did not cry. But he dropped his chin on his fists and scowled at what he saw. He was too worried to cry!

The sweeping horsemen put out a dark arm of a score of flying riders; and the little boy scampered over the top of the knoll down into what would hardly have been a hollow to a man. He ran until he was tired. His feet were scratched and he was cold. He lay down in the grass to rest and remained there for a long time, until all the noise of the shooting and all the weirdly echoing voices had ended. Then, when there was quiet everywhere, he started out to find the caravan again.

And he walked in exactly the wrong direction. He walked and walked, hurrying to the top of each little wave of ground that rose before him against the stars and then scurrying again across the next diminutive ridge, until he came at last to a great fire with a circle of dark forms swinging around it, with a whooping and barking and screaming of voices!

That racket kept Glanvil away for a moment, but the broad red face of the fire was like a singing welcome home to him. He edged closer and closer. He passed through the outer circle where boys and old women were squatted on the ground watching the dance pass between them and the blaze. In that circle beside the fire were two men who whirled bloody scalps above their heads, and every time one of those lucky warriors came in view, a shriek of congratulation was raised.

The boy had gone to this point when a sudden arm snatched at him from the side and a hard hand fell upon his tender, naked body. Not a man's hand, but a woman's— a woman's hand, hard as that of a man from much labor. She caught her victim into the air above her head and leaped up as though she would strike him to the ground.

But she did not cast him down. Instead, holding him high, she rushed in closer to the fire, the light of which glistened on the struggling body of Glanvil until his white skin shone like burnished ivory. The squaw began to dance in her turn, and her dancing seemed of so much greater interest than all else, that even those who were prancing around the fire, and those who bore the bloody scalps, and all the children and women, and old men and fierce young warriors themselves pressed around her. Eventually they

9

began dancing again, exactly as in the scalp dance, each bending over a little, lifting each leg in turn, making a little false stop with the foot as it came to the top of the step, and jerking the body. As for their song, it did not seem like a song to Glanvil.

It was a ridiculous, snarling, grunting drone interspersed with an occasional yell of exultation that fairly tore his eardrums in two. He was a little frightened, but not a very great deal, for he had never been harmed in his life. His mother and his father had loved him too much and too foolishly to discipline their boy and the harshest of the blows he had received were those which he had dealt to himself. He had had no fear in his home; therefore he had no fear in the outer world.

This would have been very good—to be swung about in the air above the heads of the other people. It would have been fun to be flaunted through the air in this fashion, with the men and the women and the children who passed him leaping up and trying to tap him lightly with their fingers. The trouble was that the squaw had him so very firmly gripped by the middle that her broad, long thumbs were threatening to cut right through his stomach. He began to gasp and wriggle with distress. And when that brought him no relief, he did not waste time in crying. He simply reached down and fastened one fist in the greasy black hair of the squaw and with the other began to beat her face.

This produced results at once.

There was a scream from the copper-faced woman. But it was a yell of delight. She brought him down to her bosom; and from this position of greater vantage he kept his clutch tight with his left hand on her short hair and with the other thumped her face with his stout fist.

Rose Tucker could never have endured such a beating without tears, I suppose, but this wild creature seemed to love the blows which fell on her. She began to laugh and scream with all her might until the others fell back from

10

her. What she said Glanvil Tucker did not know then, but he was told about it many a time thereafter.

"Tirawa, who is kind," said she, "has sent a new son for my dead son. He has sent me a son with a white skin. He has come straight from Tirawa. He has come to me naked out of the night. I, Little Grouse, saw him. I took him in my hands. His body is as soft as a buffalo calf. His body is as strong as a buffalo calf. He holds me by the hair and he beats me like a scratching badger. He says that he is a man, and that I must work for him until he is a great warrior and has many wives. He is a white badger that will grow stronger and greater than a bull. And he is mine! He is the son of Little Grouse, and Tirawa sent him!"

This was not a speech but a sort of rhythmic song, the words of which were screamed out from time to time while her bare feet beat an accompaniment upon the ground. A tall Indian with a half-starved face broke through the lines of warriors and women to watch, and then he leaped out to join her. He snatched the boy from the arms of Little Grouse and standing still, raised the youngster above his head to the full length of his left arm, so that Glanvil Tucker sat eight feet above ground, and he knew that if he did not poise himself, he would fall out of that hand and perhaps dash out his brains on the ground underfoot. So he sat still, and balanced himself. He liked this very much better than being crushed almost in two by the grip of the squaw. He could see the fire very well as it leaped and sang by itself, and he could see one by one all the wildly painted faces over which it washed its light.

He forgot his soft-voiced mother; he forgot his gentle father. At least, these people were more *fun*.

Underneath him the tall man was shouting words which Glanvil did not understand any more than he had understood what the squaw had said before. But of these, too, he was informed later.

For, in Cheyenne, the tall man was barking: "I, Rising Bull, say that Tirawa has remembered that the legs of

11

Little Grouse are cut and bleeding and her hair is short; and the heart of Rising Bull is weak as a girl's heart. See how his right hand was taken from him by the tree!"

Here he brandished the stump of a wrist covered with a white-polished scar.

"For this one hand, Tirawa now sends to me two strong hands of my new son, the little badger, the white badger without fear—"

This word struck a sudden chord out of the minds of the others and there was a wild yell which welcomed to the Cheyenne tribe a new brave in the making, no matter what the color of his skin. The son of Tommy Tucker had been thrust into the fire-flooded air of the night on the palm of an Indian brave; but in the view of the tribe he had been metamorphosed into quite a new being—White Badger, a Cheyenne "brave to be."

There was more talk, more shouting, more beating of hands and drums, more wild yelling which was constantly echoed and added to from the near distance by scores and scores of wolfish dogs waiting around the edges of the firelight.

Now, when all this was in full blast, it was ended suddenly by the appearance of a tall man with a flight of towering feathers in his hair and with his face still covered with the war paint.

He took the boy from the unresisting hands of Rising Bull, tossed the white body in the air and caught it as it came spinning down—too surprised to utter a cry. Then Red Eagle passed the youngster back.

"Our son shall take many scalps and be without fear," said he.

Which made Glanvil Tucker pass from existence at that instant and gave birth, definitely, to quite another creature: White Badger, the Cheyenne.

3

There were no clothes in the lodge of Rising Bull which would fit such a small child as little White Badger. But that lack was soon remedied.

White Badger was tucked under the arm of Rising Bull and carried into the lodge. It was only a small tepee, occupied by two families besides his own, so that, altogether, scarcely more than eight people, aside from the new boy, were to sleep under that cover of buffalo skins. There were little partitions made of buffalo robes raised between the beds. Rising Bull and Little Grouse held a reception. It was a crowded affair. Some few of the warriors preferred to stamp and chant around the fire and talk about what they had done or what they had wished to do to the caravan of whites that day. But the majority—particularly of the women and children—desired only to see the new son of the tribe.

An endless line kept ducking under the flap of the lodge and passing around the central fire from right to left. Each one—man, woman, or child—paused for an instant before the form of White Badger. And every time each person passed White Badger, something was deposited at his feet. Perhaps it was no more than a bright little pebble from the hand of an Indian girl; perhaps it was a broken play-arrow presented by some boy. Or it might be something more appropriate. There was a stock of clothes enough to last White Badger for the next six years—and fit him year by year! These clothes were very old and nearly worn out, but well-dressed antelope skin or the hide of buffalo calf takes a great deal of wearing before it rubs away. These clothes were serviceable. Also, they were fortified with dirt and grease of every kind. Other trinkets came into the heap which grew before Little Grouse, and she accepted all these presents for her new son as a matter of course and right; one might have said that she expected each to pay for the privilege of seeing a child so fair!

All that she demanded of White Badger was that he stand up and let the people see him. And this White Badger did. One of the first presents had been a strip of crimson rag and this had been knotted around the black, long curls of the boy. That flash of intense color set him off to a great advantage. It exhibited in a sharper contrast the blackness of his eyes, the blackness of his hair, and the wonderful fairness of his skin.

He stood up and laughed at the people who went by him. He laughed and waved at them. They were so ugly that they were just a step beyond the terrible—that is to say, they were ridiculous, and he laughed until his sides ached, and then he laughed again.

They tried him out by doing mimic war-dances and brandishing knives and hatchets over his head. But he was accustomed to such things. In the hands of his mother and his father, he had seen instruments of threat more than once. But those threats had never developed into anything, so the more the big warriors, the ugly hags and the bright-eyed boys made faces at him, the more White Badger laughed and laughed.

Neither did the boy care how much he was handled, whether the women stroked the wonderful softness of his skin, or the men laid hold upon his legs and with a professional eye admired the straightness of the joints and the size of the bone, or the spreading width of the shoulders. Only when a mischievous boy ground a knuckle deep into the tender ribs of Glanvil Tucker, the heavy little hand of that youngster was instantly clenched and landed upon the tender tip of the nose of the Indian youth. It brought a

14

wail of surprise and pain from the latter. It brought a yell of applause from the others.

So the procession went past that odd little family group. Rising Bull's pride began to mount and mount. His squaw—the last of his family, for the rest of his five wives had left him when his hand was lost at the wrist—sat impassive, showing her appreciation of what happened with only a single glint of fire in her eyes from time to time. But Rising Bull had too much in his spirit to contain it. His memory was still raw and wounded from the loss of his good right hand, which made him almost less than a woman in the tribe, and above that, far above it, the loss of his fifteen-year-old warrior son, Spotted Elk.

Here was the first salve for his injured spirit. His nostrils began to flare. He swayed his body a little from side to side. His breath came in soft snorts. And with his hand in constant sign language, he was saying to the procession of visitors: "He is without fear! See my son! There is no fear in him. He is a baby—but he is ready to take a scalp!"

At length, White Badger stretched out his arms and yawned. It was the most unpropitious time he could have chosen for a yawn, for at that moment Red Eagle himself, the chief, was standing above him, looking down from a towering height. But White Badger turned his back upon the chief and said imperiously, "Hungry!" and he rubbed his stomach.

Rising Bull was too delighted with this spirit in his new son to care in the least what consequences might spring out of it, but Little Grouse was first, last, and always, a great deal of a diplomat. She cast her piercing eyes up to the face of Red Eagle, and she rejoiced when a smile rippled on the face of the famous warrior. For although Red Eagle was young, he was already great, and perhaps on a day he might become grand war-chief of all of the Cheyennes! Now he squatted on his knees, and beginning with his thumbs at the root of the spinal column of White Badger he worked them up along the back of the boy to the base of

15

the neck and then ran his fingers gently over the thick, wide bones of the shoulders.

"He shall take many scalps," said Red Eagle.

And he put into the soft fist of White Badger a long, glistening hunting knife of the finest steel, with the manufacturer's polish still glistening upon it.

Here was a gift to be remembered for a lifetime—and from such a hand! Then Red Eagle left, but behind him remained what was a benediction—and a prophecy!

It spread, as all prophecies and benedictions will when they get onto the tongues of rumor. And the last of the line of visitors were chattering late that night to Little Grouse, "Look how he sleeps—he is not afraid—and he smiles! Is it true that he never cries?"

Little Grouse would wrinkle her nose in scorn and make her face, if possible, more hideous than before.

"Cry?" said she. "He is a warrior already! Does a warrior cry? He is a great chief in a little body, but the body will grow!"

And she would make a gesture tall and wide, to indicate that the growth of his frame would one day fill half the sky!

When, at last, everyone was gone, she put the boy on her own bed and lay down beside Rising Bull. The moments she chose for talking were those when some of the tribes of dogs fell into a flurry of fighting and yelling and barking— and then the scream of a badly punished dog when an enemy got a death grip.

In those moments, to such accompaniments, she said to Rising Bull, "The whole village thinks that he will not cry and that he knows no fear! Do you, also, think that it is true, Rising Bull?"

"I think it is true," said he, for it was easy for him to believe in good and wonderful things in spite of all the sorrows which had come upon him in the very heart and prime of his life.

Yet Little Grouse had doubts. It was not for nothing that

16

she had watched one son grow tall and straight and power-ful of limb, the only child of the five wives of Rising Bull. It was not for nothing that she had poured her soul and her wisdom into that fine boy, and then had lost him. Not even by a bullet, but a spent arrow, which had lodged in the hollow of his throat!

Well, such things make wisdom. Little Grouse was wise. She lay in the black heart of the night and she said to herself, "Is it possible? Has Tirawa sent to my husband and to me this great reward—a son without fear—with a per-fect body!"

No! At that very instant, while her heart was swelling with riches greater than gold or jewels, at that very instant she heard a soft whimper from the little body beside her. The heart of Little Grouse stopped! How the others in the tepee would laugh if they were wakened by the screaming of this white boy who was called fearless by a foolish foster mother!

The whimper grew. It seemed to Little Grouse that she would lose her mind, so great was her anguish and her shame. She clapped her hand over the mouth of the boy and over his nose and then, rising, she glided from the lodge.

Outside, she kicked a stone at a sleeping dog which leaped up and sank its fangs in the neck of a sleeping companion. Twenty dogs were presently fighting, growl-ing, snarling, howling. And while this war went on, she removed her hand from the nose and mouth of White Badger.

Instantly there arose a screech powerful enough to saw stout wood in two! And she clapped her hand over his nose and his mouth again. He struggled and beat at her. Yet she kept her grip until he was in a frenzied struggle. When she removed her hand this time, he gasped a second or two for breath before his yell recommenced.

So it continued for fifteen minutes, and by the end of that time, White Badger was a-drip with perspiration, but

17

he had learned his lesson and he lay quietly in the arms of
Little Grouse. Then she sneaked back into the tent and lay
down at the side of her husband.

Another woman, a tent companion, sat up, yawning,
and threw a stick on the lodge fire.

"What is it? Did I hear a child gasping, Little Grouse?"
she asked.

"Shall I tell you what has happened?" said Little Grouse.

"Tell me, then."

"I heard the dogs fighting like devils. I wakened. I
found White Badger gone. I ran out. Ah, ah, ah! There he
was setting the dogs on one another, and laughing."

"S-s-s!" whispered the other in admiration. "Will he not
be a great man if there is no fear in him?"

"Tirawa has sent him. He is a holy boy!" said Little
Grouse.

She knew that she was lying, of course. She knew that
White Badger was as apt to whimper and whine as any of
the other boys of the village, but the strange new rumor
about him had made him so great and made her and her
husband so great by mere association, that she could not
give up the splendid thought. She could not take down the
idol from its base and call it an ordinary child.

She lay down beside White Badger and waited until he
slept. She loved him more than ever because there was a
little weakness in him. She loved him most of all because
she had been forced to tell a great lie in order to maintain
the legend of his greatness.

Then a great thought came to her and she lay in the
darkness with that thought unfolding before her like a
magnificent golden flower, filled with light. She wakened
her husband at last and said to him: "Rising Bull, it is true.
There is no fear in him!"

Even to her own husband she must lie. And the secret
would lie only with herself and Tirawa and White Badger
himself.

18

4

I said to Danny Croydon, long before I began to write this history at his special request: "How could the youngster have maintained such a reputation when he lived surrounded by other rough youngsters in the Indian village, to say nothing of the mature men, and above all, the new braves, the warriors strong as men and mischievous as children? How could White Badger have lived in the very strong intimacy of Indian village life without being discovered by the rest to be no fearless creature at all, but just a spoiled white child—a little more courageous than other children—very much bolder, indeed—yet, at heart, not a great deal different from any other children who cry when they are spanked?"

I asked Croydon because, although I have seen a good deal of Indians and even have lived among them, I cannot pretend to his familiarity with their *minds*. It is all very well to view things from the outside, like so many monuments and buildings, but Croydon, to a certain extent, was able, through peculiar talents and through long intimacy with the tribe, to creep into the hearts of the Indians—or of the Cheyennes at least.

He pointed out to me that if little White Badger had been living among white men, he would sooner or later have reached his Waterloo—probably sooner than later. For the white man will not tolerate much nonsense from children other than his own; and the older white boys take a particular pleasure in distributing discipline to those who have not been kept in hand sufficiently by their parents.

However, in an Indian village there are many differences. As for the older warriors, children are beneath their attention. They will take no heed of all the noise and the disturbance which youngsters can make unless the racket grows intolerable, and then, after a solemn warning, one of the boys in the lodge will be rapped over the head with a stick. But, on the whole, the mischief-makers in such a town can be sure that the hands of the elders will not be visited upon them.

So White Badger was delivered from two dangers. There remained a greater and more intimate danger than either of these—that is to say, the danger that some among the boys with whom White Badger played would discover weaknesses in his character. Croydon admitted that it was almost miraculous that they did not, and he attributed the reason to several things. In the first place, and most important of all, Little Grouse, in daily dread lest the secret that White Badger was only an ordinary child should be revealed, took care that he be removed from the other crowds of children as much as possible. To this end, she insisted that she and her husband should go off on solitary hunting expeditions by themselves, and for months at a time they were absent from the town. It was a greater sacrifice for Little Grouse than for her husband. For his part, that cheerful brave hated to be among his fellows where they could daily look upon his wrist stump and realize that his fighting force was gone. He much preferred to be off by himself. He had stolen a few traps from a white trapper, and he had learned how to snare a few birds with simple contrivances.

In this manner he and his squaw could eke out a living, and, while they were away from the village, Little Grouse worked desperately, slavishly, to teach her adopted son the ways of the most wise and stoical Indian warriors. She taught him the language, first of all, and then she drilled into his mind as well as she could all the maxims concerning stoicism and solemn courage, and indifference to pain, and boundless pride. And, eventually, she ventured upon the most dangerous ground of all by declaring to this little spoiled youngster that he himself was a spirit gifted by the great power, the great Tirawa, with perfect courage, perfect indifference to danger!

She told it to the boy as though she herself believed it. She told it to him most solemnly. And, if she saw him tremble in the dark, or quake at the sight of a stalking buffalo or a wolf appearing among the rocks near them, she would close her own eyes to the fear in her adopted son. So that he felt she had seen nothing. Like a religious fanatic she went through the days repeating to herself words concerning the infinite courage and hardihood of her new-found son, until, at length, she began to believe what she said.

Her mind was too full of ideas, hopes, fears, schemings, to leave much room for actual fondness for White Badger. But Danny Croydon vows to me that he has heard it averred that Rising Bull would take the white boy in his arms every evening and handle him like a foolish mother, and grin down hideously on White Badger's face, and admire the two stout, mischievous little hands!

And yet this family could not spend all of its time upon the perilous plains, away from the tribe. In the long buffalo hunts of the summer months, for instance, it was necessary that they rejoin the tribe so that Rising Bull could give all the strength of his one hand in helping at the "woman work." For, since the loss of that hand, woman's work was all that he was fit to do. He could help at the skinning. He could carve meat and cut it into strips for the drying. He could scrape skins and prepare them as robes or as leather. He and his wife working anxiously to make up for the fact that together they could not make up the force of a real hunting warrior, managed to do enough to warrant the issuance to them, from the general supply, of enough robes, enough dried meat, to last them through the weary length of the winter months. But during those summer months when they went out alone, ah, how frightful was the poverty of that family which had not so much as a single pony! Instead, they were reduced to a fashion which had gone out two generations before among the fighting Cheyennes. When horses appeared, the Cheyennes became flying eagles. But here was Rising Bull reduced to the old and shameful necessity. His household goods had to be packed upon little travois, and these travois were drawn by Indian dogs! So, on foot, the family trudged across the plains while the rest of the village could whirl away on the backs of fleet-footed ponies.

But the dogs were the salvation of White Badger, if one considers that his salvation had anything to do with the maintenance of that illusion about the poor child. But for my part, it seems very clear that all the tragic story of his later days was based upon that same illusion that he was the miracle—the man without fear. I don't wish to pose as a moralist, but attitudes which are based upon lies are usually poison in the end! However, it was from the dogs that protection came for White Badger in the first place.

The story is as follows: When Rising Bull took his family away from the village for the first time that summer he harnessed in the travois a big yearling puppy which had never worked before. Most Indian dogs are extremely wolfish, and this one was almost an exact replica of his brothers who ranged wild. He was so very startlingly like them, indeed, that as he grew older he lost the knack of barking and had no voice except the terrible, wailing cry of the timber wolf itself! He was a tall, rangy puppy with a pelt of yellow-white—almost a pure white—and when the light travois was harnessed upon him he was given to White Badger to conduct across the plain.

For two days all went smoothly, but on the very morning of the third day, as they started on the trek, an ugly old dog, who was accustomed to leading the procession, took exception to White Badger, who was running gaily into the lead with the yellow puppy. An instant later the puppy was sprawling on its back and the teeth of the old dog were in its throat.

"White Badger has lost us a dog," said Rising Bull with composure, "it is the first bad luck that has come to us!"

For he knew that with one hand he could not separate those fighters. Moreover, he knew the bulldog grip of the old leader. These were things beyond the ken of White Badger, but he was fully old enough to understand that his own yellow dog was being killed. When his scream for help was not answered by the elders, he cast about him for some desperate remedy. Right at his feet the providence of Tirawa had placed a long, narrow, flinty stone. It was just small enough for the boy's pudgy hands to grasp; it was just of weight enough for him to wield it.

He raised that stone and struck with all his might. He might have pounded all day for all the old dog would have cared; but by exquisite chance the stroke lodged right over the sensitive temple and the killer dropped senseless to the ground. The white puppy had enough life left to stagger to its feet and reel towards its enemy, but White Badger did not want that. He did not want his puppy to be clamped in those terrible jaws again, so he grappled at the head of his dog—

"He took him by the jaws—an untamed young dog!" Rising Bull used to say, "and he dragged that dog away from the fight!"

It did not take much dragging, for the puppy was so thoroughly mauled that there was not above an ounce of life left in him. Afterwards, Little Grouse tried to dress the deep wounds in the throat of the young dog, but White Badger pushed her hands away. He alone should minister to the needs of his dog. *His* dog by the high right of the life which he had saved! Little Grouse sat by and showed him how to wash the cuts and then rub in some grease, which was so soothing to the puppy that afterwards it licked the legs and the hands of White Badger in gratitude.

After that, it became the unceasing attendant upon the

23

boy. All that summer it grew in bulk and in strength. It was so fleet of foot that Rising Bull, watching it skim across the plain, found a name for it bursting out of his throat, "White Hawk!"

Now the point of this matter was that when the summer was ended and the family returned to the tribe for the fall hunting, White Badger—sunburned to a brown badger by this time—walked at the head of the procession, and right behind him, freed from any indignity of the burden of a travois, strode White Hawk. I ask you to remember that the boy had just turned his sixth birthday and that this was a hundred-pound monster of a wolf-dog, young as it was, so that the head of White Hawk was as high as the head of the boy. And, as it stalked along, continually turning its head and looking first across one shoulder of its little master and then across the other, the great wolfish creature looked wild and savage enough to satisfy any Indian heart.

The whole village came out to look.

They were too awe inspired to shout; they merely whispered: "See! The White Badger has captured a wolf and tamed it with his own hands!"

I suppose that any of them with a historical sense might have remembered the tall, rangy puppy which had followed the family of Rising Bull when they had left the camp early that summer. But they believe what they wish to believe. And here was something beautifully startling. Here was a miracle for the eye to grasp. Here was a little boy with a great white wolf walking behind him, a slave to his every gesture and every word!

"He will be a great warrior," said the women to Little Grouse. "Is it true that he has not cried—all summer?"

Little Grouse remembered the time he had seen the wolf; the many times he had stubbed his toes on sharp rocks; the day he had tumbled down the steep bank into the stream. But she shrugged away all memory of the tears of her adopted son. Oh, how sweet it was to smile con-

24

temptuously, proudly, upon these other women who were the mothers or the sisters of warriors.

"I shall not speak of him," she said. "Look for yourself! See if his hands and his feet do not speak of him better than I can!"

5

Soon every man was plaguing Rising Bull for an account of how White Hawk had been caught. And all the answer they could receive from him was: "You speak to Little Grouse. She will tell—if she can!"

Mind you, there was never any malice in the lies which Rising Bull told—at least Danny Croydon vows that there was not. He was as honest as any Indian on the plains, but of course he could hardly be expected to overlook an opportunity as glorious as this for making his family and self more important. Besides, he rarely told a direct lie; he simply referred people to his wife, for he knew that she was much more capable of constructing an interesting fable.

Little Grouse herself chose to say little. Instead, she wrapped herself in an air of smiling mystery. To preserve the strange air which now surrounded White Badger she would say: "I do not wish to tell stories that will seem lies. I do not wish to have people point their fingers at me and say: 'That woman tells great lies!' I do not wish to have people point at Rising Bull and say: 'His wife is a great liar.' No, I shall not tell you any strange stories. But I show you White Hawk with the Badger. Is not that enough? *I* cannot catch a wild wolf and tame it in one summer like that. Rising Bull cannot catch a wild wolf and make it talk and lick his hand. But there is White Hawk. And there is the little Badger. Now I have not told you any story. I have shown you the facts. You go away and think of it, but do not say that Little Grouse has made lies for you to listen to! Only—ah, there he is now!"

This last explanation as the boy stalked past with the big, wolfish creature stepping at his heels.

So the gossip, gazing in dismay, would hurry off to her home with round eyes. And that night even her husband— yes, and all the men and women and children of her lodge, together with the nearest neighbors, would pour in and sit speechless while she told of how she had interviewed Little Grouse, elaborating what she had heard into the most improbable and thrilling narrative her mind was capable of compassing.

In a week Little Grouse had acted her part so skillfully that every good imagination in the village was busy coining more and more preposterous stories about the catching of White Hawk. This is the story which, at length, was told by an old man in a most convincing manner and which impressed itself so upon the minds of the Indians that all the other tales were forgotten. Before the Badger was seven, he was the subject of an enchanting story which charmed every other child in the village. Before he was eight, he himself did not know whether or not the tale was true, and by the time he was nine, he would have sworn to the truth of it.

This was the story:

One day in the summer, Little Grouse and Rising Bull sat in their tepee on the plains. The day had been hot. The night was cool and pleasant. In the dusk the Badger was playing before them. And every moment he ran back and forth, and farther and farther away from the father and mother who had adopted him.

At length, they could see him no longer. They stood up and they called to him, but the Badger did not answer.

26

They began to run wildly, one this way and one that way. They ran and they ran for a long time, calling out to him. At length their voices grew tired and they could not speak. They staggered on together. The moon came up. It turned from yellow to white. Then they saw, on a hilltop, seven great wolves, each of a different color, lying around the feet of the little Badger.

He stood up, and each of them came and licked his hands and fawned at his feet. A great white wolf was the last of all. Onto the back of this wolf he climbed and thumped him with his heels and rode him down the hill and back to the tepee. When Rising Bull and Little Grouse came back to the lodge, the wolf rose and tried to leap at their throats. It began to snarl and rage at them. But the Badger took the wolf by its long red tongue and crowded it into a corner and beat it with a stick. And the White Hawk lay down at the feet of the boy and licked them and asked for forgiveness.

And from that day it was the willing servant of White Badger!

This was the story—very much in brief—as it was told in that Cheyenne village and, after the next medicine dance, by the entire tribe. Fame was thrust upon the Badger from his very infancy.

Of course, Little Grouse allowed the tale to float away into fairy regions of impossibility. But, in the meantime, she saw that there was an earthly basis for the attachment of the wolf-dog to its tiny master. She and Rising Bull fed the dog from time to time bits of meat—with burs or some other disagreeable substance concealed in it—with the result that in order to prepare White Hawk to fly at one's throat, the very best method was to offer him a tempting morsel of flesh, even dripping with blood. From no hand would he accept food except from the hand of his master, the White Badger.

Well, I have often thought that it must have been a great thing to see the Badger strolling through the streets of the village with the great animal at his heels. If he paused, the White Hawk curled up before his feet. If a stranger approached, the snarl of the big beast was a sufficient warning. The stranger—and all people except his master were strangers to White Hawk—was forced to side step.

This went on for a week or so and then Chief Red Eagle himself decided that the white creature was a nuisance. He had a number of savage dogs, big, three-quarters wolf, and very strong. He took half a dozen of them onto the wide prairie and then he sent for the Badger. The white boy came and behind him, of course, was White Hawk.

There was no need for an extensive invitation. A word or two and the fight began. It continued in a circle of a half mile or more in diameter. White Hawk flew in front and the dogs of Red Eagle followed. It was a lovely thing, in the way of effective fighting, to see White Hawk run until the dogs trailed behind him. Then he whirled and made at the leading runner and gave him one convincing rip with his fangs. He was wolf enough to fight in the true wolf manner, which is in the style of an expert fencer armed with a saber—a dart, a slash, and then away. I suppose there is as much power in the jaws of a wolf as in the jaws of any two dogs. At any rate, one or two brushes with White Hawk were enough for the most ambitious of the dogs of Red Eagle. He killed two of them outright by knocking them down and then slashing their throats open with one cut. That seems a good deal, but you must remember that a wolf will bite and tear several pounds of flesh out of the side of a running bull! Two more of the chief's dogs were crippled and drew off. And the remaining pair decided that the white devil was extraordinarily bad medicine. So did Red Eagle and he stopped the fight.

"Now, bring this medicine dog to me," said he.

The Badger whistled and the ghostly dog was instantly at his back. He walked up to the chief and the latter held a rifle at the side of White Hawk.

"Are you not afraid for your dog?" he asked the Badger.

But little Glanvil Tucker merely tossed up his head and laughed.

"Why are not *you* afraid?" he asked. "White Hawk does not mind bullets!"

It was enough and more than enough for the worthy chief. And he went back to his lodge to sit and curse his dogs and continue cursing them. It was two days later that he told the story and averred, as his strong belief, that White Hawk was such strange medicine that a bullet would not harm it.

This odd story was carried to Spotted Ear. Spotted Ear was seventeen years old and so eager to distinguish himself that he decided that by breaking this "medicine" of White Hawk he would be doing something eminently worthwhile.

So he went out and hunted for White Hawk and the Badger. Then he rode his horse at the big wolf-dog and tried to shoot him through the back. White Hawk, however, hated to have things come up behind him. He whirled out of the way at the critical moment and while a heavy charge of powder and lead was blown into the earth he, unharmed, dived up at the horseman and brought the young warrior out of his seat with a scream and slammed him upon the ground with a double row of long white wolf-fangs fixed in his shoulder.

Before White Hawk could change his grip and tear out the throat of the fallen man, White Badger had him by the ears and took him from his victim.

It made a great noise. If the people had looked askance at the little boy and his great guardian wolf-dog before, they now stared in real awe. For Spotted Ear had to prove that he was not a mere cheap fool. So he swore that he'd stolen up behind the wolf and had held the muzzle of his rifle a foot from the back of the beast, but that when he had fired, although the blast of smoke had fanned the thick coat of White Hawk, the beast had not been hurt at all. It had merely turned and caught him by the shoulder.

So people continued to rise and stand out of the way when White Badger came too close with his attendant ghost.

Little Grouse, watching the days of the buffalo hunting drift past hand over hand, prayed to Tirawa every day, and begged that the greatness of the Badger might endure.

I believe that Red Eagle was a crafty warrior and a thinking man as well. For it was he, apparently, who was the only man in the tribe able to look through the mystery of this boy who rode wild wolves and tamed them. He appeared one day at the tepee of Rising Bull and said: "Let the White Badger bring the Hawk and tie him."

It was done. White Badger was always glad to show his mastery over the great brute. He tied the wolf until it could not stir a hair. Then the chief took him by the hand and led him down the town street, through the dust and among the crowds of other dogs. At the end of the short lane there was a group of a dozen youngsters—not warriors, but boys from twelve to fourteen years of age, every one of them able to break the little white boy in two.

"Here is the Badger," said the chief. "And now, let me see if there is really no fear in him! You may do what you please."

And he himself sat down with his chin on his fist to watch and judge and keep the fun from going too far. He wanted to learn for himself whether or not this child was a blessing to the tribe and a warrior who might help to make his own hands greater in the future, or simply a little sham which his adopted parents were making into a great story.

The youths were glad of this invitation, of course. They began to run in a circle around the White Badger. First they kept at a distance and yelled mockingly at him. Then they came closer and began to throw little sticks and stones at him. Some of the stones struck him hard and one cut his mouth and brought out a trickle of blood. But he stood perfectly still. He was so thoroughly spoiled and petted and made a fuss over that he could not conceive that this thing which he saw was real. The sting of his mouth did not hurt him as much as the numbness of astonishment. So he leaned on his little club, which was used to discipline White Hawk, and glared at them. As a matter of fact, he was coming perilously close to bursting into tears, which would have ruined the fine illusion concerning him. But, in the meantime, he maintained a very striking picture as he stood there resting on his stick and gazing at his tormentors in apparent scorn.

Red Eagle began to be more and more excited. He stood up and struck his hands together.

"It is not a baby but a man!" said Red Eagle.

At that instant the man fell from his proud estate. The eldest of the boys flicked a rawhide lariat over the head of little White Badger and there he was, rolling head over heels with the force of the tremendous twitch with which the thrower had completed his cast. Straight at the tall boy rolled the Badger.

Then he came pitching to his feet not two strides from the laughing, triumphant tormentor. Surely it seemed enough—to have knocked down the little man and rolled him so in the dust. Still the Badger did not sit down and cry. Every petted and pampered boy is filled with a rage of pride at a first indignity, although a second one is apt to break his spirit completely.

As it was, the Badger rushed at the other and hove his club above his head. To avoid the blow, the big boy drew a long knife with a threatening yell. It was too late for that excellent bluff to work. The hard little club descended and smote Goliath fairly in the middle of the forehead. Down he crashed upon his back and little David, sitting astride him, picked up the fallen knife and prepared to cut the throat of the enemy as he had seen Rising Bull cut the throat of a calf.

In the very nick of time the strong arm of Red Eagle glided around him and plucked him away from his victim.

But enough had been done. Yes, more than enough. Red Eagle carried the boy back with a solemn face and put him down in the tepee of his adopted parents.

"Red Eagle would be happy," he said, "if such a young man were in his lodge! There is a great medicine in him!"

6

I said to old Danny Croydon, on a day, "Do you mean to tell me that any normal youngster went from his fifth year to the time of his manhood without crying or showing some sort of natural weakness in the presence of other people?"

"That," said Danny Croydon, "is exactly what I *do* mean."

"How the devil could it have been done, unless he were inspired?"

"He *was* inspired," said Danny Croyden. "He was inspired with meanness. There ain't much doubt in my mind that the Badger was, take him by and large, the meanest kid that ever stepped. He was so doggone mean that it hurts just to think about how bad he was. He was so mean that it makes me double up my fist right now when I recollect it!"

Mean, of course, because he was so thoroughly spoiled. Having been given a headlong start in the direction of pure "cussedness" by a fond and pampering mother and father, his ruin was completed by Little Grouse and Rising Bull. From Rising Bull, and from many other Indians, he freely learned that he was an exceptional person, capable of subduing wild beasts and overcoming boys and men. From Little Grouse he learned that all of this was the sheerest sort of sham and that he was just exactly like every other boy, except that she, Little Grouse, had so excellently contrived matters that people would believe what she chose to have them believe about the Badger.

"But perhaps," she would often say to the Badger, "it may be true! Think of the way the White Hawk came to your hand!"

That was long afterwards, when the Badger was growing into the strength of his boyhood, in his ninth year—when he was tall and straight, but still with the promise of those wide shoulders of his athletic father not yet realized. He had forgotten how he'd really gotten the mastery over the White Hawk. He only knew that there was a thrilling story about that affair, and that other people believed the tale from beginning to end. He believed the story, except for one little grain of doubt, which made the story all the more delightful to him.

But he had understood for some time, now, that he must never cry when he was hurt, and he must never show fear, and he must never allow himself to be startled by any sound no matter how sudden or how terrible. Behold, when Tirawa himself was enraged and the thunder rolled through the heavens, and the lightnings splashed upon the drenched earth, and the boldest of the Cheyennes cowered in their lodges and wished that the morrow had come—then, peering through the flaps of their lodges, they could see the slender form of White Badger with the ghostly wolf stalking at his heels as he walked down the street of the village.

What did White Badger care for Tirawa? Nothing in the world, except that Tirawa's mighty splutterings gave him a chance to show off his superiority. He was a frightful actor, this boy. He knew that the eyes of other people were constantly upon him, and like most children accustomed to the stage, he loved this attention, and he accepted it as freely and as naturally as the air which he breathed.

I do not like to give this picture of Glanvil Tucker. But

when I talked the matter over with Danny Croydon, he vowed that the good must be written with the bad. So I have put everything down. No, not everything. It is beyond me to give a picture of the perfect insolence, brutality, and coldly centered selfishness of the Badger. I shall say, however, on account of the good that was found in him afterwards, that we must attribute most of his glaring faults to the manner of his upbringing. I don't think that any child could be systematically spoiled by a whole tribe of Indians without showing infinite bad effects.

By this I do not mean to infer that the Badger was loved by the Cheyennes—even by the band which Red Eagle led. Not a whit of it! The Indians are just as sharp-eyed as you or I for the personal faults of other people. They saw as clearly as anyone could have seen, that the Badger was an insufferably conceited young puppy and that he had about every fault of vanity and pride that could make a boy despicable. But at the same time there was a shuddering belief in him lodged in the center of their hearts. They felt that he was great big medicine of the very largest sort! And so they tolerated his follies and his pride because they felt that he was to be extremely valuable to the tribe sooner or later. And, on his account, life was made easy for lucky Little Grouse and Rising Bull, who lived now just as comfortably as though he had been possessed of both hands, for there was a constant string of presents from the rest of the village.

It was in the Badger's tenth year that he was first used as "medicine" by the Cheyennes. In the spring of the year, when the snows were ended and when the ponies were covered with the first fat of the year and the first strength of it, none other than Spotted Ear came in search of the Badger and found him down at the river, practicing dives from the bank and then swimming as long under water as there was breath in his lungs. He was all by himself. Down the river in the pleasanter spots, where the trees hung thicker from the banks and covered the waters with a greener shadow, were the other youngsters from the village, but the Badger was by himself.

For several reasons. The first of these was that he did not like to bring himself close enough to the other boys to be compared with them. The second was, that he desired to be alone while he experimented with himself and tried in various ways to improve his style. For, every day of his life, Little Grouse said as she wakened him in the morning: "Is this the day that some Indian will beat you?"

He lived under the charm of that horrible expectation. No boy must surpass him. He must run faster and farther; he must swim more easily and dive deeper and with less noise than any other youth. He must shoot straight with bow and rifle and revolver. He must develop such strength of arm that every other boy should fear him.

Very well. Practice, practice, practice would impart to him these qualities. But all the practice in the world could never give him certain gifts which he had seen and envied in the other Cheyenne boys. He could not, like them, learn to read a trail as though it were a printed page. To him the far-off thing on the prairie was still a blur when it was a well developed wolf to the companion who ran with him. Neither had he the patience to sit all day, waiting for the rabbit to thrust out its head from the burrow. Neither could he endure hunger or heartbreaking fatigue as the other boys endured these things. He might run as fast, but he could not run as far. And he knew very well that although he might carry all with a high hand until the very last moment, yet if it came to enduring torment he would never be able to stand it as the Indian boy could stand it. Indeed, the whole life of the Badger was founded upon a sham, and he knew it. He was pretending to be a very great Indian when he knew that he was a very poor one in most respects. He had to act like a cunning fox; but the fox which fooled the tribe was also gnawing at his own heart. In his tenth year, even, there was a wistful, hunted look in the eyes of the Badger, such as one sees, usually, in the eyes

35

of children who have been desperately or hopelessly ill for a long, long time.

On this day, Spotted Ear came up the river, for the other boys had informed him, with many snarling and evil words, that the Badger was much too good to play with them. They hoped that he would die a weak old man—or go to the other life with two broken legs—or enter the happy hunting grounds with an arm chopped off. For, as everyone knows, in the other life one remains exactly as one is when one enters it!

But Spotted Ear did not care to hear this chatter. He had heard plenty of it before this day, and he had uttered plenty of it himself since the time when the teeth of the White Hawk had been fastened in his shoulder. He sat down on a fallen tree-trunk and watched the swimmer dive from the bank and slide in a glimmering shadow under the clear surface of the water. But midway in his skimming dive, the Badger whirled about in the water and looked back.

What could have warned him that there was someone behind him? What could have warned him when he was so deep in the water? Spotted Ear did not notice that among the brush on the opposite bank the White Hawk had risen ominously and so given the swimmer a sufficient warning. And, not noticing this, the young brave shivered and told himself that there was certainly a great medicine in the Badger.

The latter now popped to the surface and blew the water from his nose and mouth. He treaded water until he was shoulder free.

"Have you come to sit and watch, or to sit and talk, Spotted Ear?" he asked.

"I have come to talk, White Badger," said the brave, swallowing his resentment at the hidden sneer in the tone of the boy.

"Well," said the Badger, and struck out for the shore.

He reached it in a moment, for he swam extremely well.

36

His swimming was not modeled upon the fashion of the other boys. But he had watched Red Eagle, himself the best of all the tribe in the water, and patterned his craft after that of the master. Now he leaped up on a rock and shook the water from his body and from his long black hair. Then he wrung out that hair and with a few gestures skimmed the water from his body with the edge of the hand. That body was so dark a brown that the only way of detecting the difference between him and his brothers of the tribe was in the luster of the skin itself—which was coppery in the little Cheyennes.

The Badger lay down in the grass and stretched his hands above his head. Now one could see beneath the pits of the arms a pale patch of skin. He had taken out from its leather sheath a knife which he wore day and night around his waist—a long, heavy knife of the most beautiful English steel. The first gift from Red Eagle and the dearest friend and companion in the life of the Badger, with the exception, always, of the White Hawk. Now the knife was in his hands, tumbled lightly from finger to finger; now lying with the hilt in the flattened palm, ready for hurling; now gripped dexterously by the point for a spinning throw; now with the haft in a stern, tight grip, ready for ripping work at close quarters. The eyes of the Badger were most impolitely upon his knife and not upon his companion. But then the Badger was already famous among the Cheyennes for his bad manners.

"I am glad," said Spotted Ear, swallowing an inner burst of rancor again, "that you take Spotted Ear as a friend."

"Why do you say that?" asked the boy, insolent as ever.

"Because you lie here beside me without fear."

"I have this," said the boy, grinning wickedly as he fingered the knife. "And also I have that!"

There was something in his tone and in his side-glancing eyes which made Spotted Ear jerk around. White Hawk had raced up the river, crossed it partly on a fallen log, partly by leaping and partly by swimming the remaining distance, and now he sat lolling and grinning a scant six feet behind the Cheyenne. The sight of him brought an exclamation from Spotted Ear and, instinctively, he touched the glistening scars in his shoulder.

"He will not hurt you," said the Badger contemptuously. "Here, fool!"

He struck the earth with his flat hand and the wolf instantly stretched himself on the spot. The Badger lay down at easy length and pillowed his head upon the flank of the big beast. And, as though understanding that he was now perfectly guarded, he closed his eyes and yawned. Then he sheathed the knife.

"Why have you come hunting me, Spotted Ear?"

"We are friends, however?"

"If you wish."

"White Badger, I am no longer a child but I am followed by bad luck. My good medicine turned to bad medicine from the day that your wolf pulled me off my horse. Now, when I am about to count a coup, my horse stumbles. I have never yet taken a scalp! And when I feel poor and wish to go on the warpath, the braves smile. They will not come with me—not even the youngest of the dog-soldiers."

The Badger yawned again, slowly, luxuriously, and kept his mouth indecently at full stretch with the hot sun pouring into it.

"There is a taste in the sun," he announced. "It gives a good feeling in the belly."

Then he deigned to answer Spotted Ear: "What you say is true. In war and horse stealing—you are not lucky, Spotted Ear!"

There was a very insulting innuendo in these words, but the young brave was forced to overlook the insinuation. He said bluntly: "So I have come to ask you for friendship. I have come to ask you to ride with me when I go to steal horses!"

The Badger wanted to sit up and shout. Instead, he yawned broadly again.

"You steal from whom?" he asked.

"Pawnees!" said Spotted Ear.

In spite of himself, a grunt of admiration was forced from the boy, for the Pawnees were almost the only Indians of the plains whom the Cheyennes considered to be on a par with themselves. "But why should I go?" asked the boy.

"To me you are a great medicine, White Badger. When it is known that you will ride with us, then many young braves will wish to go with me, because they know that you are medicine. We shall have the best men in the band. And we shall steal many, many horses—the best of the Pawnee horses. We shall come whirling back. We shall bring gladness into the village. Spotted Ear will stand like a man before his friends. And you and I, White Badger, will divide the best horses between us. Because it has come to me that Rising Bull has no horses behind his lodge!"

7

The way of Spotted Ear began to be easy at the very moment that the way of White Badger became difficult. For when it was announced through the village that the Badger intended to accompany Spotted Ear on a horse-stealing excursion, there was a fair scramble among the young braves to get themselves admitted among the chosen few. So that Spotted Ear could stand back and choose the best men with the fleetest horses. But when the Badger reached his lodge, the tidings had gone before him and he found Little Grouse in a panic. First she stormed at him and commanded him to stay at home. But the Badger was not one to be commanded by a woman.

He shoved the hilt of his knife into her ribs.

"Fat pig," said the Badger, "there are no bones in you, but there is a throat to be choked. Do not trouble me with your talk. I go with my friends for a little ride over the plains."

Little Grouse fell into a speechless rage. When one of these spasms came upon her, she used to run out and throw herself on the ground and beat her head and tear her hair. Her passion was so terrible because it was impossible for her to relieve herself with words. She dared not tell the world that the boy she had reared was a wicked little ingrate with a tongue like a wolf's tooth. She dared not tell Rising Bull, even!

And now, through the headstrong foolishness of this youngster, he was about to throw himself away, and throw away, in the same gesture, all of the care and the labor of head and hand which she had poured forth upon him. Yet she came back to the tepee hurrying. She met Rising Bull on the way. And she told him the story.

"The Badger must learn the ways of men," said her husband. "You cannot keep him like a woman all of his life."

She turned and glared at him. It was a continual curse to her that Rising Bull himself did not know the secret and that she could not pour forth to him all of her cares concerning the Badger. As time went on, she had a more and more potent sense of loneliness; even the Badger himself no longer realized that his importance was based upon a sham. In the course of five long years he had come to regard himself as a predestined being, strange and strong in certain respects, and strangely weak in others. His task was harder than the task of Little Grouse. She had only to talk about him; but the Badger had to make good those words. So he began to look down on Little Grouse.

When she reached the lodge with her husband she

merely said, "The Pawnees have good horses and bad horses. And we are poor. Bring back ten horses. Make us rich, White Badger!"

"I shall bring you twenty horses," said the Badger.

And he went out to meet the others. They were ready and waiting for him. In half a dozen lodges medicine had been made, and the report of it was good. Spotted Ear had a small pinto for the Badger, and as the latter leaped up into the saddle, Spotted Ear said: "This is your horse, my brother!"

How the heart of the Badger leaped in him then! He had ridden before, of course; he had learned to leap on the bare backs of the wildest ponies and cling to them in spite of bucking and in spite of threatening teeth; but he had never before possessed a pony, so frightful was the poverty of Rising Bull with his maimed right hand.

It was a fleet and dainty thing, this painted horse, and as the Badger flew across the plains with White Hawk running and leaping at his side, snapping terribly at his hip as though ready to tear his little master from the back of his mount, it seemed to the Badger that he was already a warrior and full-fledged in the tribe! So he laughed as he rode, and when he laughed, the wind of that fierce gallop hummed between his teeth.

They journeyed for three days, using the light of the sun. On the evening of the third day Spotted Ear found a herd of antelopes and he and two other warriors managed to stalk them. Poor Badger could not join in such sport. He had only a bow and arrows behind his saddle, together with an old-fashioned pistol stuck through his belt. And one rarely gets close enough to antelopes to use a pistol ball!

He remained behind to watch the fun. Two antelopes fell, and they spent the rest of the daylight cutting up the bodies and late into the night they were curing the meat, for they had started on their excursion traveling light. Through the next week, they traveled chiefly from the dusk to the dawn. In the day, they slept in some secure place, with a lookout always on guard. And then, at the last, they found a sign of the Pawnees. It was around an old campfire. The ashes were blown away; there was only the blackened earth. And when the Badger dismounted, he did as the others were doing, kneeling, or working from a crouched position, lifting and turning blades of grass, and frowning at the ground underneath it. He knew what they were looking for. But he also knew that his eyes could never see it unless it were written in what might be called capitals. A fifteen-year-old youngster who had made himself a brave by taking a scalp the year before was now the one who made the find and announced its meaning. Then the horse thieves sat in a circle for discussion. Spotted Ear believed that that sign was so fresh that in three hours they would be up with the party who had left the fire sign behind them—unless the latter were traveling at high speed. But the fifteen-year-old Running Deer swore that there was plenty of time. They might ride as hard as they chose.

Spotted Ear turned to the Badger.

"We have not used your medicine, White Badger. What does it tell you now?"

The Badger was perfectly prepared for such a question, and he knew how to answer it. He stooped and picked up a half-palm full of dust and pebbles. The dust he fanned away with his breath until only the pebbles remained. These he pretended to study for a moment. At last he tossed them into the air and announced: "Running Deer is right! We must ride carefully, or we shall be up with them before the night!"

His companions were much impressed by the nonsense of this ceremony, as he expected they would be.

"What do the stones tell you? How do they speak?" whispered Spotted Ear to the boy.

"They speak inside my ear like the squeaks of little baby

field mice," said the Badger solemnly. And Spotted Ear sighed with wonder and envy.

However, they went on now with great caution. And even while the Badger was praying that they might come upon fresher signs of the Pawnees, his prayer was granted. Spotted Ear himself, riding in the lead by a hundred yards, suddenly reined his horse back on a hummock and came hastily back to them, speaking not a word, but with both hands talking in that sign language which is the universal speech of the plains, among the Indians. He told them that he had found five Pawnees, well mounted and armed, riding ahead of them.

So they waited for a few minutes and then rode forward again, keeping the most careful watch. They rode until the dusk was gathering, and then they halted and prepared to make a camp for the night, but now, as the dusk turned to the dark, they saw far ahead of them a faint glow spotting the blackness of the night.

"Those are lodge fires far away," said Running Deer. "Come, White Badger. You and I shall ride out and look at them!"

They did not need to ride far. By the time they had crossed the first rise of ground, they saw before them the glowing light of a great village; five hundred or a thousand warriors might be in that camp. And when they lay on the ground, they could hear a trembling murmur out of the distance—a sound made up of the barking and the howling of dogs, the signs of men, the screaming voices of children—all wonderfully blended. You or I could not have heard it. Perhaps Danny Croydon himself could not have heard, but it was perceptible to the ear of our wild raised Badger, and it was very plain, of course, to the child of the plains, Running Deer.

He insisted on going closer. So they whirled on for half a mile until sights and sounds were very clear, and then they came to the edge of a wide, still water—no, not entirely still, for when they halted their ponies, they could hear the faint lisping of the current as it stirred in the center of the stream. They swept on up the stream until they found the lights faintly streaking the black water of the stream with little pools and fine brush strokes of orange.

"This is enough," said Running Deer softly. "There are enough there for all of us, are there not, brother?"

The heart of the Badger was high in his throat. For he had been congratulating himself every moment since he first saw the size of the Pawnee town; surely, he had said to himself, they will not dare to adventure near so great a place! Now he saw that he had gone out to steal with madmen for companions!

Running Deer turned his horse, and the Badger beside him, too, when a harsh voice in a strange tongue hailed them on the far side of the water.

"Pawnee!" whispered Running Deer. "Do not ride away. I can talk their tongue. Perhaps we shall play with them!"

And he raised his voice and called to them in studied indifference. A little pause followed his remark. Then a more friendly hail from beyond the water, to which Running Deer replied. He translated: "They want to know why we turn back from the camp. I tell them that we think that we have found the sign of a small party of Cheyennes! Now, listen! They want to cross and come with us—ay, they are coming uninvited!"

The other two, indeed, pushed their horses straightway into the water, and drowned the spots of orange light from the distant lodges with waves of black cast up by the knees of their horses. They came splashing out on the nearer shore.

"I this man on the right—you that man on the left. The knife, little brother, so that the village may hear nothing!"

So saying, the heart of Running Deer rose so great and so high in his throat that he began to sing aloud as he pushed his horse toward the approaching pair and the

Badger, half swooning with terror, moved on toward the other man. The two halted. One was speaking sharply and rapidly, designating the small size of the Badger with many signs in the starlight. But Running Deer kept straight on, laughing as he spoke until he was near enough, and then the Badger saw the wink of the stars on a naked knife blade.

He drew his own knife and lunged at the same moment, setting his teeth in desperation. But his hand was neither so swift nor so steady as that of the other. The Pawnee shrank from the stroke with a gasp and the edge of the Badger's knife merely slashed the front of his tunic. His own knife was in his hand at the same instant and a touch of his heel against the flank of the Badger's horse lifted it forward. The Badger felt his pinto stagger at the shock of that greater weight; he saw the flash of the coming steel straight at his throat. And then a pale streak intervened—White Hawk, lunging for the throat of the stranger and closing teeth on his arm instead. The next instant the point of Red Eagle's gift knife was buried for the first time in human flesh, in the soft hollow of a man's throat. Like a broken tree the tall warrior toppled from his saddle. As he struck the ground the body of the Badger was on top of him and the knife of the Badger was striking for his heart.

All the fear had left his heart the moment the hot blood had come streaming upon his hand and his wrist, bathing all of his forearm. He was filled, instead, with a savage joy, that made him set his teeth and shudder. He caught the dead man by the hair and beat his head against the ground and he found an Indian song of triumph bubbling up through his lips.

"I, the Badger, have seized in my claws—I have torn and rent the Pawnee—I have laid him on the ground—I shall take his scalp and his spirit shall never leave him. It shall rot as his body rots—"

"Brother, little brother," came the voice of Running

Deer, quivering with joy, choked with joy, "make haste! Make haste. We may have need of our time!"

He himself was squatting on the breast of his victim, working at the scalplock, and the Badger followed suit.

Danny Croydon can speak of this with the most perfect good humor, but it turns my stomach a little whenever I think of it. Yet, as Croydon always says: "The Badger was at that time an Indian, pure Indian, and nothing but an Indian. Wouldn't he have been a fool if he had refused to take that scalp? An Indian fool, I mean?"

One has to agree. Logic is logic—but sometimes it is devilish disagreeable stuff, you will admit with me!

I say that the little Badger, in the starlight, ripped his first scalplock from the head of the enemy and leaped to his feet and shook it in the air. But there was still other work. Like his companion, Running Deer, he had to work the dead man out of his clothes. Running Deer had finished long before and came to help and, the moment he did so, he groaned with much envy.

"I have taken a scalp from an old man—a weak man!" he made complaint. "But you, White Badger, have taken the scalp of a great chief. Feel the beading and the quill work! Five squaws have worked a whole winter to make such a suit as this! And look! There are two revolvers, one at each hip. Ah—ah—look at him even by the stars. He is a great man. He is as big as a fallen cliff. Now look at his horse, also. Ha, little Badger, there is a horse for *you*! He is taller than my own head!"

As a matter of fact, they did not need daylight to show them that the horse from which the chief had fallen was a stallion as magnificent as the gelding which the other victim had bestrode was broken down and weak. Only with difficulty could the Badger clamber up the side of this fine animal. Then he planted his feet in the leathers above the tops of the stirrups. His new loot he tied on beside the saddle. Under his knee he felt the steel barrel of a rifle on a

holster there. Certainly, as he braced back his shoulders
and tossed up his head, the air of that night turned to wine
in his nostrils!

8

If they had come with a dash, they returned like a whirlwind. And the five waiting men received them with deep
murmurs of joy and of envy. Rather than a thousand
stolen horses they would prize these two scalps. For
Pawnee scalps grow not on every bush—even for the pick
of Cheyenne warriors.

There was even one brave who suggested that enough
and more than enough had been done already to make
this a notable party of the warpath. But the others were
only the keener for the work which lay ahead of them.
They crossed the river at once, and then worked into the
low-swelling hills behind the camp. There they consulted.
The village was still full of light and noise and it was
decided that, instead of attempting to take advantage of
the noise to cover their approach, they would wait until the
big Indian town was silent for the night.

All too rapidly, in the ears of little Badger, the noise died
away. The first exultation which had followed the killing of
the unknown warrior had died away now. All that he could
concentrate upon was the task which was ahead. And even
when the town lay black and still beneath them, it seemed
to the Badger the crowning height of folly to go nearer to
the swarming danger, even when the village slept. For he
knew that a nest of hornets does not more quickly answer

47

the tap on the hive than does the Indian town come to life at the first alarm, no matter how light.

But to his horror these madmen who were with him decided that they would advance upon the town not with a stealthy approach with horses and then a wild dash to run off what untethered horses they might, but by crawling on foot to the town and cutting loose the finest animals they could find!

So much had the scalps raised the hearts of the entire party!

One man was left with the horses. Ah, how little Badger yearned to be given that post. For all the man with the horses had to do was to wait until the stampede of the Pawnee horses began toward the hills, and then cut in behind them and give mounts to the thieves. But that post was left to the youngest brave next to Running Deer. The medicine of White Badger seemed to have proved of such excelling quality that they would not have dreamed of leaving him out of the final work.

Down from the hills they went, and when they came close to the edge of the town, they flattened out on the ground and began to work forward like so many snakes. To the Badger it was like creeping into a mist, the heart of which is colder than ice. He could hardly breathe, and his limbs shook under him, and cold sweat poured out from beneath his arms, and nausea seized him in the pit of the stomach.

This he told to Danny Croydon, and also he confided in that old hunter how he despaired, at that moment, of ever becoming a really courageous brave, worthy of being a Cheyenne. Far less to become such a leader as Little Grouse wished to make of him. He felt at that moment that he was a coward. He said that he would have turned back, deliberately, even if it had meant that he would be known as a woman forever after! But just behind him slid the noiseless form of White Hawk, and he felt that he dared

48

not move back lest that wise beast should read him and scorn him!

Well, that is an odd confession to come from the lips of the Badger, as you will agree when you have heard a little more of him.

The crucial test was when they came close to the rim of the village and two braves reeled suddenly out of the flap of a lodge and came straight toward them. They had, apparently, secreted some brandy or alcohol from the rest of their lodge companions and had accumulated a glorious "edge." But when they were a few strides from the row of flat shadows on the ground, they decided, apparently, that they must go back for a farewell drink. When they disappeared behind the tent flap, the Cheyennes closed on the town with a rush and conveyed themselves behind the next tepee. There were half a dozen horses tethered there, and instantly the whisper of sharp knife-edges in leather began. Those horses were loosed, but not startled. They began to wander slowly away. Others must be loosed. And the harvest was as yet hardly begun.

The plan was now to be developed through a more dangerous stage. It was that young demon Running Deer himself who suggested the scheme. The party was to separate because they would then make much less noise. They would perform, each of them, a half circle, winding up near the center of the town. So each man cut off by himself. And White Badger wished that the end of his life might be no farther than a minute away, so sick at heart was he.

Do not imagine that he was wandering through a silent town. For when one speaks of a "quiet" Indian village, one simply means one in which a lesser pandemonium is raging. Here it was the middle of the night, but the noise swept in waves back and forth among the lodges. There were wails of children startled into wakefulness; there were flurries and scurries of dog-fighting in various parts of the town. And sometimes a dozen horses would be neighing at once.

In the midst of that confusion, the Badger stole on his way, heeding nothing in the world save *human* noises. Once or twice he cut a tethered horse free. But on the whole, he used his mind to watch the flaps of the closed lodges. And he had just passed between two that narrowly verged upon one another when he fairly stumbled upon a brave standing stalwart before the flap of a third lodge.

When I say that he stumbled on the warrior, I do not mean that he actually touched him, but terror stopped the Badger with the suddenness of a stone wall when he saw that erect, wide-shouldered figure, a statuesque being with arms folded high on his chest. Had he not heard something, perhaps?

Then in a flash he had whirled on the Badger.

Instinct, nothing else, made the Badger poise his knife at the breast of the brave, but instinct did not make him strike, and if the Pawnee had looked down to the weapon, he would have known by the tremor of the starshine on the blade how the hand was shaking that held it. But the Pawnee did not glance down. At such a time it did not become a warrior of any heart to take notice of the nearness of death. Instead, he fixed his glance steadily upon the boy-form of the Badger and the skulking white shadow of the wolf-dog in the rear.

Then he said, in very good Cheyenne:

"It is the Badger and the White Hawk. You are welcome, my brother. What will you have from Standing Elk?"

The boy could not answer, for the name had paralyzed him. Standing Elk was a chief so great that, compared with his fame, that of such a leader as Red Eagle, let us say, disappeared into the thinnest air. So great was that name, indeed, that it seemed to expand the physical dimensions of the brave. So the Badger stood dumb, unable to realize, it seemed, that the point of his knife was a fraction of an inch from the heart of the greatest among the Pawnee leaders. And the Pawnee, in turn, was reading that silence in quite another fashion. His big hands began, slowly, to close and the muscles of his arms to harden, and his arched breast commenced to swell and the iron of resolution entered his soul and he prepared himself to die, but to die struggling, at least.

Then, from the Badger: "Standing Elk, I have been looking for you through this town."

"It is good that we have met," said Standing Elk. "And yet," he could not help adding with a grim humor, "if you had asked any warrior in the village, he would have pointed out my tepee."

The Badger felt a trifle more at ease, but that did not keep him from holding his knife within the breadth of a hair from the breast of the chief. Only, from the corner of his eye, he took note that the lodge from which the chief had issued was a towering affair, twice the size of the ordinary tepee.

"The White Hawk," said the boy, "was in a hurry. He would not stop. He said that he could smell out the honest man in the Pawnee nation."

"Waugh!" murmured the chief, perhaps not a little pleased by this compliment. But, all the time, his brilliant eyes were staring at the face of the boy and trying to break through to an understanding of him, as it were. However, it was not for nothing that the Badger had spent five years in the center of the stage, ringed with the attention of the Cheyennes. He withstood this scrutiny with the greatest ease.

"Brother," said he, with the tip of his sharp knife resting in the shirt of leather which clothed the chief, "it is not time for you to die."

"That is good!" said Standing Elk.

"But it is time that you should show me the finest horse in the Pawnee town!"

Standing Elk drew himself up a full inch or two taller than before.

"Brother," said he softly, "do you speak of the finest horse or of the ten or the twenty finest horses that Pawnees own?"

But the Badger did not care so much for ten or twenty. Ten or twenty horses were the wealth that would come to the hand of Little Grouse and Rising Bull. But one horse, fleet as the wind, was for himself. And that horse would take him away from danger or into it, exactly as he chose. Surely if he could find the cream of the Pawnee stock, the very best of their famous horses—

"I speak of one horse, Standing Elk," said he. "I speak of one horse so great and so fine that its life is almost worth the life of Standing Elk."

"See, White Badger, you make me into a thief. Follow me!"

So he went stalking through the night at a measured gait. And the Badger could not help adding a soft warning: "White Hawk is behind you, brother. While you walk slowly, he does not see you!"

There was an inaudible grunt from Standing Elk who stopped a moment later before three young horses tethered with their heads close together.

"Look!" said Standing Elk. "These are three horses like three great braves. They are better than three hundred common dog-soldiers. But they are not, altogether, worth one like this!"

He led them around the tepee to the farther side and there the boy beheld, against the stars, the most glorious figure of a horse that ever gladdened the eyes of man.

I do not speak for myself, for when I saw Red Wind he was so very old that gray hairs were beginning to appear in his glossy coat, and the gloss itself was departing; but I have the oath of Danny Croydon for the truth about Red Wind. He was a three-year-old stallion when the hand of the Badger first fell upon his neck. I would have given a very great deal to have seen him by the stars of that same night. He dipped his head and extended his muzzle toward Standing Elk.

"Brother," said the boy, much moved, "do you own him?"

"I own him," said Standing Elk through his teeth. Fiercely, because he feared lest he might speak tenderly. "I could have given you one of the three, but I am an honest man, White Badger. Take him. He is the price for me! Wait here—this is the saddle—and now the stirrups are short enough—"

He flung the saddle on the back of the stallion. And all of this he did so freely and so gently that a certain spirit of nobleness came over the hard heart of White Badger himself, until he said: "Standing Elk, when I am a warrior, I shall come to find you. Then I shall fight you for this horse."

"Then Red Wind will come back to me. Deal kindly with him, White Badger, as I have dealt honestly with you."

The Badger gathered the reins, and gathering them, he felt all the speed and the delicate intelligence of the horse like electricity in the leather which ran to his hands.

"Farewell, Standing Elk. I shall not forget."

With that, he twitched the reins to the side and that perfectly trained horse answered with a side-leap that carried him behind a tepee and out of sight of the Pawnee chief. The latter, at the same instant, raised a war yell that pierced the ears of the boy and brought an answering wail instantly from every sleeper within hearing of the shout.

9

As the Badger wheeled his horse into the first open space within the lodges, he saw a swirl of men issuing from the flaps of the tepees—most of them more than half naked, all yelling at the top of their lungs, some with weapons, and some without, and all huddling and jostling each other this way and that. To increase the confusion, there was the clamor of the dogs, which were darting in every direction through the mob, and adding as much to the disturbance as they did to the noise.

But in the meantime, there was a shout in a familiar key, and he saw Running Deer whip onto the back of a beautiful bay mare and drive into the press of people, yelling like a madman. And behind him scurried five other men, each seated upon a horse of some sort.

The Badger was instantly among them, and as they swept into the crowd together, knocking down women and children and making the warriors leap to either side for safety, they imparted a movement and then a heady impetus to the other horses which were already loose by the score and were rearing, plunging, biting, kicking like so many demons. And, in an instant, the whole mass of horseflesh had whirled off down the street with the robbers flattened on the backs or clinging to the sides of the mounts they had chosen.

But all of this happened in the snap of a finger. There was barely time for the Pawnees to know that enemies were in their midst when, like dust and leaves sucked up by a whirlwind, the whole herd of horses and the yelling Cheyennes among the rearmost, were shooting through the village and away from the open country beyond!

Not without a pursuit behind them. The Pawnees were on the naked backs of their horses in a twinkling and flying after the fugitives. For they were wild with rage. In the memory of their oldest man there had not been a horse raid executed upon them with such boldness and with such amazing success. The reason for the success was that very boldness. It was incalculable—not to be guarded against! But how hot were the Pawnees on the trail! Every man was on horseback; every man was whipping and kicking and yelling his way on the heels of the fugitives.

However, there is a tremendous impetus in flight itself. Nothing can match the first mile or two of a really frightened horse. And the stolen herd shot away with a dizzy speed, the thieves only gradually falling back from the unburdened horses.

But what amazed White Badger was that there was no need for him to fall back. He was sitting, indeed, in the midst of the wind itself. Only a strong pull on the tender mouth of the stallion could keep him back or, in another moment, he would have darted through the midst of the racing herd. But, as the Badger sat him with tight reins, what power, what gigantic power there was in the legs which spurned the ground and turned it to flowing black quicksilver beneath them!

There was only one danger, and that was to the guard who had been left with the horses among the hills. He had remained on his own pony, which was not overfleet, and now the leading Pawnees, and particularly one big man whom the Badger believed to be Standing Elk, began to gain rapidly. But a Cheyenne never abandons an imperiled brother. Every man among them dropped to the rear and sent a blast of bullets whirring back toward the pursuit, while one brought up a splendid animal—the horse which had gone to the Badger as a partial reward when he took his first scalp. That horse was brought alongside the brave on the failing pony. He made the change from running horse to horse with a wonderful courage and speed that brought the heart of the Badger into his throat—and then away shot the Cheyennes again, with bullets now humming everywhere about them. Here a horse squealed with pain, and there one fell; but starlight shooting from the back of a running horse doesn't make for the most accurate marksmanship in the world.

They had a vast advantage, those fugitives. They had the sweep of the herd before them to carry their horses along, and the pursuit faded and faded. And when the dawn came gray in the eastern sky, the horses were staggering, but the Pawnees were not in sight.

Running Deer and the Badger—because their mounts were the freshest—turned the herd and headed them toward the river. They crossed it before sun up, and now they were well on their way toward the Cheyennes.

They had been ten days on the downward journey; they were six days rushing back. For victory makes the heart light. They drove before them six score of horses, the cream of the Pawnee herd—nearly twenty horses for every man in the raiding party! And, sweetest of all, they carried two scalps at their belts.

There was joy enough for all, you will say, but most of all was there joy for Spotted Ear. He had led forth his first war party, and these were the spoils. Let the others have shares greater than his own, if fate would have it so. But even when Running Deer and the Badger, in days to come, told of the taking of those scalps and the counting of the coups, they would have to begin: "On a day, Spotted Ear led out a war party—"

That was glory enough for him! From this point on, his word would be listened to with perfect attention in the most weighty councils of the nation.

All the way, they never once sighted the Pawnees behind

them—for the very good reason that the day after the horse raid a great band of the Ogallalla Sioux came down to harry the Pawnees with war, and they had to give up the horse thief chase and turn back to sterner battle.

But, on the sixth day, the seven thieves rode very slowly. They rode slowly partly because all the horses were tired— except that unwearying miracle of flesh, Red Wind—and partly because they hoped that they would be sighted in the distance by some Cheyenne scout who might bear the good news to the town and cause a welcoming escort to pour out around them. But here I must pause to say that the thief among the Indians was not like the thief among the white men. He who stole from an enemy was a glorious hero, the more of a hero the greater the theft. And the more of sneaking skill with which the theft was accomplished, the more the exploit could be boasted of. So the seven, driving all those fine ponies ahead of them, were tremendously pleased.

And, because no mature man can be as happy as a boy, the happiest of the lot was the Badger. In fact, he had reason to rejoice. He had the two finest horses of the entire lot. Upon one he rode, and upon the other there was a fine saddle, together with a beautiful new rifle, two excellent new Colt revolvers, plus pounds and pounds of ammunition! Ay, and a scalp at his belt—in his tenth year, a scalp at his belt.

It was a prophecy of blood, but it was a prophecy which thrilled him to the soul, I assure you!

Presently a swarm from the village came out—men with their ponies at full speed, unsaddled and unbridled, and they themselves, like circus riders, clinging to the side of their horses and yelling their savage joy. They circled whooping around the herd of captured horses, pointing to the finer animals, and waving their arms, filled with deviltry, merriment, and vulgar enjoyment of life. The gravest person in the entire crowd of them was the white boy, the

57

Badger, who sat on the back of Red Wind, which was dancing sidewise, with his chin tucked almost back to his breast in the excitement.

He was so beautiful that even Indians grinned with joy at him. And these first Cheyennes, after they had congratulated their friends and their relations who were on the expedition and after they had poured praise upon the head of Spotted Ear, naturally gathered with a greater wonder around the youngster who rode the finest of the herd and who carried on a little pole a great scalp, newly sun-cured. He and Running Deer alone! But Running Deer had not the horse, or the shining new rifle.

Oh, yes, with all of his gravity, the Badger managed to draw the rifle from its holster—the finest of the breech-loading type—and show it to the admiring Cheyennes, and when they begged for a touch of it, he thrust it slowly, smiling, back into its holster. Then, one by one, he took out from their holsters of polished leather, two new Colts, perfect and brilliant with newness! These, the fine horse at his heels—led on a rawhide lariat—and the glorious Red Wind beneath him—there was no question as to who carried off the palm of this expedition.

They paused just out of reach of the town, where the women and the old men were seething on the outskirts, their yells of triumph wavering across the plains. And the boys and the girls—light-footed as the males, for all of that—came charging out to meet them. Here they split the herd deftly into seven equal sections and they went in one by one, Spotted Ear first, as the leader of the expedition, and then the eldest warrior following him, and last Running Deer, with the Badger behind him.

Ah, what a climax it was; the two boys of the expedition had gathered in the richest fruits. And how rich a fruit a Pawnee scalp is to a Cheyenne cannot be taught from a page of cold print!

Yet most of the yelling was for Running Deer. Well, he was a beautiful creature, that Indian. And in his boyhood

58

he must have been an Indian Apollo. Besides, he was so good-natured that the entire tribe loved him. And when they shouted for him, he was continually turning and waving with both hands and a wide smile toward the Badger, as though to tell the tribesmen that the real homage was due to this man-child who had outdone them all.

He could not persuade the others, however. And they looked with only a mild satisfaction upon the splendid loot which the Badger had brought with him. Do you ask us why? Because, simply, a man who is in league with mysterious powers does not deserve so much credit as does the man who works by the power of his unassisted naked hand.

And if there had been doubts concerning the youngster before that day, there was not the slightest doubt after the scalp dance which terminated it.

The Badger was an enchanter, one to be respected and feared. But who could love, really, one so young who dealt with the dark powers and derived benefits from them through, who could tell, what dismal contracts? There was no question as to the very great bigness of the medicine of the Badger. But there was a sizable doubt as to the *goodness* of it!

Only two hearts were too full for doubting. Little Grouse and Rising Bull. Little Grouse wept with purest joy as she tied up the horses and ran to borrow lariats to tie up more of them when her own leather gave out. She cried again with joy when she saw the guns and the scalp and the two fine steeds which had fallen to the share of the Badger. But when tears ran down the face of Rising Bull it was from sheer satisfaction because White Badger had come safely home to them.

10

They held the scalp dance at once in a haste which did not make it less significant. There was only one awkward dance on that occasion, and the awkward one was, of course, the Badger. He was used to being in the eye of the people, but he was annoyed beyond measure to have to prance up and down with a ring of other braves, the six who had accompanied him on this expedition. The little circle faced inwards towards the dangling pole from which the two scalps dangled, and as they chanted their song the mass of people who watched and listened maintained the most perfect silence. It was only when one of the dancers whooped—for those yells of exultation were all that distinguished this dance from any other—that the crowd joined in heart-thrilling shrieks of triumph. Presently Spotted Ear leaped to the inside of the circle and began a loud chant of his own, telling how the thought of starting on that warpath had come to him, and how he had gone to the Badger and found him lying asleep on the breast of the river and called to him, and the Badger had swam ashore and sat on the back of the white wolf and listened.

This was merely a proper beginning for Spotted Ear's narrative which became more wonderful every moment. Spotted Ear went back to the circle of dancers with shouts of high applause ringing in his ear. One after another the rest of the party sprang to the inside of the circle and each had some marvel to tell of the work which he had done. Last, Running Deer, with a shriek and a bound, touched the scalp which he had taken and began the narration of what he had done. And, as he shouted and chanted and acted out the story, quick wine began to wriggle through the veins of the Badger. For it seemed according to the tale of Running Deer that it was not an old man he had slain but a youth, a giant of stature and strength, and they had struggled mightily together until at last with the strength of his grip Running Deer had broken the wrist bones of the other.

"The knife fell out of his hand—whoop-e-e-e!" screamed Running Deer. "I snatched it out of the air as it fell. I drove it into his breast and through a rib and into his heart. The blood leaped out on my hand and my wrist, and the Pawnee fell to the ground. I sat on his back and I took his scalp that the Cheyennes might be more glorious and the lodge of Running Deer might be pointed at by other men—by warriors!"

Running Deer sprang back to his place, and the Badger had come to his turn. To miss that turn was to proclaim oneself less than a man and miss half the sweets of victory. But the Badger had no intention of missing his chance. Naked like all the rest except for the single crotch-piece, he leaped into the center of the ring with the light glowing on the sun-polished bronze of his body. He stood with his hands flung above his head, his head raised, his body strained upward on his toes, and his arms rigid with exultation.

"Listen to me, brothers, I am the White Badger. By the black water I found a great chief. The lights of Pawnee lodges were on the river beside him, red lights, like his blood. He was about to die. He did not think of that. He came riding to me as tall as a tree. I ran at him. He saw the stars on my knife and raised his own arm to strike."

He paused to tilt his head still further back and laugh and weave his body from side to side. And men and women and little children strained forward to hear him.

"Then I caught his arm by the elbow. He thought that

his elbow had struck on a rock, but it was my hand, and his knife hung helpless in the air like an icicle in the winter that hangs from a stone by the river. So I held up his arm. I struck him between the bones at the bottom of his neck. His voice became a sound like a bubbling stream and he fell and rolled on the ground. I took off his scalp while he still lived. Then I stabbed him through the back and stripped him of his clothes, because he was a great chief. His clothes of beadwork and of quillwork are now in my lodge. Go to Little Grouse and ask for them. Go to the Rising Bull and ask and he will show you a new rifle, and revolvers and much powder and much lead for bullets. He will show you, too, how Tirawa was kind to the White Badger and led him into the camp of the Pawnees and covered the eyes of their men with sleep and turned their great warriors into stone. They saw the Badger coming and they trembled and they reached for their guns, but Tirawa covered their eyes and put them in a fog and turned them to stone. And Tirawa led the Badger through the camp to the center of it and showed to him a horse so bright that he shone even under the stars—the stars shone in him as if he were a pool of water. The Badger took that horse, the Red Wind. He took the best horse in the Pawnee nation. He took the horse of Standing Elk and rode away and brought back all that he took in the battle to Little Grouse and Rising Bull to make them happy."

The entire tribe went mad with joy when they saw that a boy like this had actually taken a scalp of a great man among the Pawnees.

How great they did not know until the next day when word came in from the Pawnees that the first man killed by the Badger had been no less a person than the brother of Standing Elk, a warrior hardly less celebrated than that chief. Clouded Sky was his name.

That part of the news was delightful enough; for it was known, at the same time, that the whole tribe was mourning for the death of Clouded Sky. But the second part of the story which was carried to camp was not so delightful. Red Eagle himself came in the evening to talk it over with Rising Bull and Little Grouse and the White Badger. He came in, agreeable to fixed custom, passed in the right direction around the fire, and was asked by Rising Bull to take a seat next to him on a folded buffalo robe which Little Grouse spread for the guest. It was noticeable, now, that though there were three families and two efficient warriors in that lodge, yet so great was the prestige which the Badger had gained in this latest exploit, that Rising Bull had been granted the place of honor just opposite the flap of the tent.

At his side Red Eagle sat down, but his eyes were fixed upon the Badger.

He told them the story softly, slowly. How the same report which came to him of the death of Clouded Sky brought also with it the unlucky tidings that Standing Elk, the most dreaded enemy of the Cheyenne nation, had been at the mercy of a Cheyenne knife which had not struck home but, instead, had chosen to accept a bribe, and the price of the life of that terrible chief was taken in the form of a horse! And then the guilty Cheyenne had dared to come back to his tribe; only he had been wise enough not to tell the story of that night's work in full!

So, speaking softly, the chief detailed the wicked story of mercy given to a foe. And his gloomy eyes were fixed upon the face of the boy so steadily and so ominously that White Hawk stood up and stepped before his young master and growled in the face of the chief.

"What is the soul of a man who values riches more than glory?" asked the chief in the end.

It would have been hard to tell whether shame or wonder most filled the eyes of Little Grouse and her husband. But there was fear in Little Grouse, for she felt that she had made a painted image and the painted image had turned into a man! She had dreamed of a great, a terrible warrior, and the mighty man of war had become a fact!

63

"He is new on the warpath!" she told Red Eagle gravely.

"He is young, but his brain is old," said the chief. "Let him come with me and speak for himself."

He beckoned to the boy who cast a single praying glance at his foster mother. When she nodded, he rose without a word and walked out of the lodge behind the chief, White Hawk gliding at his heels.

They stepped alone through the black of the night, and the hand of Red Eagle rested on the shoulder of the youth.

"Tell me," said Red Eagle gently, "that you have been very wrong."

It occurred to the boy that, if he admitted error, all would be forgiven though a lesson might be preached to him. But he did not feel like admitting error. Nothing, indeed, was farther from his mind.

"I have done what Tirawa told me to do," said he.

Red Eagle spat into the dust with fury.

"Did Tirawa tell you to spare the life of a Pawnee that lay under your knife? Do not say it, my son, because then the ghost of the next Cheyenne who is scalped by Standing Elk will come to haunt you and moan in your lodge in winter nights and make your wives barren and fill you with unhappiness!"

"Well," said the boy—and now the white brain began to work in him—"he stood there in front of me as close as you are. When he turned at me, I had the point of my knife an inch from his heart. What would you have had me do?"

"Stab—strike home!" cried Red Eagle savagely.

"I can stab, too," said the Badger with sufficient egotism. "Did I not kill Clouded Sky with my own hand, so that the heat of the blood went spouting up to my elbow? But Clouded Sky was ready to fight. How could I kill a helpless man?"

Red Eagle stopped with a gasp of purest wonder.

"Is it not better," he asked, "to kill without danger to yourself?"

"There is no pleasure in that," said the boy.

"Do you mean that?" asked the chief, striking a hand across his forehead, because he felt that he was listening to madness.

"Consider this," said the boy. "If White Hawk had been caught in a trap so that I could safely beat him almost to death and teach him to obey me, would that have been a thing worth doing?"

"Answer me!" said the chief, still unwilling to believe his ears. "If you could creep into a Pawnee camp and if you could find ten men lying on their backs asleep with their throats naked, would you not cut their throats one by one?"

The Badger, unaware of the deep significance of this question, paused and yawned.

"Bah!" he said at last. "That would be better work for the White Hawk!"

"Answer me!" cried the chief. "Would you not do it yourself?"

"Consider this," said the Badger. "Are you glad to dry scalps in the smoke of your lodge?"

"Yes," said the chief, "we are glad to take scalps."

"But do you take the scalps of buffalo calves when they are hurt and cannot stand up to help themselves?"

"That is a foolish question," answered Red Eagle with some sternness. "Why should one scalp a calf?"

"Ah," cried the Badger, for his nimble wits had worked quite around the Indian and then back again. "You will admit that. And I say that the pleasure in a scalp is knowing that it came from the head of a fighting man who struck bravely but not straight enough. But who will want the scalp of a sleeping man? It is nothing! It is the scalp of a calf which was helpless! I could not take it. Tirawa would stop my hand from making the circle. That is the truth and it is right. You yourself will now say so!"

"Boy—child—" The chief was about to add "Fool!" but he hesitated and changed his mind. For one could not tell about this strange youth. At any moment he might give a

65

sign to the wolf-dog, for instance, and the teeth of that monster would be in the throat of Red Eagle. It was very well to handle this youngster with a considerable caution. One could never tell what might happen from one who dealt with spirits and powers of another world!

"Go back to your lodge," said Red Eagle at last, "and tell your father that I must speak to him in this place at once!"

11

There was hardly a more important crisis than this in the entire life of White Badger. When Rising Bull came to Red Eagle he was told briefly that his son must prepare at once to leave the village and journey to the main section of the tribe where the chief medicine man Black Antelope was to be found.

"Because," said the pious Red Eagle, "this boy had in his hands a greater chance of doing harm to our tribe's enemies than he may ever have again, and he did not take advantage of it for one of two reasons: either he was too covetous of that famous horse, Red Wind, or else he was not properly instructed in what is right and good for a warrior to do."

"Ah," said Rising Bull, "my wife and I talk to him words that are like iron. Also, he is still young!"

"Brother," said Red Eagle gently, "I know that your heart is good and I think that the heart of Little Grouse is good also. But I am sure that the mind of the White Badger is growing up in a strange way. We must send him to a man who will teach him better ways. Tomorrow he must start!"

Rising Bull went back to his wife and said to her tersely: "We are all in danger. It is said that wrong thoughts are in the head of the Badger. Therefore one of us must have put them there. The life of Standing Elk was under the point of his knife—and he let that man live! Will you think, Little Grouse, of what his fame would have been before he became a warrior if in one night he had killed two such chiefs among the Pawnees? I do not know what has been teaching him strange things. Tomorrow he starts to live at the feet of the Black Antelope. His mind will be made good if it can be done. In the meantime, remember the things which you have taught him!"

He said this with a frown which made Little Grouse tremble and remember, though he had never struck her, that there was more weight in the one hand remaining to him than there was in both of hers. She took the White Badger aside, therefore, and asked him first in a voice filled with trembling fury why he had not slain the great chief when the golden opportunity was at hand.

"Look!" said the impertinent young rascal. "I have ridden and talked with warriors. Why should I answer the questions of a squaw?"

"Ah, little devil!" cried she, and took him by the nape of the neck.

There was a great deal of muscular power in the lithe young body of the Badger, but since his foster mother once had him in her hands—those hands so strengthened and hardened by work—it was very doubtful whether he could escape from her grip—at least before he had received a stern drubbing. He did not intend to risk the fight if there was no need.

"Mother," he said through his teeth, "you are a fool. Take your hand from me or I shall have the White Hawk rip open your flabby old throat. Or if he misses that, I have a knife in my hand!"

She released him instantly.

"There is no good blood in you," she told him savagely.

"There is blood which you do not know," said the Badger.

At this, Little Grouse trembled. It was only very rarely that a word escaped the lips of the boy concerning his white skin—sun-bronzed as it now was to the darkness of any Indian.

"Ah, little Badger," said she, trying to fondle him, "you have never loved me!"

He struck her hands away.

"I do not wish to be mauled by a woman," said he. "What have you to say to me?"

And she trembled again. The only love that she had for him was the love of the riches which, she was convinced, would flow from him upon her husband and upon herself. For the rest, she partly distrusted him because he was not of her blood, and partly hated him because he had once been a tool in her hands and was now something more!

So she told him, briefly, what Red Eagle had decided concerning him.

She said, "Black Antelope is a wise man and a good man. Some people say that he loves wealth. I cannot tell. You can tell when you put your bright eyes on him. Go sit at his feet. Watch him. Speak gently when he speaks to you. Remember what he says. Look at me, White Badger! Will it do you any harm to learn by heart even those things which you do not believe?"

The Badger shrugged his shoulders. And he countered on her, "Why have you told me so many lies? Partly about myself, and partly about other things, so that I cannot tell what to trust! I have to learn everything over again from the beginning for myself! But I tell you this, that you or Red Eagle or Black Antelope could not make me kill a sleeping man!"

She shook her head at him. This sort of reasoning was far past her comprehension.

68

"I may have told you strange things and taught you some that were not true. But I never taught you such folly as this, White Badger!"

"*You* have not told me. I cannot tell where I learn things. Perhaps from Tirawa," said the Badger, as insolent as ever. "As for going to Black Antelope, I may leave Red Eagle, but I may not go to Black Antelope. There is much room on the plains, and there are many tribes!"

He turned his back on her sharply, but, in his heart, he felt that she had given him the very best of good advice. Furthermore, no matter how he wished to stab her with his cruelty, he would have been the unhappiest boy in the world if he had not been able to think of himself as a Cheyenne, heart and soul.

He prepared for his departure in the morning, therefore, and when the time came, Red Eagle himself came and made a picture of the way he was to travel. It was an art which all of the plains tribes possessed in the old days. These drawings were crude enough, but they could represent trees, rivers, hills, and other things which the traveler would meet by the way. And so Red Eagle made out the map and instructed the boy in the way he was to travel.

"Sit at the feet of Black Antelope," he said. "Learn much. Become wise. If I could leave my village and go to him to learn as you are to learn, I should be very happy! You go not like a boy but like a great warrior, with two fine horses and with many guns!"

For while young White Badger rode one of the horses which he had captured from the Pawnees, he led Red Wind behind him, to keep that fine animal ever fresh and strong in case of times of sudden need.

Little Grouse came to weep for him; Rising Bull rode out with him a short distance into the prairie; and so he was gone and presently he was all alone. All the plains were green, and all about him seemed a rolled lawn running to the horizon incredibly far and pale. And looking up at the immensity of the pale sky and down to the height

69

of the strong horse of dead Clouded Sky which he rode, it seemed to the boy that he had shrunk very, very small indeed! He was almost nothing, in fact!

It was only when he remembered a certain scalp hanging in the lodge of Rising Bull that his heart expanded again. And he rode on singing a soft Indian chant which had no particular meaning, except that it fumbled with the idea of what happens to the seed in the ground when the wet of the spring and the warmth of the spring sun comes upon it, and it told of how the green shaft rises from the ground, of how it climbs slowly and steadily, and of how the fruit comes at last. He did not think of the meaning, however. He thought rather of Black Antelope—and rather than of Black Antelope he thought of the glorious lawn upon which his horses were stepping. His horses— and his guns!

You will understand why he was happy again very shortly as he sent his horses ahead across the prairie. He was half a day away before he found a thing worthy of comment. Then he came upon a streak of black ashes over which sprung ribs of iron, and iron tires from great wheels lay upon the ground. He rode up and down this streak of black, which was in the form of a great semicircle.

He knew well enough what had happened. In a surprise attack, some lucky band of Indians had thrust in between the too slowly closing ends of the caravan, and this was the result; plunder, murder, scalps, and then the fire! How many scalps, however! And particularly, how many scalps were there like that one which hung in the lodge of Red Eagle—of long, black, silken tresses! His heart always leaped when he looked at it. He promised himself such another, on a day!

Do you wonder at the unnatural heart of this boy, who knew that he was white and yet wanted nothing so much as a white scalp? And the scalp of a white woman above all? Well, for one thing the only whites he had ever seen were occasional traders—and a greasy, sharp-eyed lot they were!

70

He had never laid eyes upon a white woman! For the rest, although he knew that he was white, he knew it in a very surface fashion. He knew that his skin was white, but he never pondered upon that subject. His heart and his soul were red—all red—all Cheyenne red, he told himself. He felt no kinship with any other people!

So he exulted over the ruin of this caravan. It might have been a trader's possession. Or it might have been a train of settlers' wagons, slowly treading west and west. The Badger never knew, but he remained to wonder over it. For his part, he hoped that the train was of the latter kind. He had heard much concerning the white women, and everything that he had heard was disgusting. It would have been pleasant to see so many of them as might have belonged to this outfit, running and screaming—

I do not care to step any farther into the ugly mind of the Badger on this topic. I only dare to say that he was smiling and even chuckling to himself as he cantered away across the plains again.

It was on the third day that he saw, in the distance, a pale band of mist streaking toward the sky. It was close to the evening. He waited until the coming of the dark in the hope of locating the fire by a little spark of light, but when the blackness settled there was nothing against the ground except the bright, big faces of the rising stars. He started off in the direction from which he had seen the mist— which might be smoke. When he had gone forward a certain distance, he dismounted and secured the two horses. Then he went ahead on foot.

One never could tell. It might be a party of more than three. In which case, he would have to retreat as fast as he could. Or it might be a party of two, in which case he might try two shots from his rifle—or one, when the victory was certain. Or, again, it might be Pawnees—

Nevertheless, his heart grew bigger and bigger with joyous excitement as he crept forward, pushing the rifle before him. He went slowly and cautiously, and yet a real

Indian would have gone just twice as slowly and with three times as much care.

It cost him all of an hour. And then he came on a thing worthwhile, indeed—a flare of red so thin and so faint that it would not be visible a hundred yards away, so misty was that light. But, as he came closer and closer, he could see well enough. The skillfully built fire of buffalo chip had been so screened that the light was shut away from all but one side. And there was a dim scent of food in the air to the sensitive nostrils of the Badger.

The fragrance of tobacco smoke overrode all else, however. The Badger came closer and closer and more and more behind the white man. Oh, how beautiful was the snaky stealth of his movements now! He melted through space. The grass dared not rustle beneath him. And, at length, he came to a halt a scant six feet behind the stranger. Here he lay on his belly and snuggled the gun against his shoulder. The small of the back—or between the shoulder blades—or the neck—or the back of the head. How could one make a selection among so many tempting targets? He decided, however, that a bullet through the head might spoil the pure beauty of the scalp, which promised to be a rare one, for this man had long, fair hair, almost like the hair of a white woman.

But now, as he sat with his back to the murderer, he clasped his arms around his knees and tilted back his head and began to sing, softly, and then more loudly.

No Indian would have cared for that music. For what the Indian loved in music was a droning chanting with many a yell to spice it, and a broken, staggering rhythm. And something to sing about, too—death, victory—such themes as these. But I tell you that the Badger, lying in the dark of the plains, and understanding not a word that was said, found the melody so sweet and so sad that tears stung his eyes.

He was suddenly afraid that, by enchantment, this man was about to blind him! For you must remember that it was

72

many a year since the Badger had known tears! The tears cleared away. He crept closer, and made surer of his aim—and then the solitary victim began to clap his hands together in a lively fashion and sing a jig tune.

The Badger found that it was all he could do to keep from laughing, and the muscle of his heart loosened, and he was very happy. He waited until that song ended, and then, smiling, he curled his finger on the trigger.

Then a thrill of very real terror ran through him when he found that he could not pull that trigger! Look, look! There were half a dozen ponies in the train of this traveler, and their big, bulky, promising packs lay on the ground. And there were guns, too! More than one, to be sure! Here, indeed, was enough wealth to break the heart of every Cheyenne with envy. And yet the Badger lay stretched behind his man and could not shoot!

12

He was frightened, as I said before, by this thrill of humanity and the desire to give fair play to the other. And I suppose that I may claim the sense of fair play as the prerogative of the white man from this one instance, if no more! At least, it was an emotion which burned the heart of the Badger.

He reached a trifle forward, and the muzzle of the gun touched the back of the man by the dying fire. The latter stiffened a little, a very little, and then he spoke in English. There was no answer from the Badger, who of course had forgotten every syllable of that language. The stranger tried French and Spanish with no better result.

"Be quiet!" said the Badger at last. "And raise your hands!"

The other obeyed, and the Badger, taking a Colt instead of a rifle, held it close to the back of the stranger. The latter sat quite still, his arms raised well above his head. And the Badger went rapidly through his clothes. He took a revolver and a hunting knife—there were no other weapons. He took, also, a wallet with some papers and a little gold in it.

"Now," said the Badger, as he stood back, "build up the fire a little."

It was freshened instantly and obediently by the other, and the Badger noticed that though the stranger worked without a sign of haste or a suspicious movement toward the weapons on the ground, still he did not appear to be overcome with fear.

The fire, being freshened, showed a tongue of flame, and by that flickering light the Badger looked into the face of a man who was to mean much in his life—a wide-shouldered man, thirty years old, with sun-faded hair, and a good fighting American face. I can think of no better way of describing it. He had a pair of bright, keen eyes which some men had already learned to fear greatly, but the Badger was a little unused to the thought of fear, connected with other men.

Besides, he was angered by the cheerfulness of the white man.

"Well," said the traveler, speaking the Cheyenne tongue so perfectly that the Badger heard him with a violent start, "do you want the fire as a signal to your friends?"

"I want the light," answered the boy grimly, "so that I can see how your scalp looks—while it is on your head!"

The other merely laughed, and rubbed that same scalp complacently.

"I think it will stay there for a long time yet," he answered.

"Waugh!" snarled the Badger, and the Colt jerked in its muzzle in his hand.

To his great astonishment, the white man showed not the slightest alteration of countenance.

"What is your name?" asked the Badger.

"Dan Croydon," said the other.

He, in turn, was a little disappointed when no sign of recognition appeared on the face of this gloomy boy. For though Danny was now only thirty, he had been on the plains for the past half of that life and through the last dozen years he had been spreading his reputation rapidly. It seemed hardly possible that there could be a Cheyenne who did not know of him. But he did not know the peculiar solitariness with which the Badger had been raised.

He presently had his own enlightenment concerning the identity of the little Cheyenne, however. White Hawk had been strictly ordered not to leave the horses, but now curiosity had proved too strong for his wolfish heart and he had hurried up to trail his master. He appeared out of the dusk—a glimmering form, gigantic, and looking, as the firelight touched him, purest white.

"Ah!" breathed Danny Croydon. "The White Hawk— and you are the famous boy of Red Eagle's band—you are the White Badger!"

I know that Danny has a way of throwing an immense cordiality into his voice, and these simple words, from him, must have sounded like a great tribute to the Badger.

He grunted, but he acknowledged the tribute by sitting down suddenly cross-legged, the muzzle of the Colt still carefully turned upon the white man. He spoke sharply to White Hawk, and the wolf-dog trotted into the dark. He spoke again, and Croydon had the uncomfortable knowledge that a grown wolf squatted behind him, ready to break his neck at the word of his young master. It was apparent that the Badger knew this, also; for he laid his revolver aside and sighed with a bit of relief.

75

He was much intrigued by this white man. This was one unlike the whisky vending traders whom he had seen hitherto. This was a face more akin to those other faces of white men which moved through a dim mist of his distant past—ghosts of faces, and ghosts of voices. Every year, now, his memory of that distant time was clearing and two people in particular were standing out more and more brightly for him: Tommy Tucker and Rose Tucker—though still they were to the mind of this boy nothing more than undiscovered emotion, unseen mists and not faces at all. However, he recognized that in the man before him there was an entirely new type which was worthy of study, at least.

"Why do you look at me so hard?" asked Croydon, smiling.

"Because I wonder why I am not sitting on your back, sawing at your scalp," said the boy.

"If you'd meant that," said Croydon, "you would have crashed a bullet through my spine. No, there's no fear of that. But—"

Here he paused, for it seemed to him that there was something in the face of the youth which was worthy of more attention. Hitherto there had been thick shadows upon it and Croydon had noticed only the long black hair and the black, bright eyes, and the high cheekbones. As a matter of fact, the Badger was about as ugly as any Indian that I have ever seen, but here the fire tossed up a glow of light and the first thing that Croydon found missing from the makeup of this "Indian" was the coppery-red color in the skin! Then he looked closer and saw a certain delicacy in the carving of the lean, square chin—

"By God!" said Croydon.

"Stranger," said the boy, "I shall be rich with this pack and these horses."

"You will not take them," said Croydon.

"So?" said the boy, and grinned like a wolf.

"Does a man steal from his own tribesmen?"

"Are you a Cheyenne?" asked the boy, a little staggered, because indeed the Cheyenne tongue was perfect on the lips of Danny Croydon.

"I am white, and you are white," said Danny Croydon.

The boy sneered.

"I am Cheyenne," he said. He grew a little excited, for the stinging thought was working under his skin. "I am all Cheyenne. My father and my mother are Cheyenne."

"Your real father and your real mother," said Danny Croydon, "were scalped and murdered by the Cheyennes."

It was a staggering way to put it. This truth smashed against the face of the Badger and made his head swim. Of course Danny was only guessing, but it was not hard to guess, now that he had noticed the truth. This boy was white! His eyes, and something nameless in the quality of his voice, showed his blood.

"Did you see them scalped and killed?" asked the boy.

But Croydon countered: "Did your mother give you to the Cheyennes for nothing—for a song? Do white people sell their children to the Cheyennes?"

"Much talk is bad!" said the Badger.

He was beginning to grow very sick in the pit of the stomach.

"I am all Cheyenne!" said he, but his voice was only a gasp.

Croydon merely smiled, and he saw a glint of tragedy in the face of the boy. His own smile went out. He began to be sorry.

"You are all Cheyenne while you're a boy," he admitted to the Badger. "But after a little while the Badger will be a man. Unless the Pawnees get him first. And Standing Elk will try his best, eh?"

"You have heard even of that?"

"I have heard."

"You have made me sad. If I had pulled the trigger, you would not have been alive to talk to me!"

"You could not pull the trigger, you see, because a white

77

man cannot shoot from behind without a warning. It is not fair!"

"Ah!" cried the Badger. "*You* understand!"

"I do. And not a Cheyenne in all your tribe could tell you why you could not pull the trigger!"

"No!" sighed the boy. "They could not tell!"

"I can take you, White Badger, where thousands of men will understand because they feel just the same way about it that you do. Will you come with me?"

"I go to see Black Antelope and hear him talk, because I did not stab Standing Elk."

"You had a chance to do that? I thought Clouded Sky was your man?"

"I took the scalp of Clouded Sky," said the boy, and he struck his chest. "By the edge of the water, I saw him with the lights of the lodges—"

Croydon appeared to recognize the tone of this narrative, for he broke in suddenly: "Very well! You killed Clouded Sky and then you came on Standing Elk—"

"Before his lodge—by chance. He turned around, and there was my knife at his breast. But Tirawa caught my arm by the elbow and held it and I could not strike!"

The face of Danny Croydon must have lighted then.

"Good boy!" said he. "Will you come with me, White Badger? Will you go back to your own people with me? You shall have half of my packs—and they are filled with the finest furs. There will be a little fortune in your half of the stuff!"

"It is all mine if I wish to speak with this," said the insolent boy, and he touched the gun beside him, "or if I speak to the dog. It would all be mine, then."

"You could not do it, White Badger," said Croydon. "I have never harmed you. I have traded fair with the Indians, or else I trap my own furs. You could not rob me, my friend. Tirawa would chase you with thunder. But if you will go with me, you will be a brother to me, Badger. And half of what I have shall be yours—and there will be a way to fix you up with schools—you will learn something—"

"Why should I leave my people?" said the boy. And he stood up suddenly and moved a long step back into the encircling darkness.

"Because they are *not* your people. They've murdered your people, White Badger. Get the truth out of them!"

"I am all Cheyenne in my heart!" groaned the Badger.

"If you were Cheyenne, my scalp would be at your belt, and you would have my packs spread open!"

"Ah," sighed the boy, "I wish that I had never seen you!"

"You cannot help hearing me, White Badger, and if you steal away now, it is because you are afraid of meeting the truth about yourself! Is that true?"

"It is a great lie!" cried the Badger.

"You will never forget what I say. Listen to me, White Badger, for I know! The day will come, sooner or later, when you will strap your pack behind your saddle and come riding to me or to other white men. You will wash the paint off your face and come to us. And I hope by your God and mine, White Badger, that when that time comes there is the blood of no white man on your hands. For if there is, then the line is drawn, lad. Remember! You could never come back to your own kind then—"

But the White Badger, with a sort of frightened moan, had fled into the dark of the night, and the wolf-dog whisked after him.

13

From that white self which Danny Croydon had called up so vividly before him, the Badger fled through the night and to the horses. And then on the back of Red Wind, he flew away on his journey and traveled half of the night. He was hungry, now, to reach the end of his journey and to converse with Black Antelope. For that purpose he pushed ahead, without mercy on his horses. For he felt that the great medicine man, that link between Tirawa and common men, could easily drive away the doubts which tormented him and could make him the thing which he wished to be—all Cheyenne—Cheyenne to the heart. And yet, as he pushed away across the plains, again and again the voice and the face of Croydon cut in between him and his goal and an instinct in him said: "Wait and hear him again. For he can convince you!"

But all men know that there is a magic in the tongues of white men and that they can say the thing which is not so with wonderful ease and make others believe also.

So felt the Badger, and he rushed on until he came to the main village of the Cheyennes, where the medicine lodge stood in which medicine dances in times of peril brought down to earth the decisions of Tirawa in a palpable form.

The thoughts of boys are not the thoughts of men. What the Badger wondered at as he rode into this permanent camp was the frightful amount of female labor which must have been needed to pound and to scrape the tons and tons of hides of buffalo cows which had been used in the making of the lodges.

He thought that by this time he and White Hawk must be known through the Cheyenne tribes, and to the boys, most of all. But there was one ignoramus who did *not* know. He sent two big half-breed dogs to tackle White Hawk and the Badger drew rein to look on and laugh with a malicious pleasure while the Hawk took those dogs one by one as they rushed on, sprawled each on its back with a shoulder-thrust, and then slashed the throat across. He left two struggling, dying bodies in the street of the Indian village, and then he rode on. And behind him he heard the wail of the boy for his two champions!

The Badger did not care for these things. He went to the lodge of the great medicine man. There were other men of the same profession in the nation, of course, but this was the great one, the peculiar spring out of which Tirawa chose to pour his wisdom upon the sons of men.

When he tapped at the flap of the lodge it was thrust aside and a hag's face looked out at him. She gave him only one glance and then caught him by the neck with a long and powerful arm and dragged him inside. She flung him down on the nearest buffalo robe and instantly proceeded with the work at hand.

She was assisting her husband. And that husband was Black Antelope. The boy had seen him before but never so close—never with a wish to be so close. An old, ugly face, with a great mouth that twisted up at each corner and was wreathed around with wrinkled skin, as though he smiled. He was covered with paint, now, and he and his wife were in the act of purifying themselves with smoke. A small quantity of sweet grass was burning on the coals of the fire and with this smoke the pair were rubbing their bodies and heads. At the side of the lodge, reclining on a robe with a most desolate expression upon her face, was a squaw of middle-age, shuddering with the chill which comes over a fevered body when it is exposed to the open air. She was very sick—very sick indeed, and yet she kept burning eyes of hope fixed upon the medicine man and his wife. The latter, having purified himself with the smoke to his own satisfaction, now took a roll of skin, and, carefully unfolding it, brought out a long pipe stem.

At the sight of this holy of holies, the boy shuddered and crouched lower in his place.

Black Antelope held the pipe stem up to the sky.

"Hear me, Tirawa," he said. "Be good to us. Be good to your people, the Cheyennes, and when you look down on me, see this sick women who is standing so close to me. See her here, at my hand, Tirawa. She is sick. There is a black spirit in her. Her legs are weak. Her knees bend under

81

her. Her eyes are dim. She has a pain in her belly, where food will not stay."

Having prayed in this fashion to Tirawa, he went over to the body of the sick woman with the stem of the pipe, rubbing each part in which she had complained of suffering. After all of this, she stood up and walked lightly from the tepee with a smile on her face. And to the wondering eyes of the boy, it seemed that half of her illness had disappeared at a stroke.

He stood up as the eyes of the wonder-worker fell upon him now.

"Stand close to me, my son," said the medicine man, "and I shall tell you where you are sick—in your body or in your heart!"

He stared fixedly down into the eyes of the boy. "It is a sickness of the heart, White Badger!" said he.

There were two wonderful things about this, in the belief of the Badger. In the first place that, without White Hawk nearby, the famous healer had been able to recognize him and know his name. He, a child, and Black Antelope, the greatest man in the tribe. In the second place, that he should have known that it was for no physical illness that he had come to him.

"How could you know all of this?" asked the Badger. "Has Red Eagle sent a messenger ahead of me?"

The medicine man shook his head and smiled indulgently at the youth. He led him to the flap of the lodge and pointed into the sky. A dim and circling speck, an eagle, rode on the upper currents of the air.

"If I speak now," said Black Antelope, "do you not think that the eagle would hear and come to me?"

"Do it!" cried the boy. "Do it, and you shall have that horse—no, not the red one, but the other, with the good saddle on his back!"

The medicine man licked his lips, and in each of his eyes there was lighted a little fire.

"Shall I call the eagle out of the air over the lodges,

where an arrow might fly at him from the hand of a fool?
No, but I, Black Antelope, walk out every day and am
alone on the plains; and every day an eagle stoops out of
the wind and tells me the things which I need to know!"

Here the boy gaped indeed.

"That blackbird on the top of that lodge, cocking his
head at us, does it speak to you, Black Antelope?"

"It speaks to me," nodded the old man.

"What does it say?" breathed the boy, entranced.

"That you have come from Red Eagle to me and that you
have come very fast!"

"Ah!" cried the boy, "as fast as two horses could bring
me. But how could that bird be talking when it makes no
sound?"

"Do you see the feathers of its throat quivering? It is
speaking inside its throat, and that is the way most birds
and beasts speak to me. What I hear, no other man can
hear. And yet, any man could learn to do so!"

"How?" cried the Badger, now trembling with delight
and with wonder.

"By spending thirty years in prayer to Tirawa," grinned
the old Cheyenne. "Are you ready to spend that time?"

"Waugh!" snorted the boy in disgust. "I shall be dead
long before that year comes!"

"That is good," said the medicine man. "If one cannot be
wise, it is best to die young! But why has Red Eagle sent
you to me?"

"Does not the blackbird tell you?" asked the Badger,
cocking his head up like the bird itself.

"It will if I ask it—no, it may have to fly far back to the
city of Red Eagle and ask there and then fly here again. It
was sent with only one message—to tell me that you came
straight and fast."

It was enough to convince the boy. These definite par-
ticulars about the missions on which well-identified birds
flew in the service of the medicine man quite overwhelmed
him. And he poured forth the sudden tide of all his sins:

the mercy which he had shown to the great Pawnee, and the second mercy which he had shown to the rich white man, who also had been in his power, he and all the ponies and packs of that trader and trapper! But, last of all, he ended with a great wail: "Oh, Black Antelope, make me what I want to be—all a redman, all Cheyenne to the heart of the White Badger. I want to be all Cheyenne! Make me that!"

The Black Antelope retired to the deeps of the lodge and there he stood shaking his head, as though the difficulties of this task were too great for him.

"It is a huge task!" said he. "First you must be forgiven for your sins. Next you must be taught over again all that a good Cheyenne should know. But while your heart is filled with wickedness for the bad things which you have done, no teaching can get into you. For your heart is filled with badness!"

The Badger was filled with terror which he swallowed as well as he could.

"Can I be forgiven? But how?" he asked.

"Why did you let Standing Elk live? For the sake of a fine horse!"

"No!" cried the boy stoutly, and a flush of red blood showed through the tan of his cheeks as it never could show in the face of a true Indian. "It was not for the horse, but because I did not wish to kill him."

"There were two reasons," said Black Antelope. He raised his withered, great-jointed hand. "Do not tell me which was the greater reason. Black Antelope has been inside your head. He knows your thoughts! And the horse was the greatest reason. And your sin will be forgiven by Tirawa—I hear the blackbird say it!—if you give away that Red Wind! Give him to another man—to the wisest man you know!"

The life left the eyes of the Badger. He went to the flap of the tent and looked out with a sigh on the young stallion. Then he turned back to Black Antelope.

"I'd rather die now," said the Badger. "If death can catch me when I am on the back of Red Wind!"

From the eyes of Black Antelope's wife there shot a red ray of anger.

"Tirawa will fill your bones full of aches, and double your back like the back of an old man!" she barked at the boy.

Black Antelope intervened.

"There may be another price," he said.

He was very angry, but he was too thoughtful to throw away a fine gift simply because he could not get a greater one.

"There might be the price of the poor horse—and a good gun—a pistol in the holster!"

The Badger bit his lip and flinched. This was a high price for a service which was not yet performed.

He said: "I am not born Cheyenne. Will you make me all red for that price?"

"I shall make you all red for that price!"

The Badger left the tent and led back to the entrance of it the horse of Clouded Sky. He gave the lead rope to Black Antelope and presented him, at the same time, with a Colt revolver, of a shining newness.

"I shall speak to Tirawa," said the medicine man. "I shall make everything well for you, my son!"

"I shall watch and wait," said the boy. "I have paid you a great thing. Make me all Cheyenne, Black Antelope, for that price. Make me hate the white men. Or else the White Badger will come and try his medicine on the Black Antelope. And White Badger has very strong medicine, too!"

14

There is no doubt that such talk had never been used before to the face of Black Antelope by any chief, young or old, to say nothing of such a nameless boy as this. The wife of the medicine man was ready to put a knife between the ribs of this daring child, but her husband dissuaded her with a gesture.

And he said afterwards in her ear, when the boy had left: "He still has a rifle and another revolver and the finest horse that ever stepped in this land under the eyes of Tirawa. Shall we be fools and let him go with such things in his hands?"

The squaw could not help agreeing to such words as these.

And the very next day the lessons began. They consisted of taking a walk to a nest of rocks above the river, where the boy was forced to sit on a little amphitheater when it had been well heated with the sun. And every time the Badger wanted to look into the face of the medicine man, he had to look at the sun also. So that each lesson left him half-blinded, dizzy and dazzled. And he went reeling back to the lodges with his brain a-whirl, for it really seemed to him that the lessons which he received were of more strength than those of a mere common Indian. Sometimes little dark doubts like wriggling snakes came across the mind and the reason of the youngster, but, after all, he was only ten years old.

His work was to listen and repeat—listen and repeat—until he had littered his mind with a stock of maxims.

"When should a man die?" asked the medicine man.

"When he is at the strongest point of his life."

"Why should he die at that time?"

"Because as he is then, so will he be in the other life forever."

"Suppose that he dies by scalping?"

"Then his soul will stay around his body or fly away to haunt the man who killed him."

"Can those we scalp hurt us?"

"They can shoot invisible arrows into us which cause us no pain, but afterwards, we are sick."

"Suppose that a man dies by hanging?"

"Then his soul has to stay with his body."

"Why is that?"

"Because the soul leaves the body by the mouth and the throat when the body dies. And if a man is hanged, the soul dies in the body and stays in the body and rots with the body, and when the body is dust, the soul is in that dust also!"

In this fashion the boy would respond to the questions of the Black Antelope. He had reached such a point that he could repeat this sort of wisdom for an hour at a time. And he had discovered that it was wise to attend carefully to the word of the healer. Because a slipshod lesson would cause the great healer to make him sit for a long time in the broiling sun, until the blood swam up into his head and he almost fainted with exhaustion. The Badger grew thin and weaker during these lessons, but he grew more sun-blackened, naturally, as he sat naked every day for hours in the blast of the open face of the sun.

There was only this trouble in his mind. That he had by this time promised to the great enchanter not only the horse which he had won by the risk of his life from Clouded Sky, but also both of the new Colt revolvers, which he had sworn to give in the same way.

"And now," said the boy at last, "I have learned enough of the law, have I not?"

He had worked for three months, whenever the Black Antelope had no better thing to do. And all of those months the Badger had to hold himself in readiness day or night because he could not tell when the great medicine man would be ready to pour out inspired instruction. And, during these months, he had not played, except to run out in the evening over the plains with White Hawk to romp with him.

One night, half wild with the joy of trying the speed of his feet across the grassy prairie, he sped away for a full three miles from the camp, and ran and ran until he saw suddenly before him an ominous thing—the newly risen moon, a pale and sickly scimitar of light, floating above the eastern hills and floating also in the broad, flat face of the river.

He could remember now that the medicine man had given a warning that evening that he intended to walk in this direction and that no man, under the heaviest penalties, must presume to come near the river in that direction.

The Badger had had no mind to break that rule.

For it was said that one man who had broken in upon the chosen seclusion of Black Antelope had been cursed with a sickness of scabs such as comes to little boys who fail to keep the fire alive in the lodge on cold winter nights. These scabs were worse with this man, however. He grew very sick. And in a fortnight he died, dragging himself about at the feet of Black Antelope and begging him to forgive him and to heal him. It was also reported what Black Antelope had said upon that occasion.

"It is not I who put the curse upon you, poor brother. But Tirawa, who loves me, watches over me and keeps me from harm, and he struck you, friend, with this sickness. I am sorry for you!"

So that the Badger looked up, and not down, as he stood back from the river side. He looked up and marked the darkness of the sky, dimly streaked across with red; he was so intent on the sky, wondering if Tirawa's dreadful and unknown form might appear at any moment, that he swung far to the left and crossed a little crest of rocks. As he stumbled on these, he looked down, and he saw beneath him the venerable form of the medicine man, Black Antelope, wrapped comfortably in a great buffalo robe, and sound asleep.

He waited to see no more. In fact, it was the last thing in the world which he wished to look on, for the watchful Tirawa might have seen and the plague might be descending inescapably at this moment upon his shoulders!

His way back to the village was fleeter that night than his coming out had been. And he forgot the hunger in the pit of his stomach which had been like a hand of fire before. He wanted only to crawl into his buffalo robe and lie shuddering and begging Tirawa for mercy, because he had not looked upon Black Antelope intentionally.

When the morning came, he could not wait to leap up and speed away to the edge of the river. There he tore off his scanty clothes and dove into the water. When he came up, he examined himself minutely, forgetting even to shiver in the chill of the early morning wind. There was no sign of an itch breaking out on him, however. He spread his hands towards the nameless one in the sky. The prayer that was in his heart was too devout for his lips. He had no words, so great was his thankfulness as he went back toward the village.

And when he met the magician later in the morning he hardly dared to begin their conversation in the usual way, for he rarely missed a morning opportunity to ask the great man what birds or beast had come to him to answer his questions or, unbidden, give him information, the night before. Sometimes it was the eagle or the vulture; sometimes it was a field mouse or a ferret. Sometimes a lumbering bear rose upon his haunches and muttered thunderous prophecies to the wise man. The heart of the boy had been stirred many and many a time by such tales, and he would have given anything if he could have eavesdropped during one of those miraculous interviews. However, on this morning though he dreaded to speak of such a thing, yet he felt that it might be a suspicious thing if he did not ask the customary question, for then Black Antelope would begin to think, and he might ask Tirawa to tell him everything!

So he said as he gave the morning greeting.

"Who spoke with you last evening, father?"

The old man removed a pipe from his toothless gums and grinned and nodded.

"It is very well that you were not there," he said. "You would have been frightened, my child! Even the White Badger, who is not afraid!"

The Badger sat down, cross-legged, and dropped his chin on his hand, prepared for a marvel, prepared, also, to believe every word that he heard.

"It was just before darkness," said the medicine man. "There was only a little paint left in the sky and I sat on the rocks and looked in the river and saw the face of Tirawa forming there, very dim, like something rising out of the water. And I said: 'O Tirawa, send some creature to speak your words to me. Do not speak with your own voice, for the thunder of it frightens me!'

"Then the face began to disappear in the water."

"Were you afraid?" asked the boy.

"Tirawa is my friend, and yet I was afraid. For few even among the medicine men can see his face! But I have seen it often, though never without terror!"

The boy listened, entranced. At the very hour of the day of which the Black Antelope spoke he had himself looked down upon the wise man! No doubt, a great sleep followed the appearance of Tirawa, and perhaps a dream in the sleep.

"Then," said Black Antelope, "when the face had disappeared, I heard a howling in the river and out of the water leaped a great wolf, and at the shoulders he was twice as tall as a man!"

"It was in a dream, father, was it not?"

"A dream? Child, I saw it as clearly as I see you now. When he shook himself, some of the water from his fur flew into my face and left a smell there, like wood smoke."

The Badger broke in: "Surely it was in sleep that you saw it!"

"Young fool!" said the medicine man darkly, "am not I the Black Antelope and do I not know truth from falsehood and sleep from waking?"

The Badger bowed his head; but only to think the more, for he could not have been mistaken. His eyes had showed him the medicine man stretched in sleep among the rocks and suddenly he knew that even the great Black Antelope was capable of lying, and of lying most broadly.

15

It is hard to exaggerate the importance of this fact in the education of little Glanvil Tucker, now the White Badger. He had felt before this moment that the Black Antelope was a very wise and certainly a holy man, although, it was true, a very grasping person. But now that the talk turned upon daylight glimpses of wolves that rose out of water like fish—wolves that were twice as high at the shoulder as the height of a man—ah, that was a very different matter! The Badger bowed his head, as I have said, but it was because he did not wish the old man to see the hard light in his eyes.

"This wolf," said Black Antelope, "climbed up the side of the bank and up among the rocks until it stood over me. Its tongue hung from its mouth and the saliva that dripped from the tip of its tongue was burning like bits of flame. Look where one of those bits of flame touched on my robe!"

He indicated a smudged place on the edge of his buffalo robe. Ah, Black Antelope, had you been able to look into the mind of this boy! This was the proper time to stop! For it seemed to the Badger that he recalled the exact moment when a living spark had leaped from the fire and settled on the fur of that very robe.

But he only said: "You were very much afraid, then, Black Antelope?"

"I am afraid, yes; but only of the face of Tirawa, which has been seen by what other person of Indian nations? But of everything else—no! I knew by the size of this wolf that it came either from Tirawa or from the underwater people. So I said to it without fear but very politely: 'Why are you here?'

" 'Wise and noble Black Antelope,' said the wolf, 'I have come to tell you that there is a great danger in the way of the life of a little friend of yours.'

" 'Kind wolf,' said I, 'tell me what the danger is?'

" 'One of the little wolves who make their prayers to me,' said the great wolf, 'is going to meet him on the plains and kill his dog and then kill the dog's master!'

" 'Ah,' said I, 'but who can this be?'

" 'It is the young boy who wants to be a Cheyenne. It is the White Badger!'

"There, Badger, do you hear how I drew all that knowledge out of him? It is your life that is in danger!"

The Badger kept his head bowed and stared upon the ground. Now, however, he shuddered, and the medicine man imagined that it was with terror. It was only scorn and disgust.

Black Antelope continued foolishly: "I said to the great wolf: 'How can this danger be averted?'

"'It can be done very easily,' said the wolf. 'All that the boy has to do is to give you the rifle which he keeps. For you yourself will meet that wolf before the wolf meets the boy, and with that rifle—which is strong and shoots straight and far—you will kill that wolf, and so all the danger will be gone from his way.'

"And that, White Badger, is the whole story!"

"What became of the wolf?"

"I told him that I would try to do what he had advised me to do, and he wagged his head like a calf and grinned at me.

"'Turn your head away from me,' said he.

"I turned away my head, and when I looked around the next moment there had not been a sound but in the river I could see a whirlpool, and away from the whirlpool a wave of water a step in height rushed for the shore and crashed against it!"

"So!" said the Badger, heaving a great sigh.

"That is the way the wolf left me!"

"And he told you that I must give you the rifle?"

"He did not say that," said the medicine man with some wariness. "But he said that that was the way for me to kill the wolf!"

"Well," said the Badger, "I suppose that I must think about it very hard. You have my two revolvers already."

"I have them," nodded the medicine man. "I would give one of them back to you, I suppose, if you gave me the rifle—but this is all work for your own sake, and not for mine, of course!"

"Of course," nodded the boy without enthusiasm. "Let me see those two revolvers, Black Antelope!"

Black Antelope gave a glad glance at his wife, who had

dropped her face down on her hands. The knuckles pushed up a great fold of flesh under each eye and in this manner she was masked against all observation. But her eyes flamed! There were no other rifles in all of the Cheyenne nation as new and as strong-shooting as this one, which the Badger had brought among them. And many a warrior's heart had been swelling with the desire to put hands upon it.

So, in all haste, the medicine man brought the two revolvers, each, as though it were a big medicine, wrapped in a piece of soft beaver skin. The Badger took them in his hands and turned away.

"Come with me, Black Antelope," he said, and he led the way out of the tepee and to the rear of the tent where both the horse of Clouded Sky and the Red Wind were tethered. Without a word he put a saddle on the back of Red Wind and stuffed the two revolvers into the holsters of the saddle, which was of the finest leather and all chased with silver which had shone when it was first a prize—though now the silver was tarnished black.

"What is this for?" asked the Black Antelope, going half mad with greed and with joy.

For it seemed to him that he understood, and that the boy, out of vast gratitude because his life was to be saved by the medicine man, would now give him not only the rifle but Red Wind, also. Or, at the least, that the young fool would offer him the rifle in exchange for the stallion! Laughter began to form in the throat of the medicine man!

"I shall tell you what this is for," said the boy, "this is for riding away!"

"So?" asked Black Antelope. "And for whom to ride away?"

"For me!"

"But not with the two revolvers which belong to me!"

"Little mouse!" said the Badger. "Old, dying, stinking mouse, why did I not step on you and leave you squashed on the ground? Why do I not knock out the brains so that they run down your neck?"

The medicine man thought of one thing only—madness! And he drew back a step only to see a revolver come into the hand of the Badger.

"Stand still," said the boy. "I am very gentle. I do not hurt old men, but you are not a man. You are a filthy buzzard; you are a snake; you are everything that is unclean. My belly wriggles at the thought of you!"

It was the time for Black Antelope to keep very still, but after all, he was a very old man. And now fury and the prospect of the loss of those two guns drove him out of his senses. He began to dance up and down.

"You will die by hanging!" gasped Black Antelope. "You will die with a rope twisting your neck, fool! You will die, and your soul will die with your body, and it will never be free to rise out of the dirt. Your soul will pass from your bones into the stomachs of vultures and eagles! Oh, a hundred painted buffalo robes would not be enough to pay for this thing that you have said to me. Not to me, but to Tirawa through me!"

"Old fool!" smiled the boy, showing flashing white teeth. "Is this as true as the truth that you saw the great wolf?"

The medicine man stopped and gaped.

But still his rage was a great wave which carried him on and away most recklessly.

"You shall not leave the town!" he shouted. "I shall call for the chief. I shall call for the war leaders and for the old men for council! They will take all that you have and strip you naked and send you away with bare feet!"

The Badger, as I have hinted in a few other places, was not of a reverent nature; neither did he possess any inherent respect for old men. And now his temper had been raised several degrees—several violent degrees! He stepped closer to Black Antelope and laid hold upon him—even I cannot help trembling when I think of the sacrilegious brutality of it! But he laid hold of Black Antelope by the loose, wrinkled skin of his breast, and then he shook that old man until his toothless gums clapped violently together.

"Listen to me, old dying vulture, old molted eagle, old buzzard!" said the Badger. "I should wring your loose neck from your shoulders, but I cannot. I rather leave you to be laughed at. But now I ask you what you will have me do.

"Will you stay here quietly and take that fine horse which was once the war horse of the great Clouded Sky among the Pawnees? Will you take that horse and let me ride quietly away? Will you take that horse and let it be known that I am perfect Cheyenne in body and soul? Will you let it be known that the White Badger is a good Cheyenne and worthy to be made a warrior? Or will you have me go to the center of this city and call the old men and the old women and the children and the old warriors and the young dog-soldiers—and then will you have me tell them the story of how I saw you sleeping by the side of the river? And then shall I tell them the great lie that you gave me when you wanted to steal my rifle but did not have the courage to steal it with your hands and wanted to steal it with your wits—your moldy-sided, knock-kneed, blind, loose-lipped, roach-backed, cow-hocked wits? Tell me, Black Antelope, what shall I do?"

The Black Antelope cast a wild glance above him, making a great and swift prayer to Tirawa to send a bolt of thunder from the heavens and consume this impertinent young demon. But alas, the sky was clear, and although the greatest medicine man among the Cheyennes offered up silent prayers, that sky showed no desire to employ the rage of Tirawa. Not so much as one poor cloud appeared over the edge of the horizon!

So the Black Antelope looked down to his young companion again.

"However, you leave me the horse which Clouded Sky once was proud to ride!" he said.

96

"I leave it," said the boy, "so that the young boys and the warriors may say: 'White Badger is generous to the old men. He is free-handed and kind to Black Antelope.'

"In the meantime, while I ride back to Red Eagle, if I hear a word that Black Antelope is telling lies and speaking foul names about me, I shall come back on Red Wind faster than lightning riding down from the sky. Then I shall tell the chiefs and the town how you lied to me. Then I shall take you by the flabby skin under your chin—"

He suited the action to the word, and with a cruel wrench he brought the seer to his knees, floundering and groaning with pain and with fear.

"Then," said the youngster, tight-lipped with rage, "I shall take a whip of rawhide and I shall flay the skin from your back. And after that, I shall take a rod and beat you till you beg!"

The great medicine man, even in his agony and his fear, with the feeling that his head was being lifted every moment from his shoulders, stared feebly upon all sides, to make sure that no man saw this atrocity. For, though they might rescue him, they would also expect him to blast the boy with the thunders of Tirawa. And by late experience Black Antelope knew that Tirawa was not always a dependable deity.

"Go!" he gasped at length. "Go in peace. All shall be as you wish. All, little brother! But go! go and take the horse of Clouded Sky also. Only, go quickly, before the children or the women should see—"

"Waugh!" said the boy with a sneer, and he turned up his heel and with his toes he scratched up half a handful of dust into the face of the enchanter.

Then he stepped to Red Wind and was presently flying across the plains with White Hawk at his heels.

16

There was never a better chance to test the speed of the Red Wind than this, and it seemed to the Badger, as he let the stallion take his head across the plains, that there was no draining of the strength of his horse. And between dark and dawn the fine animal kept up as steady a pace as the Badger had been able to maintain when he'd had two horses and changed them twice a day. Rather, the red horse seemed to grow tougher and hardier with more use, and they whirled away steadily. It was not always galloping, for the Badger had learned that whereas the Indian pony seems most at home at that gait, this taller and finer limbed horse could strike out a swinging trot that ate up the miles smoothly enough and seemed to fatigue him no more than walking. A hard pace to sit on most animals, but the supple fetlock joints of Red Wind cushioned his legs against the shocks of the hoof beats.

It was a fine trip—this homeward journey. And yet it was a bewildering one, too. For the Badger, having gone to the very fountainhead of sanctity among the Cheyennes, felt that he had simply looked inside the nature of Black Antelope and found there simply a cunning, greedy old man's heart. Something, then, lay behind and beyond. What it was he could not tell. It might be that the white man was right who had smiled at the Indians. It might be that the Indians were right and that Black Antelope was a rascal who did not do justice to his cause. Certainly, there was much wisdom in some of the things he had said!

However, the Badger was only ten, and he decided that he had given enough time and attention to these matters. Time itself could take care of the rest. And, in the meanwhile, he was busy with his new weapons. He had worked with them enough, before, until even Rising Bull had cried out that his son shot away in practice the price of a buffalo before he made a kill!

The Badger did not care for this. He understood without teaching what the Indians could never understand—that constant practice is required if they are to hit a target with a gun. They knew it well enough with their bows and arrows, and the Badger shuddered when he considered how his skill with the bow lagged behind that of every lad of his age in the village! But when it came to guns—well, to the Indians, they remained part of the white man's "medicine," part of his magic. One leveled the rifle and it was more or less expected to do the rest. Besides, bullet and powder cost too much!

But the Badger did not care about that. He knew that he had in his hands a rifle which would shoot three or four times to the muzzle-loader's once. Moreover, the man who handled the muzzle-loader had an awkward performance to go through after every shot, whereas with the breech-loader he simply clicked his weapon open and, without changing his position or the line of his fire, snapped in another charge and he was ready to fire again—with his eye hardly off the target for an instant!

The average Indian groaned if he discharged an actual bullet at other than living game, but the Badger was quite prepared to shoot twenty times in practice in order that when he did fire, it would strike the mark. If it cost money to buy cartridges, he would find money to pay for them! And there were the two revolvers, also! Every day during these three months, he had found time to get off on the prairie with his horse and work with all three weapons. And still, as he rode homeward, there was always a revolver in one hand or the other—or, with the reins hooked over his shoulder, he would be throwing himself along the side of the horse, his body supported at the shoulders with a loop of leather thrown over the pommel of the saddle. And so he could present this rifle under the throat of his mount and take steady aim on some object beyond the horse—a shrub, a rock, a discolored patch of ground—not quick, casual aim such as an Indian takes, with a prayer rather than a real glimpse of the target through the sights, but a steady and patient effort, until he attained that right flash of the target. Then, in imagination, he pulled the trigger!

How many times had he seen the Indians go through that maneuver and fire instantly, but how often had he seen them strike the goal? For his part, he was determined to have results, and if it took longer in the aiming, he would take that length of time. He was eleven years old now as he started back for his home town. And it was still two years at the earliest before other boys would be expected to show themselves men, but he had already stepped into a mysterious and important rôle in the life of the tribe, and therefore he must be ready at any instant to step out as a man, prepared to carry on a man's duties.

Had he been an Indian, he would have been simply wildly delighted at the thought. But he was not an Indian, and the brain of the white man working steadily in him gave him warning of the hard times to come.

In the meantime, he had this rare, rare outfit of weapons. What murder of murders had Clouded Sky committed to get such an armament? Or what treasures had he paid to purchase them? Above all, here was beneath him a horse which would take him whirling away from danger faster than other horses could follow, or again, here was a speed which would make him overtake any enemy!

But at the present time he did not wish to overtake any enemies. He wished only to keep out of the way of danger until he felt in his bones the reality of manhood. Meanwhile, there must be constant sham; constant evasion; and constant practice to fit himself for the crisis!

These were sobering thoughts for a youngster like the Badger to take along with him. You will not wonder, then, that every time he raised his rifle to his shoulder he did it with a concentrated grimness. For a boy in his position, it was not hard to imagine that the other outline was a mortal foe!

And he practiced pointing his guns a hundred times for every shot he fired. Merely pointing has an excellence in practice that is all its own. And it brings about, at last, a sort of mental certainty which most old hunters have and recognize—if they are highly organized, nervously—the instant their finger presses the trigger and before the bullet leaves the gun the certainty that they are to make a hit at least. And some have told me that they *feel* the kill before the beast drops. Such certainty is a matter that lies entirely within the senses and has little to do with actual firing of shots. And this priceless experience was what the little Badger was accumulating.

How heartily I, for my part, wish that he had not had that long journey to the Black Antelope! How heartily I wish that he had not had those long, solitary months of experience during which his guns were his constant companions! For it was during this time he learned the essentials of true marksmanship. It was during this time that he established in his mind a sort of mental ideal of what the perfect marksman should be in speed and in accuracy. When a man has established an ideal, it means that he can never be self-contented—which also means, if he has practical energy, that he is halfway to the goal at the first stride!

Now the Badger had fired away a small fortune—in Indian ideas—in the way of powder and lead. And as he came to his eleventh year, on one of those days when he was riding back toward Red Eagle, he achieved a beautiful synchronization of hand and eye and gun. Had it not been for that perfection, I know that he would never have tumbled into half of the tragedies which lay before him. Because I never have felt that the Badger was your true hero, insensible to fear. Half of his deeds were inspired by the knowledge that reputation *forced* him to step out in front of the other warriors in the tribe to redeem his repute as "the fearless." And another portion of his deeds—heaven alone can tell how great a part!—was inspired by an immense confidence which naturally came to him when he saw how far his skill with guns exceeded that of other men.

He had reached a point when he began to know that death had commenced to reside within the crook of the forefinger of either hand; and on the same day, he reached the last ten bullets for his revolvers and the last five for his rifle. He had begun as a rich man, and he was coming home poor—in ammunition, at least. The heart of Rising Bull would swell with much sorrow when he saw the depleted store of provisions. But the Badger did not care. He had the skill which he wanted, and it was more than gold to him. So he rode hard and fast.

He was still more than an hour's riding from the village when he saw a form walking across the plains, bent over, dragging something which was hitched to his back. An Indian, even at that distance, would have been able to distinguish the exact article. But the Badger could not see. He did not have to. He knew that the ceremony of initiation had taken place while he was away, and yonder was one of the would-be initiates dragging behind him a buffalo's skull.

It made the Badger close his eyes and shudder. Someday he would have to confront the same ceremony. Someday, when his deeds were considered numerous enough by the tribe to warrant his testing as a warrior, the braves would vote upon him, and then he would be taken from the town by Rising Bull. Perhaps the incisions would be made in his breast; two deep incisions almost to the bone in either breast, deep enough and long enough to permit a three-quarter inch rope to be passed through the hole. That rope would be knotted at the other end to the top of a pole and he would remain there without food or water until the flesh had mortified and the rope broke through, or until, by heroic nerve, he tore the rope through the trim, strong flesh and came back, long before he was expected, to his father's lodge, there to be received joyously, as a hero. They would inspect the wound, make sure that it had been fairly torn, and then they would dress the tear skillfully. From that moment, he was a full member of the tribe.

Or, again, as in the case of the poor wretch he now saw, the incisions might be made above the shoulder blades, in which case the sufferer walked restlessly across the plains, dragging the buffalo's head behind him.

No wonder the Badger grew sick at heart!

Yet there was an easy and an instant release. If the boy so much as whimpered when he saw the knife in the hand of his father, the ceremony ended that instant. Or if he cried out as the rope was knotted in the raw wound, the proceeding stopped that instant. And, finally, if his nerve gave out after the ropes had been attached to him, he could at any moment cut or untie them, and so be free from the torture.

But, ah, if he freed himself in that manner, what a life remained for him! From that moment he ceased to be a man. He was a woman. He lived among them. He did their work, universally despised. He could not hold up his head among the braves. Even the little boys bullied him and whipped and stoned him and mocked him. And he dared not raise a hand in his own defense!

Shall I tell you what often wakened the Badger from his sleep at night? It was the terror lest he, the "fearless," should not have the courage to tear the ropes through the new wounds and so come home first of all when the day of his initiation arrived!

He rode up to the suffering boy and found that it was a strapping fifteen-year-old boy, Loping Calf, the son of none other than Red Eagle himself. He turned and met the Badger with a smile on his weary face and a careless wave of the hand—a wave which must have cost him an exquisite pang.

He inquired the news of Black Antelope, but the Badger put these questions aside. His very heartstrings ached for the tormented boy.

"What day is it, Loping Calf?" he asked.

"The third," said the latter.

His lips trembled a little as he added: "I have not been very brave, brother! I have seen three of my friends go home before me, but my father took a great width of the flesh when he tied the ropes! They seem . . . they seem . . . tied into the very bone, White Badger!"

The Badger dismounted, took a leather water-pouch from the saddle and held it without a word to the lips of the other. Loping Calf drank with a wolfish eagerness. When the pouch was half emptied, the Badger got a handful or two of dried meat and offered that.

"If you are seen, White Badger, you will be shamed!" said Loping Calf.

"I shall not be seen," said the Badger.

He went behind the other.

"Your father was drunk when he tied these ropes!" he said.

For the back of Loping Calf was a frightful spectacle. A whole handful of flesh seemed to have been gathered under the rope over each shoulder blade. Now the back was a disgusting sight. Flies buzzed around the cuts; and the flesh was fearfully corrupted.

"I have a sharp knife!" said the Badger suddenly.

"Ah, ah!" groaned the other boy. "I have prayed for that. My heart is turned to water. I am like a sick woman. There are tears in my eyes. You have a sharp knife, but have you a tongue that will not speak?"

104

"I have a tongue that will be more silent than a rock," said the Badger.

"Can you cut so that no one will suspect?"

"I shall cut from the rope out, and let you tear the rope through the last film of flesh and skin."

"Ah, White Badger, you have made me a friend who will never leave you!"

"Loping Calf, stand still!"

He ran the keen end of his hunting knife—that old present from Red Eagle—between the rope and the flesh of Loping Calf.

"This is a knife your father gave me; think that it is your father's hand that cuts you now, brother!"

"I shall think it. Cut, cut, White Badger!"

And with a sick heart the Badger cut on either shoulder until there was only a narrow stretch of skin and flesh remaining between the rope and the surface.

"Now!" said the Badger.

A single twitch and the boy was free. And he clung to the Badger with the tears running down his face.

"See, White Badger. I was almost a woman—I am almost a woman now! You have saved me! What is my life? It is nothing! It is dirt under your feet, my brother!"

The Badger said not a word. In fact, he was too sick to speak. And what he saw was not Loping Calf, but himself two or three years hence with such a rope knotted in his flesh, and no one near.

"When the same time comes for you," said Loping Calf, "I shall remember you! But no, I forget what you are. I forget that you are without fear and that you have a medicine against pain. Forgive me, White Badger!"

So did the Badger's reputation close the door of help in his face! Oh, how sick and how thoughtful he was as he rode back toward the village!

17

I have said that the Badger rode homeward fast. But I did not say that he took a most roundabout course, for he chose, instead of striking across country, to cleave close to the bank of the river, which he knew would take him to the same place after many windings, and the result was that a messenger from Black Antelope reached that village before he did. He knew it the instant his gaze fell upon the face of Red Eagle. That chief, when the boy came into his lodge, grunted out a greeting and then nodded to a folded robe as an invitation for him to sit where the Eagle could keep a sharp lookout upon him.

The Badger did not like mysteries, except those of his own making. He merely yawned, then sat down cross-legged and stared most impudently into the face of the chief.

"Black Antelope has sent a word of me before I came," said he.

"You rode Red Wind. Did it blow slowly?" asked the Eagle, with much meaning.

"Red Wind goes sometimes faster and sometimes slow— as I wish," said the Badger.

And he maintained a stolid silence, looking upon the chief with dull eyes of unconcern.

"Shall I tell you the words that were sent to me about you, White Badger?"

"For three months or four—yes, for four moons I have heard nothing but the talk of Black Antelope."

"He is the wisest of the Cheyennes!"

There was much anger in the manner of Red Eagle and then he added with a sneer: "Unless the medicine of the White Badger is stronger than his medicine!"

A dozen responses came to the lips of the Badger. But he felt that the time had not yet come when he could afford to be frank. If Black Antelope had traduced him, then he would turn loose the truth against that old man in the most blasting form. In the meantime, it might well behoove him to sit patiently and learn what had happened to his reputation.

"I have seen wise men and wise men," said the Badger solemnly. "I did not need to see Black Antelope to know wisdom. I have known a man who was a gift-giver, but he was wise, also. He gave me this!"

He snatched the big hunting knife from his girdle and hurled it with all the whip-like force of his arm across the lodge. It struck a solid, well seasoned lodge pole, but it sank in the wood halfway to the haft. The chief followed the flash of the steel with a careless glance which did not betray the leap of his heart.

"The young warrior cannot know what the old warrior has already learned and forgotten," he said more gently. "But I have loved you, White Badger, although I cannot altogether understand you. I have loved you, and my son, the Loping Calf, has loved you. He, also, does not understand you. However, we know, and all men except fools know that there is medicine in the mind and the hands of the White Badger. And now the Black Antelope sends word to me that there is a fire in you and that if the fire is well used it will burn down the lodges of the enemies of the Cheyennes. But if it is not well used, it may burn down the lodges of the Cheyennes themself. Do you hear me, young brother?"

"I hear you," said the boy.

"And he says that he has taught you much truth, and he says that scalps will come into your hands and that you will become rich and that you will lead Cheyennes in battle."

There was an appreciative "Waugh!" from the boy.

"But also he tells me that we must watch you every day and watch you every night. I tell you this, young brother, so that you may know that the doors of the heart of Red Eagle are open. You may look through them!"

It was very much to be spoken by a great war chief to a child and the boy was stirred.

"I have come to you before I went to my father and my mother," he said.

"I knew it," said the chief, with a smile, "because I see that your belly is empty, and if you had been to that lodge first, Little Grouse would have filled you as round as a bear. Go to her now. She will hate me if I keep you long from her."

The Badger, accordingly, went straight across the village and dropped from the saddle at the lodge of his foster-father. He entered and there was a wild cry from Little Grouse. She ran toward him halfway and then she stopped with an exclamation of dismay.

"Look!" cried she to another squaw in the old lodge. "Look! He has come back half man; half of the Badger is dead!"

Rising Bull seemed to notice the difference, also. For, that night, he talked with confidence, gently, to his foster-son.

And he told him, for the first time, how he had lost his hand, and though the tale had, of course, been told by Little Grouse before, there was an effective simplicity in the narration of Rising Bull.

He said: "I was among the trees, by myself. I had a bright new hatchet. It was magic to me. With a jerk of my wrist, I could sink it the width of my palm into hard wood. That night I cut up brush to make my fire small and hot and then I saw a beautiful young tree, tall and straight. I thought: Suppose that tree is left, it will become a giant. But I, in three minutes or five can kill it forever. I took my hatchet and cut it, but when it was cut almost through and as I jumped out of the way, a strong wind that was blowing threw it across me. It fell so that all my body was free. But my left hand was caught!"

He paused here and filled and lighted his pipe, and as he told the tale, he paused from time to time to shiver and then to puff at his pipe. Time had made the story delicious to him. Its pain was tempered and flavored by the drifting years. It was the keenest pleasure that was left to him before death stole him away with his useless hand to roam through the other world, scorned and mocked by the strong spirits who roamed there also, hunting and scalping as they did on the plains of the earth!

"It was the autumn just before winter. The night was very cold. I kept the fire burning. By stretching out my body, I could take bits of wood between my feet and throw them on the fire. Then, with my left hand, I could chop down saplings and shrubs near me and feed the fire. For three days I fed it and waited, and did not freeze during the three nights, but on the fourth night I knew that I would freeze. Also, I knew that I would die even if I did not freeze, because my right arm had no feeling to the shoulder.

"I waited until the midday. Then I built the fire very bright and tall and hot. I waited until that great fire burned down, and while it burned down I whetted my knife until it was sharper than the wind that blows through the finest sieve. When the fire had burned down to coals, I took that sharp knife and cut away my right hand at the wrist, and as I cut, I knew that I was cutting away my happiness. I could never shoot an arrow again; I could never shoot a rifle; I could never throw a knife; I could never skin a buffalo. I could do nothing. I could not even handle a fast young colt that has no sense! Therefore I said to myself: 'I am cutting away the best half of myself. I am making myself into a ghost before I die!'

"Still I wanted to live. I do not know why. But I wanted to live!

"I cut that hand away and while the blood was leaping out of it and I was growing faint, I finished the job, and I went to the fire and put the stump of my wrist among the burning coals. I did not feel that fire for a moment. But then I *did* feel it. And sometimes I wake up at night, now, and feel it again! However, that wrist was made so that it would not bleed any more. It was all a great thick crust of black, and the crust began to crack the next day as I rode back to the village.

"Well, that is how I lost my hand. Because I killed a tree that Tirawa loved. There is always punishment when we kill for no reason!

"Very well, I cut off my hand, and I made myself a woman!"

He shrugged his broad shoulders as high as his ears and spurted the smoke out through his nose and his set teeth, so that he looked dragonlike and terrible.

The boy stood up and came to his foster father and laid a hand on his shoulder.

"Listen to me," said he, "you have been a father to me. So long as you live, I shall never leave the Cheyennes. I shall be to you like the right hand which you lost. This, my father, is a great word, and I shall never forget it."

18

All had, hitherto, gone very well for the Badger. Not the least of his exploits had been the visit to Black Antelope. When he returned to the tribe of Red Eagle, he said not a word of what had passed between him and the great medicine man. Nevertheless, rumor will be born out of a very ghost, and before long the word was on wings across the plains that in the months he had spent with Black Antelope, the Badger had taught at least as much as he had learned from that great man. So that the Badger was respected more than ever.

But he was not loved. Precocity may be admired but it is never loved. I may use Little Grouse as an argument. She was the only one who was on the inside of the secret of the boy, and yet he had grown even past her powers. I show you the Badger, now, in his twelfth year, a long, lean, lithe creature, with knees, hands, elbows and shoulders that looked much too big for the rest of him. His neck seemed too long for his head, and his head seemed too big for his body, and his jaw seemed too big for his head. One of the neighbors and friends of Little Grouse called him The Frog, and that nickname quickly became popular and for several years he was called nothing but that—behind his back, of course. Little Grouse enjoyed that derogatory name more than any of the others did, because she hated him the most. He had been for seven years in her lodge and yet he had never spoken a single tender word to her. And, besides, she chiefly hated him because he refused to make of her a confidante. She was never sure what was sham and what was real in him.

So that she looked upon the Badger as an interloper. A necessary one, however. He had come to them while they were in the midst of absolute poverty and when the tribe, having grown accustomed to the weak and sad condition of Rising Bull, was no longer as open-handed toward them as it had been before. But now poverty was banished from their tepee, since the day that the Badger brought home to the lodge more than twenty of the chosen horses of the Pawnees. But that was only the beginning of good fortune. In the strange brain of the Badger there was found an inventive quality. He had watched her at work scraping the buffalo robes to a proper thickness with her dull tools, and

111

he discovered a stone which would serve extremely well as a grindstone. With this she sharpened her tools, and after that, she dressed two feet of skin, or three, for every one which she had dressed before. Nor did all of the benefits coming from him cease at this point. There was the new gun! He and Rising Bull went off hunting together and they worked in the following manner: When game was sighted, Rising Bull patiently worked himself to the farther side of it; then he showed himself and it fled away, usually straight toward the boy, who, of course, remained in covert until it was almost upon him. Then he began work with his breech-loading gun. He became so expert with it that when a herd of antelopes rushed at him, he could drop four of the fleet creatures before they passed him in their lightning flight.

Neither did the blessing from young White Badger end with this point. Suppose that an extra fine robe were to be painted, what was the purpose in allowing Little Grouse, who had no talent for such things, to take weary, weary days upon the execution of it? One winter night, when the nights are longest and the days are coldest, the Badger pushed her to the side roughly—for he was always rough with her.

He began where she had left off. She had been painting, with infinite difficulty, the first of a string of wolves who were about to walk across the length of the robe. But this work took on new shape with the Badger. He made these outlined animals with a tenth of the labor and with ten times as much reality. He made White Hawk stand for a miserable hour as his model and when White Hawk was allowed to curl up by the fire again, five very lifelike wolves stalked across the robe. Little Grouse was filled with admiration—and envy. The entire tribe was brought in to be shown the masterpiece, and during the winter, the Badger painted half a dozen more of these sketchy creations. His eyes saw clearly and his hand put down what his eye saw. He could show a great wapiti striding out of a forest and into a glade. He could give you the shrinking ferocity of a puma drinking at the lip of a pool. He could show you a dog stopping to listen in alarm, with one foot raised.

When these robes were taken to the trading post, the result was amazing. Enough finery and luxuries were secured to make every woman and brave in the tribe envious of the lodge of Rising Bull. But the only pay which the Badger required for his art was bullets, bullets, bullets! For he lived with that gun in his hands—that or the revolvers. And he needed much costly fuel for them. So great became the prosperity of Rising Bull that he was urged to take other wives and increase himself still more and more, but this he refused to do even when Little Grouse pointed out to him that the time had come when she was a little tired of bearing the entire brunt of the drudgery for two lounging men!

"One wife, one trouble," said Rising Bull. "Two wives, two troubles. Rising Bull is growing old!"

Such was Badger and his family in his twelfth year, when trouble first descended upon him in the shape of sickness. It was a common fever that struck him. And he was given the usual prescription. He and two other sufferers, swathed in heavy robes, were placed in the sweat-house. There the medicine man uttered a prayer and a chant to Tirawa in which they joined to the full of their strength. After which the fire was drawn from the surface of a number of great stones over which it had been built. Upon these superheated stones, water was poured until vast clouds of steam filled the tepee. And after that more water was poured and the steam became more heavy until the sick could endure it no longer. Then they staggered out into the open air and, still swathed in their robes, they were allowed to run, or they were helped down to the edge of the river. There they threw off the robes and plunged into the snow-cold water.

On the first day when the boy took that treatment, one old woman was taken out dead. The medicine man explained that she had not prayed with sufficient earnestness to Tirawa.

Indeed, many were benefited by these rigorous treatments. But the fever of the Badger was strangely obdurate. The medicine man had many meetings with his foster-father and his foster-mother, for surely there was some dark spirit in the boy!

In the meantime, the Badger grew weaker and weaker. And, finally, it came into his mind that the sweats and the cold plunges were slowly killing him! That thought came to him in the middle of the night. Before dawn he was on the back of Red Wind and away from the camp.

He left no farewell behind him. They did not find his outward traces. And when ten days had passed and he had not returned, the medicine man excusably declared that Tirawa had been angry with this boy for trying to learn things that were beyond his years to know. Therefore he had reached down a hand and snatched him away from the earth—horse and man!

But that was not in the mind of the boy. Since his visit to Black Antelope, he had the most mixed emotions concerning that mysterious deity, Tirawa. What he himself wanted, most of all, was to get away from the sweat and cold bath torment. And he rode across the river and far up the other bank and then up a forking tributary until he was at the foot of the first hills. There, in a close hollow, beside a tiny stream, he decided to fight his battle for life.

He was dizzy and sick with weakness by the time he arrived at this place. But he used the remnant of his powers to cut for himself a bed of tender, fresh boughs. He let Red Wind go free near him, for Red Wind was sure to stay close. He had White Hawk to protect him. His rifle was stretched at his side under a robe. His revolvers were tucked into his belt. Above him was the open face of sun, wind, or icy night.

He dropped into a state of coma which endured for three nights and days. Sometimes, when he wakened, he

114

had wits enough to reach for his water bottle and moisten his lips with its contents. And sometimes he was too far gone to know the world on which his rolling eyes looked.

Once, in the deep of his fevered dream, he heard a vast snarling and a sound of struggle, and then he heard the agonized whine of White Hawk, pouring out his life as he fought. He wakened enough to see the old white wolf, now with weakened fangs and weakened body, in the grip of an upreared grizzly. The teeth of the wolf were in the throat of the monster, but the hug of the bear was crushing all life out of the smaller animal.

Clear sense came back for a fleeting instant to the brain of the sick boy. He sat up and dragged that heavy rifle to his shoulder. He aimed his shot just under the raised jaw of the grizzly and fired. It seemed to him that a mountain toppled toward him; and then unconsciousness poured back across his eyes and his mind.

Once he awakened and made a vain, vague effort to struggle free from the incubus above him.

Once he was wakened by the neighing of frightened Red Wind, who stood above him, calling vainly to him. And, before senselessness came to him again, he held out his hand to the fine animal; and he had wits enough to wonder how the stallion could have conquered his dread of even a bear's carcass to come so near to him. Then he slept again.

And at the end of what seemed an eternity, he felt the great weight being tugged slowly, painfully, from across his legs.

He wakened with wonderful clearness restored to his brain. First he saw the bright faces of the stars above him.

And then he heard the most hateful language in the world—the harsh murmur of the Pawnees, the wolves of the plains!

19

What the Badger knew, above all, was that his life was in such peril that he could count it almost certainly lost. What he knew in the second place was that the fever had left him. His brow was covered with cold sweat. His body felt ridiculously thin and light and weak. But the sickness was gone, only at a time when he was delivered into the hands of his deadliest enemies. And now he saw a familiar outline leaning above him under the stars.

He saw broad shoulders and a stern face, dim in the night, and he recognized both, as well as the gleam of the knife which was above him.

"Standing Elk," said he, "my knife was once closer to your heart than your knife is now close to mine. And yet you are still alive!"

There was a deep exclamation from the Pawnee chief. He uttered a few rapid words in his tongue to the men around him, and from a half a dozen throats came a yell of exultation.

"For your scalp, boy," said Standing Elk, "I promise you that the Pawnees will dance and will give up thanks to Tirawa. That is enough honor for you."

"I am honored enough," said the Badger, still faintly fighting for his life. "But what honor is there in Standing Elk?"

"Starved dog of a Cheyenne," snarled the chief in sudden rage, "your knife found the heart of my brother, Clouded Sky."

116

"He struck for my life and I struck for his. It was fair fight. Now Tirawa has made me sick and weak and I cannot raise a hand."

He realized instantly how absurd was his speech. Was he not enunciating as a reasonable principle the very thing for which Red Eagle and all other good Cheyennes had cursed him? Was this not heresy, this doctrine of fair play? As for Standing Elk, he merely laughed, and the knife quivered in his hand with his eagerness.

However, he was willing to exchange words. First he spoke over his shoulder a few rapid words in Pawnee, but the Badger had picked up enough of this language to be able to understand that he said: "The Cheyenne is about to beg for his life. Come closer, brothers, and listen to him like a squealing deer!"

He added to the foe: "For my life, O White Badger, I paid with a horse."

"For my life," said the boy, " I shall pay with a horse."

This brought an exclamation of another sort from the tongue of the chief.

"Red Wind! Is he near?"

"Listen and look!" said the boy, and he raised a faint and shrill whistle.

There was a snort up the canyon and then the matchless swinging beat of the hoofs of the stallion as he came in answer. Then a clamor from the Indians.

The Cheyenne war chief was in an ecstasy. He beat his hands together. He leaped into the air. And then he ran, calling softly, towards Red Wind. The sick boy, turning his head, could see everything. He saw Red Wind pause with lifted head. Then the stallion whirled and was off!

"Ah, White Badger," said he, "you have put a devil in my horse and now he does not know me!"

"Hear me," said the boy. "Carry me to the village of the Pawnees. I, the White Badger, will call the stallion after us as we go. When Red Wind is safely in your hands, then will the price be paid?"

117

"Waugh!" snarled the chief. "How long will you live in the lodges of the Pawnees who know the things you have done? Their last chief is dead; his scalp dries now in your lodge and his spirit will rot with his body. Their finest horses have been driven away and now the Cheyennes mock us, riding on their backs!"

"It is true," said the Badger. "However, a man can die only once. I am ready to go to the other world. Or, if you take my scalp, I shall die contented. There is no grief in White Badger! But Red Wind shall be lost to you!"

"I shall catch him when the day comes, little fool," said the chief. "Why should I buy him with your life?"

"Wait for the morning and then try," said the boy. "Wait for the dawn. It will be very good to see Standing Elk, like a fool, run his horses to catch Red Wind. Is not my spirit in the horse? Does he not know my voice and come when I call to him? He has lost the Pawnee tongue, and he has learned the Cheyenne. You will need time, Standing Elk, to have him know you again. Think, my friend, and then speak to me."

And Standing Elk, in turn, sat down on a stone and bowed his head on his hand.

One of his warriors came up to his side and whispered, but loud enough for the boy to hear.

"The Badger makes medicine. Do not let him put a strong medicine on you, Standing Elk!"

"That is foolish talk!" said the war chief angrily.

And, forthwith, he gave command that they should bivouac for the night in that place. There were seven warriors in that party following the chief; and they were equipped for war, riding their finest horses. This the boy could tell as he noticed the sleek bodies of the animals in the flare of the fire, which the chief built recklessly high. There they made their bivouac and there they ate. And the Badger ate with them—but of his own meat. In the meantime, his guns, his ammunition, were in their hands, and those well-cleaned, well-oiled weapons were passed about from hand

118

to hand, the subject of rapidly chattered commendations.

"The guns of Clouded Sky," sighed Standing Elk. "But the Badger by a great medicine killed him with a knife and kept the guns in their covers. Not a shot was fired! Ah, Clouded Sky!"

He came back and rolled down his blankets at the side of the Badger. Then he tied the legs and arms of the Badger to his own, to make sure that the captive should not escape.

"Tell me," he said when he lay down again, "does the Badger come here alone, to die like a sick dog?"

"I come here alone that I may be near to Tirawa," said the Badger with a matchless effrontery. "He speaks to me, and I hear him, and his voice has made me well."

"The bear," said the chief with some emotion, pointing to the great, shadowy heap of the monster. "It was your shot that broke his neck?"

The story was simple enough, but there was no reason why a miracle could not be made of it. The Badger closed his eyes, mustered his thoughts, and replied as follows: "How many scalps hang in the lodges of the tribe of Standing Elk?"

"They are like crows hanging in the sky."

"That is good. But how many claws of the great bears are in your village?"

"It is true," said the chief. "There are not so many."

"Do you think," said the youngster, "that the White Badger, when he is sick, could sit up and kill a great bear?"

The chief was silent.

"I shall tell you how this thing happened," said the White Badger. "While the White Badger lay here sick—"

"You have lost that name, brother," said the chief. "When you die among the Pawnees, they will call you Lost Wolf, for here you are lost with a wolf and a bear dead at your feet!"

"It is good," said Lost Wolf, and as he turned the words in his mind, he knew that the appellation would stay with him, through a long life or through a short one. "Here I

119

lay and I heard a sound, and I wakened and there was White Hawk clinging to the throat of the great bear, like an ant to a claw of an eagle. I tried to lift my rifle. It was too heavy. My hand trembled on it and I could not lift the gun. I called on Tirawa, then, to help me!"

"So!" grunted the chief. And his heavy breathing, as he lay quietly, told the boy that the tale was taking effect upon him.

"Then, after I had made a quick prayer to Tirawa, I saw no face and no body. But I saw a white hand as wide as the barrel of my rifle is long!"

"This is wonderful!" whispered Standing Elk.

"It lifted my rifle and it placed it at my shoulder and when I looked, I saw that it was pointed straight at the throat of the great bear. So I pulled on the trigger—but see what weakness was on me! I could not pull the trigger home!"

"And then—"

"And then I thought that a great breath like a wind of ice blew on my right hand, and my finger curled on the trigger and the gun went off. The bear fell, but before the great hand disappeared, it put the gun away beneath the blanket.

"I felt a great weight roll on me. I thought to cry to Tirawa for help. I called: 'Tirawa—'

"Then I saw a great form, taller than the tallest tree that I have ever seen. It stood before me, but it was misty and I could see the flash of the brook through his sandals. I heard a voice thick and deep, like an echo between hills.

"'Little son,' said the voice, 'what will you have?'

"I tried to tell him that I wanted him to roll the body of the bear off me. But I was too sick and too weak. My throat was closed, also. And while I lay and watched, I saw the great form get thin, like a mist that comes out of the ground on a summer morning. And then it disappeared. This is all the truth!"

Over this prodigious lie, the chief pondered for a moment. Then he sighed.

"It is a great wonder!"

He raised himself on his elbow and his deep, strong voice rolled over the quiet between the hills.

"Listen to me, my friends. I have heard of a strange thing—" and so on to the end he talked with many pauses, and at the end, while the appreciative grunts of wonder from the Pawnees were still murmuring faintly to Standing Elk, he leaned over the form of the boy.

He raised his head again and spoke once more, whispering: "He sleeps! Even with us all around him, and his scalp hardly on his head more than a feather is on the wind, he sleeps! There is a great heart in this boy. Surely the mind of Tirawa sees him!"

20

So much, however, could not pass entirely unchallenged in such a brain as that of the Pawnee chief. The boy slept like a stricken person all the night and wakened with half his strength returned and all his wits about him. He found that his legs and arms were free. Only the chief sat upon his heels at his side and watched his face.

"When did you see Tirawa?" asked the Pawnee softly the instant the eyes of Lost Wolf were open.

But crafty as was the chief, his wits did not move quite so fast as the brains of the white man sharpened by his years of life upon the plains. And the answer of White Badger, alias Lost Wolf, was instant: "Two days ago, brother!"

"If Tirawa answers your prayer and kills the bear for you, why does he not answer your prayer now, and free you from the Pawnees? To Tirawa, even many Pawnees are as nothing. He could free you from them as easily as he freed you from the bear!"

"Ah, Standing Elk," said the boy smoothly—for had he not prepared himself for that question even before he fell asleep the night before—"I have prayed to him, and he does not send me an answer!"

The gravity with which he spoke apparently shocked the Pawnee more than the most complicated lie could have done. For it seemed, indeed, that the heart of the adopted Cheyenne was broken because of the negligence of Tirawa.

"Why does he not help you, then?" he asked. "Has he turned his face away from you?"

"I cannot tell," said Lost Wolf. "It may be that he has turned his face from me. He has seen Pawnees die under my hand. Perhaps he is angry because I allowed myself to fall into their grip this time!"

So much of scorn he allowed himself to speak, watching eagerly all the while askance, and he saw the leap of rage in the face of Standing Elk.

"No," said Standing Elk, speaking aloud, "it is better to keep you for the knives of the squaws, for they will make you last much longer than I could manage it! But Tirawa has turned from you at last, boy!"

"How can we tell?" asked Lost Wolf, with the most apparent frankness. "It may be that he is sending me to the Pawnees because he loves you and your people and wishes you to be given some great gift through me. Might it not be that? Perhaps he led me away from the Cheyennes and brought me to this place so that I could fall into your hands, and he made me sick, so that you would be strong enough—you and your men—to take me!"

To this sublime egotism, Standing Elk replied with a savage groan.

122

But there was too much of interest in what this boy had told him, and so long as Lost Wolf, alias the Badger, remained a prisoner, was it not better to keep him? Also, in case he could decoy Red Wind to the Pawnee camp?

Here, however, the scheme was found to contain a flaw. It was agreed by all of the followers of Standing Elk that in capturing Lost Wolf the war party had done enough to warrant a triumphal return to the village. And particularly if they could recapture Red Wind through the boy. But when Lost Wolf, accompanied by Standing Elk, went down the valley slowly and called to the horse, the stallion would not come closer than fifty yards. If they tried to steal up on him, he would whirl and be off in a flash.

"You must let me try to take him by myself," said the boy.

The chief grinned broadly.

"Ah, Lost Wolf," said he, "I remember that I have lost a brother and a great horse through you. Do you think that I shall still act as though you were a fool? Neither am I a fool. On the back of Red Wind, you would be away like a flash of red lightning through a black sky!"

"Surround me with men and horses and guns," said Lost Wolf. "Then let me go to Red Wind."

"Tush! Perhaps Tirawa would put down his hand and turn away our bullets. And besides, it is not easy to hit a running horse—and he is the running wind!"

"But am I not weak, brother? Could I sit long on his back even if I wished to run away?"

"You are weak in your body, but your wit is not weak," said the chief. "No, brother, you must stay with me. We ride back to my city, and Red Wind will follow you if you call!"

This was the way it was arranged. The boy was mounted on a spare horse, which was tethered to the pommel of an Indian's saddle, and Lost Wolf himself was tethered to the body of the Indian. Behind, Red Wind followed. Sometimes he would swoop away towards the horizon in the rear, as though determined to run back to the Cheyenne

Camp, but he always returned, coming with that effortless and beautiful stride that made him seem to be winging tiptoe across the plains. And once he came within ten yards of the rider to whom his master was tied. All those Pawnees watched with eyes of fire, each with a lariat ready. It was Standing Elk himself who whirled his horse, at last, and attempted to make the cast. But it was like throwing a rope at a wild cat. Red Wind doubled away in the winking of an eye and was off, shaking his tail high, as in mockery of their efforts.

Standing Elk was in a tremendous fury. He came back and rode at the side of Lost Wolf.

"What have you done to him?" he asked. "He would come when I called, two years ago!"

"Yes," said the boy, "it is two years. Well, I shall tell you. I have never slept more than five feet from his nose. I have petted him every day. I have ridden every day, even when I was sick, except the last three days of all when the hand of Tirawa was upon me. I have spent half a day teaching him his name. I have made him come when I called. I have made him learn my whistle. I have taught him to kneel and to rise for me. He will lie down on his side and roll over. He watches my hand and my eye. I do not have to speak to him, even. It is enough if he sees in my sign and in my eye what I wish of him. That thing is done instantly. So you see, Standing Elk, that I have used him as if he were my brother. Did you use him so?"

"Do the Cheyennes leave such horses in the hands of such boys?" asked the chief.

The answer of Lost Wolf was instant and dry: "Only boys who bring home the scalps of great Pawnees, and the horses of the greatest Pawnee war chiefs!"

It brought the usual snarl of hatred from the tall Pawnee, but he mastered his rage and cast a backward glance, where Red Wind was following at a light trot that was able to match the steady canter to which the Pawnees pushed their ponies. And Lost Wolf felt that his secret was safe. While he called to the stallion with his voice, the red horse was receiving a still stronger signal with the hand to go back!

Five days they wound across the plains, and on the evening of the fifth, they came into the village, the same which the boy had raided two years before, but moved far into another section of the prairie. They saw the war party returning, and returning too soon—but they saw also a ninth member of the group. Presently there was a wide-flung light cavalry swooping around them like a flight of eagles; men on saddleless horses, some without bridles, even. And they caught sight of the boy with a wild shrieking like the crying of birds of prey swooping into battle.

Lost Wolf—who felt himself lost indeed—could hear and partly understand as Standing Elk said over and over again to the fiercely questioning faces of his tribesmen: "Only until Red Wind is captured. He is the bait for the stallion. After we have the horse, then—we shall enjoy him. We shall let the women do what they can to him. And the women have many ideas. More than wolves!"

However, Lost Wolf was only twelve years old, and he trusted in the tigerish agility, the speed, and the hairtrigger wits of Red Wind to keep from captivity for a few days at the least. And before the capture of the stallion, was it not possible that he, Lost Wolf, could contrive a means to escape?

I have heard how he looked as he rode into the town, with his head high, smiling disdainfully as he turned from one side to the other—with his two black braids, of more silken hair than ever an Indian wore, sliding like two small snakes over his shoulders, and hawk feathers braided into them.

He was so lean from the fever and from the frightful ardors of that long, steady ride, that his stomach clave to his backbone, and his chest was the chest of a starved man.

125

The flesh on his arms and legs was dried, lean, and tough, also. And his hands and his feet looked more gigantic than ever.

The Pawnees felt that they had captured the greatest medicine that existed among the terrible Cheyennes, and they screamed and danced like demons in front of their captive.

I have all of these details from one who was sure to see them with care and to appreciate them in a fashion a little other than that of the Pawnees.

This was Danny Croydon, who was in that town in the capacity of trader. He, leaning on his long double-barreled rifle, saw these things and recognized the starved youth as the one who had pressed the muzzle of a gun against his back, two years before.

21

They tied my poor friend, who had become Lost Wolf through his latest exploit, to a pole in the center of the village, and the whole populace came crowding around him. He made a sufficiently imposing figure.

I have forgotten to say that the claws of that great bear had been cut off and now the whole twenty of them were arranged in a great necklace which the generosity of the chief permitted the prisoner to wear, whether from real admiration, or simply because Standing Elk wanted to make his own greatness appear still more imposing through the significance of his captive. For at first glance it looked as though the captive was no more than a mere overgrown youth!

The string of great grizzly claws around his neck made an essential difference, and when it was learned that the boy had sat up from a sick bed and killed the brute when he was too weak to hold up a rifle, the wonder, of course, grew; especially when it was learned that Tirawa had interceded directly and forcibly in his favor—and that his own eyes had seen the gigantic form of Tirawa like a fading mist.

All through that evening they crowded around the post where the boy stood tied, and their delight was increased to an absolute madness when it was known that this delightful morsel—this white and famous Indian—was to be turned over to the women in the end, that his death might be as protracted and as generally pleasant all around as possible!

That night he was taken to the lodge of Standing Elk, and there he slept until almost the next noon. When he wakened, he was ravenously hungry, and his guards—for the Elk considered him of such importance that two mature braves were kept at his side day and night—gave him the meat pot. He ate until his stomach was as hard as a rock and big as a balloon. Then he rolled over and slept until the next morning, when he yawned, stretched himself, sat up, and asked those around him if he were to be starved.

He ate again, immoderately. And by this time he was well. No wounded dog ever crawled into a hole, licked its hurts, and recovered more quickly than did Lost Wolf, alias the Badger. His ribs were not half so prominent; his stomach filled. He asked for a pipe, and receiving one, squatted on his heels and smoked.

And then, raising his head, he saw a white man standing in the open flap of the lodge—Danny Croydon himself. He had not marked the trader and trapper as he'd entered the village two evenings before.

"How!" said Danny Croydon at the flap of the tent. It was apparent that he was most welcome among the Pawnees, for he was at once asked into the lodge. He stood by the fire and looked at the boy, but without the slightest sign of recognition.

"This boy," he said to the chief presently, "is he strong?"

"So?" said Standing Elk. "This is Lost Wolf—the White Badger! Go ask in the village, friend!"

"I need a servant," said Danny Croydon, "to follow the trap line, and take out the pelts. What price for this boy?"

The chief merely laughed.

"Twenty ponies could not buy him," said he.

The trader smiled with perfect good nature. "But here is a gun," said he. And he thrust the double-barreled rifle into the hands of Standing Elk.

The eyes of Standing Elk flared with fire.

"But the whole village has seen him brought in," sighed Standing Elk. "Besides, brother, I cannot cheat you. You could not make a servant of him. He is not yet a brave, but he has done more than warriors, being still a boy! He killed Clouded Sky. He took Red Wind from me. He would cut your throat and steal all that you have!"

Danny Croydon took a quirt which was attached to his wrist and slapped his leg with it.

"I come," said he, "from a south country where we train our servants with the whip, as you train *your* horses. I know the way to train them so that they come along softly when you speak to them. And this boy is young. He can be taught!"

Suddenly he added: "I have five rifles in my pack! Go call in your wise men!"

Standing Elk was so staggered by this prodigious offer— for one of those rifles cost fully a hundred dollars, even at a reasonable rate without exorbitant profit—that he could barely get himself out of his lodge. He returned half an hour later with two sub-chiefs and three old men.

"Brother," said Standing Elk, "we have talked. For ten guns you may have him!"

But the trader shook his head.

"I have named all the fine guns in my packs!" said he.

"Eight guns!" said Standing Elk, holding up that number of fingers.

The trader turned to walk out of the lodge.

He was at the open flap when the trembling hand of an old man caught at his shoulder.

"It is enough," said the seer. "Five such guns will give us many scalps. And who can count scalps in money? Make this trade, Standing Elk!"

And that trade was made.

Lost Wolf—feeling lost indeed—had followed only the high points of this talk, but he had managed to follow along closely enough to keep him fairly well in touch with things. And when the rifles were placed in the hands of Standing Elk and the sub-chiefs, he had wit enough to protest when they gave him, with hobbled legs, to a new master.

"Look!" said he to Standing Elk. "You give me to one man. Can one man keep me? And when I finish taking his scalp, shall I not be coming back to take more among the Pawnees?"

"If we are fools," said the chief, "why do you tell us about it? No, no, Lost Wolf. You hate to serve. That is why you tell me this, but you are bought and paid for!"

22

There was only one point of possible argument remaining, and that was whether or not the trapper should be allowed to start away at once. The chief settled this. He pointed out that if Danny Croydon started now, the great stallion, Red Wind, would see him and would come flying after him.

But if he started during the night, the famous horse would not have a chance to take the trail and so he would be left wandering around the Pawnee camp. And, in the latter case, Standing Elk had no doubt as to his ability to capture Red Wind.

So it was in the dark of the early night that the trapper came into the lodge of Standing Elk and murmured to the boy in Cheyenne: "It is time, my son. You travel with me!"

"Suppose," said Lost Wolf, pretending the utmost distaste for this journey, "suppose that I refuse to go to be a slave to you?"

"Then," said that little man, "I shall take you like this."

With that he laid hold upon the boy and in a trice had him over his shoulder, like a sack of wheat—helpless, because the wrists and ankles of Lost Wolf were securely tied. In this way, surrounded by the exultant shouts of the Pawnees, he was carried to a horse and there his ankles were freed and he was put in the saddle with his feet tied again under the stomach of the horse.

The Pawnees were in ecstasies of delight. They whooped and yelled until the camp was crowded with an uproar, such was their delight at this summary treatment of an enemy.

"He will become less than a white man's dog—and there is nothing less than that!" said Standing Elk. "Besides, we have five good guns for him. Are they not better than his scalp?"

There was such a whoop of approbation from his tribe that he knew he had not lost by this transaction. Certainly they were not apt to accuse him of a heart too soft! The men and finally the boys accompanied them for a mile or more from the camp, shrieking their insults and their exultation into the ears of Lost Wolf, but when they were beyond that distance, the last of the Pawnees turned back. Still for half an hour the little train went on.

Two things were filling the heart of Lost Wolf. The first was that this man had remembered his own act of generosity so firmly that two years later he was willing to pay down five costly guns—each almost as precious as the life of a warrior! The second thing was that so small a trader had dared to pass into the camp and then out again!

For there were five mules and three ponies loaded with packs in the caravan of this trader, and each pack was doubtless crammed with valuables. Yet the man had dared to venture alone into the presence of Standing Elk and had come out again unscathed. This was something to be wondered at—not to be understood! But, as he remembered the keen, steady gray eyes of this white man and his resolute front, like a front of a rock, he felt that there were new sidelights thrown upon him. Perhaps Dan Croydon would have done the same thing with equal ease in the camp of the Cheyennes themselves!

He waited a little longer until they were safely out of reach of the village. Then he said: "This is far enough!"

Croydon had been riding in the rear of the procession. Now he closed up instantly and came to the side of the boy.

"You called to me?"

"I called. It is far enough now, I said."

"Far enough for what?"

"To set me free."

"To set you free?"

"Did you not buy me?"

"With five rifles."

"Was it not to set me free?"

Danny Croydon laughed heartily.

"Do you think," said he, "that I can afford to pay down five of the finest rifles in the world for the sake of setting a Cheyenne free from the stake?"

Lost Wolf digested this news sullenly, amazed. Yet he did not believe that there had been any bad purpose in the heart of the little man.

He said at last: "Is it true that you have taken me in order to make me work?"

"That is true!"

131

"Well—" said the boy, and let his voice trail away.

After all, this was better. Had he been set free, it would have meant that he would be under an obligation to Danny Croydon. But, as it was, it was much, much better. All he had to do was to take the first opportunity to slide a length of knife into the body of the trader. After that, he would take this caravan and lead it back to the lodges of the Cheyennes. He would be a greater man among them than ever. Far greater, indeed!

In the meantime, he hurriedly revised his opinions of the little man and of the entire white race. All the justice and the kindliness of which he had been accusing them in his heart of hearts was removed. They were simply like the Indians, though with skin of another color. Now he must bide his time, with Indian-like patience!

No opportunity came that night, where they camped on the open plains. His arms were now joined wrist to wrist by two manacles and a strong steel chain about three feet long. It gave him a great deal of freedom. He could work according to the bidding of his new master—his first master. Also, he could use either revolver or knife with that amount of freedom—if the chance offered!

That chance was not presented during the night. The packs containing weapons were handled by the trader alone. And that night, when they lay down, he was tied to the side of Croydon. At that, the heart of the boy rose into his throat. He was himself about five inches over five feet, and Croydon was hardly any more. To be sure, the weight of matured strength was in the white man, and the width of his shoulders, the depth of his chest suggested that there was much power in him. Here was a time when White Hawk would have answered an excellent purpose—stealing up to tear wide the throat of the trader! But White Hawk was dead!

In the meantime, no matter what the strength of the trader, Lost Wolf could fasten his thumbs in the neck of the man. Would that be much less efficient than the teeth of White Hawk?

He lay pretending sleep until midnight, at which time he was sure that the white man beside him slept. Then he began to move—as a hunting panther or an Indian moves. It required, perhaps, half an hour for him to change his place and roll upon his side, leaving his hands free to get at the other. But, when the time came, the slowness left him. His hands moved with the speed of darting snakes' heads, straight at the bare throat of Croydon.

They found their marks but, an instant later, as the white trapper wakened with a gasp, it seemed to the boy that hot steel bands gripped at his wrists. His hands were torn from their grip. He himself was whirled suddenly upon his back and above him was the furious, contorted face of the trapper. He found both of his hands taken in the incredible grasp of one of the trader's hands. And the cold point of a knife tickled his throat.

"You Cheyenne murderer!" grasped Danny Croydon. "Is this your game? Then, by God, I'll go back and see what the Pawnees will pay me for your scalp!"

The boy lay still. No words came into his mind. Besides, he had a feeling that almost anything he said would act merely as an invitation to thrust that knife into his throat. So he lay still.

Presently, with a snort of disgust and of hatred, Danny Croydon stood up. He put two more pairs of chains upon the boy and having tied his hands and his feet together behind his back, he went back and rolled himself in his blankets.

Lost Wolf lay quietly through the rest of that night, telling himself that there was one mercy granted to him by Tirawa. It was, that this humiliation had not happened to him in the presence of any witnesses. And the memory of that disgraceful manhandling could be removed only by knife stroke or bullet.

133

In the meantime, it was a most uncomfortable night for the boy.

He had to lie with his heels drawn far up toward his head. After a time, his backbone seemed to be giving way under the pressure. He tightened his stomach muscles all he could to relieve the strain on his back. But the stomach muscles gave way with something like a snap. And then his back sagged in.

If you doubt the agony of that position, try it in only a mild form. Hold it for five minutes. And then try to stand up.

Well, Lost Wolf had to remain like that for five hours. And during the last three of those hours he prayed for only one thing: death before he weakened so much that he had to groan or make a single sound of complaint.

In the first dawning of light, Danny Croydon waked with a yawn and looked across comfortably at his captive. Then something made him get up in haste and hurry to the boy. He loosed the binding chain, and the hands and heels of Lost Wolf snapped a few inches farther apart.

The trapper called harshly: "Up! Up! Are you still sleeping, Cheyenne?"

He saw a ripple of effort run through the body of the boy, but that was all. Not a limb stirred. And Danny Croydon bit his lip. He had meant punishment, to be sure, but he had not meant torture!

He slowly straightened the body of the boy and laid him on a buffalo robe on his back and stretched his taut arms by his side. But still there was no stir from Lost Wolf, except the slow heaving of his chest, and no sound from him except the faint gritting of his teeth as he struggled to keep back the groans.

But now that there was a human eye to behold him, Lost Wolf made his face a mask and forced even his eye to be calm.

"Little fool!" said Danny Croydon. "Yell! Howl! It'll do you good!"

There was no slightest change of expression.

"Pure Indian!" sighed Danny Croydon, and sat down to examine his captive in his thoughts.

23

Wrenched as though on a rack, crushed with a heavy agony for long hours together, there was still such toughness in the body of Lost Wolf that by midmorning he was able to sit on a horse, and then the trader reined back his horse beside the pack pony on which the boy sat.

"Lost Wolf," he said, "because I suppose that people will forget White Badger and call you by the new name—Lost Wolf, I intended to make you remember that you tried to throttle me while I was sleeping. But I didn't mean to torment you, lad. Will you believe that?"

Upon the trader, Lost Wolf turned an Indian's eye, blank, dull, without a thought showing in it. And Danny Croydon sighed, because he knew that hatred was stored in the heart of the boy and that years would be needed before that hatred would be expended.

A moment later, his thoughts were taken in a different direction, for coming at a lightning gallop out of the horizon, like a point of red fire—so did he shine in the sun— Red Wind swept upon them and then careered around and around the little caravan, whinnying, as though to stop them, and shaking his glorious head at his young master.

"Call him, Lost Wolf!" said the trader.

But Lost Wolf turned upon the other a blank eye again, as though there were no meaning in his mind.

Danny did not need to assure me, afterwards, how the anger surged up in his heart. He rode close to the boy once more and spoke to him savagely.

"Lad, you and I are going to pass a long spell together. I've a hope that we'll get on well together before the end. But if we don't, it'll be hell for both of us, but most of all, for you!"

There was no reply from the white Indian. And they trekked on across the plains.

It must have been a grisly journey for Danny Croydon, traveling with no hand to help him, and with a chained panther with a human brain in his company. On the fifth day, they met with a big trader's caravan hurrying out into the Pawnees' territory. Croydon left the boy secreted in a hollow and drove his train in among the caravan.

It took a scant two hours to dispose of his wares. He was an expert. The skins which he received were twice as good as the average. And the whole of his packs made up a considerable treasure. But he got what he wanted.

A good part of it was gold. The remainder consisted of a fine saddle horse, and a quantity of powder and lead, together with a number of the best steel traps of all sizes. He traded away his good mules, also, and took in their places a number of sturdy ponies, picked for strength, not for speed, though any Indian pony could run fast enough!

He got from the caravan, also, a quantity of flour, baking powder, yeast, and some bacon, sugar, and coffee. These articles all are hard to come at in the West—at least, the West of those days, when an Indian would trade a painted buffalo robe for the sake of a few cups of sweetened tea!

In this manner he returned to Lost Wolf and found that boy sitting cross-legged, his face as great a blank as ever. Then they began to trek again and pegged wearily away at it until they were among the foothills, and then foothills changed to the northern mountains. There, in a valley blackened with enormous evergreens, Danny Croydon made his camp. He was on the headwaters of a river down which he could float on a home-made raft when he chose to move from this place. Meanwhile, he intended to camp here and trap as long as the furs came easily to him. And here, also, he would have the boy to himself. What he intended with Lost Wolf, in a word, was the redemption of that tigerish youth from barbarism to civilization.

I cannot tell the tale as Danny Croydon told it. I lack his oaths, for one thing; and he has a great store of them!

In the beginning there was the making of a clearing and the felling of trees to make a cabin, for they would live here for a year, at the least. On the first day, he shackled the legs of Lost Wolf with a padlocked steel hobble-chain. Then he gave him an ax and told him to go to work.

Deliberately, he turned his back on Lost Wolf through that first half day. For his own part, he was busy watching the great heap of provisions and weapons, and all the miscellany which had been removed from the backs of the Indian ponies. Then he had his own ax-work to perform. But, at the end of the half day, he went hunting for Lost Wolf. And the boy had disappeared!

What chills went through the body of the trader when he discovered that, without foot tracks in any direction, Lost Wolf was gone from all ken! There was only one possible explanation.

Danny Croydon began to seek eagerly for signs, looking not on the ground but in the trees, for no matter how big the "medicine" of this boy, he could not simply melt away to thinnest air. At the end of a long search, he spied the boy by merest chance in the fork of a great pine a full mile from the place where he had started. Using his powerful young arms alone, he had worked his way from tree to tree, swinging from one to the other at the risk of breaking his neck a hundred times, no doubt. Nevertheless, there he was, a mile away. He had covered that distance and he had spied the pursuer and hidden himself well, had it not been that a mischievous blue-jay, that extraordinary envoy

137

placed by the devil upon the earth, hovered about the tree, setting up a great chatter. So the trader found his man in the crotch of the tree and put a bullet into the trunk a few inches above his head.

Lost Wolf came down, and stood with folded arms at the bottom of the tree.

He said to his captor with dignity: "I cannot work. I am a Cheyenne. A Cheyenne warrior cannot work like a squaw. Kill me, white man. I shall not work like a woman."

"Will you go back to the camp?" said Danny Croydon.

"Kill me," said the boy. "I shall not go!"

And Danny Croydon carried him back to the camp! A mile through heavy brush and thick timber; but then Danny was Danny. There was never another like him. He had a hundred and seventy pounds compacted in his five feet five inches; and he had little to show the enormous power of his body except the long, dangling, odd-looking arms, like the arms of a monkey. He carried the boy back to the camp and put him down and chained him to a tree.

He left him there all of that day but, the next morning, he went to Lost Wolf again.

He said, cheerfully: "Did you sleep long, Lost Wolf?"

Lost Wolf did not reply.

"I give you still another chance," said Danny Croydon. "I set you free from the tree. I fix this heavy chunk of iron on your chain so that you cannot run or climb very far. I give you this ax again, and here is a jug of water. Now you can work if you please. But until you have cut down a tree, you cannot have food!"

Lost Wolf said not a word.

And for three days—five days—seven days, he continued his fast. There was nothing but water. All day he sat motionless as a stone, or lifting his eyes, perhaps, to see a leaf falling from a nearby tree.

But on the eighth day, Danny Croydon heard the faint sound of an ax in the forest on the far side of the clearing which he had made. His stern heart leaped. He dropped his ax and listened. Again came the sound. It was feeble, indeed. At intervals, the noise continued for three hours. Then there was the crash of a tree.

Danny Croydon hurried to the spot and found that Lost Wolf was so weak that it had required all of this time for him to moil and maul at a tender little sapling. But the sapling had come down!

So Croydon picked him up over his shoulder and brought him to the temporary tent where he was living, and put him on a buffalo robe and placed food beside him.

Lost Wolf maintained the air of a perfect stoic, except for a violent working in his throat. And Croydon knew that this muscular constriction was a mute way of expressing the agony of shame, of grief, of despair which was wringing the soul of the boy because he had allowed his flesh to conquer his spirit! And yet he had maintained his fast for eight whole days, with the tempting smell of cookery in his nostrils each day! I cannot see how any normal creature could have endured even for a single day, with a mountain-air built appetite struggling against him!

However, this was the first step of the tragedy, if you choose to call it that. Danny Croydon decided that no matter how far he might be able to progress with the young wild man, there would never be anything but hatred in the soul of the latter.

Nevertheless, Lost Wolf accepted the first lesson. Accepted it in frightful silence and bitterness of heart. He worked as much as his returning strength allowed him to work. He even allowed Danny Croydon to come and work beside him, and he picked up the lessons in axmanship which Croydon bestowed on him.

Until, finally, the result of that fasting was gone, and the body of Lost Wolf was strong and plump again; and Croydon, watching, could see that Lost Wolf was rejoicing in the rhythmic labor with the ax, or in the more exacting process of clearing the logs of branches and then squaring them. Even at that time, says Danny Croydon, that boy worked with the strength of a man and the eye of an Indian. On the third day he could square a log with more precision than his master.

So, working hard, but living on the best of game, it would seem impossible that Lost Wolf would not find his spirits rising, but Danny Croydon found in the eye of the boy only a constantly waiting shadow of hatred—a vast spirit greater than a mere hatred. And, for twenty days, Lost Wolf spoke not a single human syllable!

24

He sat down in front of his captive one night and spoke to him in the following fashion: "Steel is stronger than your muscles will ever be. And steel is smarter than your wits will ever be! Now, Lost Wolf—or whatever your real name is, Smith or Jones, or Brown or what—as long as you keep your mug shut and won't talk, and try in every way to make things mean for me, just that long will I keep the steel on you. But I'll tell you what I'll do. If you'll give me a promise not to try to run away, I'll trust to the promise to keep you here. Just gimme your word and I'll take that word that you'll not knife me in the night for the sake of revenge, and my scalp, and my ponies, and all of the stuff in the camp—besides Red Wind to float away on, and a pile of gold in the saddle bags that'll buy twice as good an outfit as all of this is! Now, Lost Wolf, I'll take that chance with you if you'll simply give me your word, and shake my hand and tell me that you won't try to get away. The steel comes off your legs, and you're free to go and come around this here camp as you please—except that you got to do what I tell you to do!"

Through the major portion of this speech, the eyes of Lost Wolf grew greater in size and in brilliance; but with the last sentence the brilliance was snuffed out of them and they were as black and as blank as ever.

Croydon saw that he had failed again. He took a turn up and down the camp and relieved himself with a little freehand swearing. Then he came back to young Lost Wolf.

You must remember that the three weeks in the shadows of the trees had taken off so many coats of tan from the face of Lost Wolf that it was plainly a white boy who sat and watched his captor. And Danny Croydon fired a last shot.

"If you'll give me your word to stay and do what I tell you to do," said he, "I'll give you *my* word for another thing. The minute that you're able to stand up to me and put me down so that I can't get up again—fair wrestling or fair fist-fighting, whichever way you want it—well, Lost Wolf, the minute that time comes, you're a free man to go wherever you damn well please!"

The mouth of the boy opened with an incredulous gasp. And he covered his lips quickly with his hand, which is the Indian's usual sign of wonder and of delight.

For the first time in twenty days he spoke: "I give you my word and my hand!"

They shook hands, and two seconds later the ankles of Lost Wolf were free. He straightened himself on his tiptoes. But he said not another word.

There began a fortnight of the most frightful anxiety for Danny Croydon. He did not keep his eyes closed for ten minutes at a time during the day or the night. And when a brief moment of sleep *did* come to him, he wakened into a nightmare in which he saw the homely face of the pseudo-Indian leaning above him, and the strong hands of Lost Wolf reaching for his throat.

In the meantime, he used his best endeavors to open a

regular system of schooling for the youngster. The program was somewhat as follows:

In the morning they traveled the trap-line. It was eighteen miles long in all of its curls and twists and windings. That gave them each a walk of a nine-mile radius. It was a four-hour swing, aside from any trapped creatures which they found, and any skinning they had to do. It was in the chill of autumn, and there were not too many hours of daylight to work in. When they got back to the shack, it was middle afternoon and there were various things to do—such as the thousand and one little odd jobs around the shack, or sharpening of axes, or strengthening of the wood shack, or stretching of skins, or the curing, perhaps, of some meat against a time of possible winter famine. Or else Danny Croydon would take the boy down the valley to some meadow lands where tall, rich grass was growing. There was only a sickle in the packs of Croydon, but that sickle was enough to lay down a great quantity of the grass. It was then kicked into windrows and finally forked into shocks with a wooden fork designed and made by the expert hands and knives of Danny Croydon, who was as handy as a sailor! When that hay was cured, it was heaped upon an improvised sled and dragged up the valley to the stable which had been built adjoining the dwelling cabin. There was space here for all the Indian ponies to be herded in and fed during the same famine days of winter. There was also a stall arranged for the permanent accommodation of Red Wind.

On the very first day of the freedom of the boy, Croydon saw him start down the valley at the true Indian's gait, long-striding and frictionless. A little later, he saw a wink of red light on the top of a hill.

"I'll never see the rascal again," sighed Danny Croydon.

But in an hour, the stallion came back with Lost Wolf on his back and was carefully introduced to Croydon. This was an odd performance; Lost Wolf kept one hand upon the neck of the stallion and Red Wind behaved very amica-

142

bly about the matter. But the instant the hand of the master was removed, Red Wind leaped back and flattened his ears. So he remained to the end. Croydon could never put a hand on him!

So the days were filled busily enough, but the nights remained, and the nights rapidly began to grow longer than the days. The moment the darkness came, the single room of the shack was lighted by rags dipped in tins of grease. By that light they cooked the second and main meal of the day, and after he had eaten like the wolf after which he was named, the boy invariably curled up and slept half an hour. It was a custom from which nothing could break him. Thereafter, he wakened, cleaned up the dirty tins, and was ready in a trice for the most grueling torment of the entire program.

He had to learn to read and to write; he had to learn his numbers, his geography, his history, and all from Danny Croydon. But, after all, Danny was not such a poor teacher. He had enthusiasm for his work, in the first place. In the second place, he had been in the plains most of his life and therefore what he read in books about the rest of the world, even about the East and the West of his own country, was as wonderful as any fairy tale to him.

He did not read a great deal, of course, but he had a Bible, out of a sense of necessity; just as he always kept a bottle of good whisky in his camp as a medicinal need! He had a *Pilgrim's Progress* and a *Robinson Crusoe*, both well studied. He had a little history of the United States and a common school geography, in which he read with a ceaseless delight. In mathematics he had nothing but a schooling in the simplest arithmetic. This was the sum total of his equipment to teach Lost Wolf; yet he made up for his lacks by a tremendous enthusiasm for his task.

It was a grisly struggle! Lost Wolf sat down with a drawn and haggard face and stared helplessly, in an agony, at the letters which his companion drew out with pencil and told him to copy. Yet he began to pick up that art with truly

143

amazing speed. His hand was already partly educated in his practice at painting on the buffalo robes. It soon learned to form the letters with precision and speed. In the meantime, he was picking up a knowledge of English very rapidly.

For two hours at reading, writing, and numbers, the brain of Lost Wolf struggled every night. Then he sat exhausted by the fireplace and listened to his companion talk.

Men have to talk when they are in the woods. I have heard a great many people speak of the taciturnity of woodsmen and pioneers in general. As a rule, I have found them a good deal like the Indians. They do not talk until they are with friends, but the moment they find themselves in agreeable society, they rattle away at a great rate. Each man has the floor by turn. He narrates as he chooses, usually with great detail, all that he has heard and seen and done connected with the story at hand.

There was only one conversationalist in this camp. That was Danny Croydon, but it was no frightful handicap to him. To this day Danny can outtalk almost any three men I know. In the day he sticks close to his work. In the evening he sticks still closer to his pipe and his talking. And through his yarning in the evenings in that cabin, Lost Wolf learned a background of what the life of the white man really is. He listened acutely. What he heard, he never forgot—to the frequent dismay of the trader.

This continued for a fortnight, as I have said, and Croydon was growing more and more exhausted with the nervous tension, never knowing when the young tiger would turn and rend him, when all came to a climax one day in the forest.

He had slipped into a muddy spot as deep as his waist, and he found the stuff a blue-mud, wonderfully tenacious—almost like glue. As he struggled to draw himself out of the entanglement, something like a flickering shadow went across his mind.

144

He managed to turn himself about from the gravelly bank, and on the farther side of the stream, he saw Lost Wolf, naked to the hips, as usual except in freezing weather, and with one of the trader's fine double-barreled rifles slung across his arm!

25

For a matter of eight or ten seconds, the boy remained there, grinning wickedly across at the helpless trader. There was no doubt that he realized what was passing in the mind of the other. But then he raised the rifle to his shoulder and the muzzles snapped into line on Danny Croydon.

"You Cheyenne devil!" shouted Croydon.

Lost Wolf laughed softly. The muzzles rose and bore upon the tree above him. Then one barrel exploded. Down from the tree tumbled a tiny squirrel and the bleeding body fell a matter of inches from one of the hands of Croydon. The head of the little creature had been blown neatly away.

"It is good meat," grinned Lost Wolf, and with that turned away.

As for Croydon, he had received a lesson which enabled him to close his eyes in peace that night. Nothing was ever said between them concerning that meeting and the death of the little tree-climber; but Croydon had a fairly definite conviction that all of this had been done by the boy merely to convince his companion that there was no longer any cause to fear him. Certainly he never again lost an hour's sleep over that question.

In the meantime, the winter was closing rapidly over the mountains; then the first snow came, and when the trees were loaded with white, Lost Wolf settled down beside the fire wrapped in a buffalo robe and looked at Danny in wonder when the latter ordered him to be up and stirring. For, in an Indian village, the white of winter is a sign for all life to stop except for the uncontrollable scampering of the children and their wild, unceasing voices. As for the men, their time is given up to feasting. A feast may be given at any time of day and it consists of nothing more than the ordinary meat diet or whatever other items are current in the camp at that season. They sit about—the host together with his bidden friends—and tell stories, laugh and chatter together. All of this continues, unless their store of provisions proves too small. Then the tribe may starve before it comes upon game!

But after eight years of this living, Lost Wolf could not consider the white man serious when Croydon told him that their work must continue as usual.

He went trembling and stiff with fear of the cold into the open morning. There the rousing voice of Croydon seemed to cheer him a little, and presently he was off on his line of traps as swiftly as ever.

It took a scant week to acclimate him to such a life. Work, he found, drove away entirely the little tremorous touches of cold which used to prick him all winter long in the Cheyenne camp. Work made his blood leap humming through his veins. Work arched his chest, and above all, work began to robe his shoulders, arms, back, hips, and thighs with neatly coiled muscles. And, rising every morning, he stretched himself and felt his stature increasing, and felt the other diminish by contrast.

They had snowshoes—homemade—after a time. And now, as the white grip of the winter settled on the mountains, with the Indian ponies trembling and starving in the valley and coming twice a week to the stable shed for hay, and with Red Wind constantly housed, the income of furs

146

suddenly jumped. Danny Croydon had not chosen that spot by chance. His line of traps extended across the lower part of a natural mountain pass, and every fox who roved in that territory was apt to start out for the morning or the evening hunt in the heart of the pass. There were four little beaver streams, also, in this valley, and they produced a growing stock. Fox and mink and beaver were the principal harvest for Danny Croydon. And he reaped that harvest thick and fast. They were busy every evening, now, with the preparing, cleaning, and stretching of skins. But still there was always the necessity of the two hours of slavery for the boy in the dark of the night.

Custom made it a little easier for him. He could write, now, and he could read. He attacked his tasks with a savage energy. And Croydon found that the way to get the most out of him was not to condemn him to a certain period of labor, but to set him a job which had to be done. Then, no matter how long the task assigned might be, Lost Wolf attacked it with fury. Perhaps, in the end, he won only ten minutes from his rule of two hours. But those minutes, marked carefully upon the ticking watch of Croydon, meant more than gold or diamonds to the boy! He lolled in ridiculous triumph during that won time and refused all work—even the replenishing of the fire.

So the progress of Lost Wolf became a staggering thing to Danny Croydon. The zeal with which he fought his tasks of book knowledge was all inspired, perhaps, by the desire to get done sooner with the torment for that single day, but Lost Wolf was striding forward through heaps of accumulated facts. And Danny Croydon, watching the good work proceed, wondered, and rejoiced.

Another matter was progressing also. With better food than he had ever eaten before, with constant work each day, and with an ideally healthy life, Lost Wolf was growing in height and in bulk. And as the winter softened into spring and the boy approached his thirteenth year, he halted one day in the trail at the side of Danny.

He stood exactly five feet and six inches in height—a full inch above Danny. And he weighed exactly a hundred and forty pounds! It was a big height and a bigger weight for such a youngster. And Lost Wolf, with the glory of his strength swelling in him like sap in a young tree, looked fiercely into the eye of Danny on this morning.

The trapper had paused and in the eye of his companion he saw what was coming. Now Danny loved a fight, I suppose, better than any creature in the world—except Lost Wolf himself, in his later days—but Danny, knowing his own strength, felt a touch of rare pity.

"Lost Wolf," he said suddenly, "you are thinking of fighting me now for the sake of your freedom, are you not?"

"Why should I not?" asked the boy.

"I shall show you," said Danny with a smile. "I have been teaching you a great many things this winter, but I've forgotten to teach you how to fight—hands or fists! Try hands first, Lost Wolf!"

"We wrestle?" asked the boy.

"First!"

They closed instantly—and suddenly Lost Wolf found himself stretched softly on the ground, face down.

"You see?" said Danny Croydon. "Then I put this hand under your shoulder and so up and behind your neck—and the other hand under your other shoulder and behind your neck—I press down—I could break your neck, Lost Wolf. But that is only the first lesson!"

He stood up and allowed the youngster to rise, and the brow of the youth was dark, you may be sure; he swallowed his expression of sullenness, but Danny knew that bitterness stuck in his throat!

"There is still the hard fist!" said Lost Wolf.

Danny sighed.

"Listen to me, lad, and I'll tell you a story. When I was a lad your age I could lick every boy in my home town. And I used to read about the great prize-fighters. I wanted to be like those chaps. And so I used to practice and try to make my hands and my feet fast, and make them keep time, too. Well, son, I worked hard every day for four or five years learning the tricks of the trade. When I was fifteen, I came onto the plains. But I've had enough training in fights, since then, to keep me pretty supple. Do you think, Lost Wolf, that you can give me thirty pounds of a man's strength and all of four or five years of steady training—and then beat me?"

Lost Wolf bit his lip and the fire leaped from his eye. But he swallowed the agony of his desire. He was fierce enough for any work, but he knew that Danny Croydon was not lying, and he knew the weight of Danny's hand. So he said no more!

However, a new era dawned for the pair of them. After this moment they worked together each day for an hour or more, striving eagerly at one another. And the long arms and the hard hands of Danny Croydon taught Lost Wolf all their craft of boxing and wrestling.

When he could snatch a moment from the work or the study of the day, he was forever begging Croydon to tell him more and still more; and show him how that hip lock was managed, and how the arm hold succeeded; or again in what posture foot and hand must be; and how the balance of the body must be maintained as two boxers dexterously advanced or retreated from one another. Moreover, when Croydon could not teach him or box or wrestle with him, he would spy out the boy working by himself eagerly, patiently, untangling point after point that had baffled him in the bout of the day before.

Thirteen is a tireless age where there is a real zest for the work at hand, and a real zest was assuredly in the heart of young Lost Wolf. For he struggled not only to master a manly art, but because that art was the means whereby he hoped, one day before many months passed, to conquer his captor and set himself free.

And he said to Danny Croydon, on a day the latter found him sitting in a brown study by the fire in the shack:

"Speak to me about one thing. Why do you show me the way to beat you?"

"Because," said Danny Croydon, carelessly, "I have never been beaten, and I never will be until I'm old!"

It was a hasty speech, and when he looked down at the black face of the boy, he regretted it with all his heart!

26

Now I should like to be able to go into detail as to how this strange pair lived together in the cabin. But though Danny Croydon found much to tell me about that time, it was such stuff as does not appear interesting in a history. There is a saying that the country is happy whose annals are short. And the vital annals of the next four years in the life of my Lost Wolf were brief indeed!

The program was the same, year in and year out. They lived in the cabin always. In spring and autumn and winter, Danny Croydon took the products of the traps down the river in a boat which the two of them had built with the most infinite trouble, and during the summer, having sold the pelts, he trafficked with the Indians. Not with the Cheyennes or the Pawnees any longer, but north-ward with the Dakotans.

And the prosperity of Danny waxed wonderfully. As he told me afterwards, from the day when he first met with Lost Wolf—then called the White Badger—to the time when he left that boy—perforce—his affairs never were in a backward state, but he went from one stage of prosperity to another, in the most amazing fashion. He could afford, among other things, to bring out a little library of books to the cabin where Lost Wolf waited for him.

"Who are the books for?" I asked him in the second summer.

Danny Croydon dropped his broad chin on his hard, black fist.

"One of these here days," said Danny, "I'm coming down out of the mountains, and I'm gunna turn loose a man-sized tornado on your little old town. But up to the time that I do that, I don't want to answer any questions."

"You've found a wife, Danny," said I. "And that's why you look so contented. Because you have someone to keep you contented at home. And what's this I hear of the balance that is growing in your bank account?"

"I've got someone at home that keeps me busy," said Danny. "Yes, and contented, too, in a way!"

And he laughed in such an odd fashion that I confess it made the blood leap in my heart. And a little cold chill twisted down my back.

"What do you mean?" I asked him.

"Oh, I'll show you—unless I get torn to pieces by the tornado before I'm able to show it to you!"

After that, he resolutely dodged all talk with me about the thing which he had done.

It was only long afterwards that I learned how he had taught the boy until there was no longer any room for teaching, because Lost Wolf could turn about and teach him—so far as book knowledge was concerned. For five long years that boy was in the hands of an inexorable teacher and for five long years Lost Wolf sweated by day and studied by night. I suppose there is a way of understanding why he was able to boil down so much in even such a compass of five years. Two or three hours a day is not much, you will say, but those hours were of absolute concentration and they were applied *every* day—not five days a week, seven or eight months of the year.

Lost Wolf was changing rapidly—very rapidly. He had lost some of his very dark sun-stain. That forest life so many months of the year had weathered him to what should be called a lighter grain of mahogany. But he was not really as good-looking as he had been when a boy—and as a boy he had been ugly enough.

See him, then, as Danny Croydon saw him at the threshold of his seventeenth year: a youth standing an inch or so above six feet, with perhaps a hundred and eighty pounds of bone and muscle distributed over him carefully—I mean, at the points of most important leverage. You see a thick-chested, ample-shouldered, long-armed, gaunt-waisted youth. You see him with an efficient, rather than a beautiful body. You see a big, heavily corded neck, meant to carry and support through any battering a head ideally suited to be the head of a warrior—with a broad, square jaw, a high, cruel nose, and black, rather slanting, Oriental eyes.

How under the high heavens did such a child ever issue from the marriage of Tommy Tucker and Rose? Well, I cannot pretend to answer. Lost Wolf was not like his parents. And if he was like his grandparents or any of his ancestry—God pity that ancestry!

For there was ample trouble ahead of our young Lost Wolf!

Thinking of him, so tall, so powerful, so well trained in the finer arts of wrestling and of boxing, I often wondered why it was that he allowed five whole years to slip away without making an attempt at his fighting teacher, Danny Croydon. For Danny was thirty-seven years old now, and his body seemed almost as strong, his arms fully as long and almost as agile as ever; but there was a difference. Something of the tough leathery quality of youth was gone from him and would never return except in moments of hysteria.

Danny himself said that he was equally puzzled. Sometimes he thought it was because the boy really feared him. Sometimes he thought it was because the young devil had an idea that there was still something which he might learn from Danny—something about the management of guns, or the use of fists in stand-up fighting, or of the whole body in wrestling, or some necessary craft of hand, useful to the plainsman.

On the whole, Danny inclined to the second opinion. He did not believe that there was much sentiment in Lost Wolf!

Ah, well, that goes to prove that even a sharp fellow like Danny can be foolish in certain matters.

But, as I say, the dawning of the seventeenth year of Lost Wolf arrived, and then Danny Croydon said to him on a day: "Will you go down with me to Zander City?"

"Do you ask me or do you tell me?"

"I ask you, Lost Wolf. If you wish to go for the fun of it— in the big boat with me—"

They built a new boat each spring, you must understand, and Croydon went floating down the river on it, steering it with a sweep, because it was a good deal too big to respond much to oars. Only when the weather was fair, he could hoist a rude sail that would push up a heavy bow wave on either side of the awkward craft. But it took a sizable craft to carry all that Danny had for the traders every winter!

"Is the boat large enough to carry a horse?"

"Certainly not! You know the boat as well as I know it!"

"Then I cannot go."

"But why?"

"I cannot go without Red Wind."

"Is that it? Damn it, lad, if the ponies can get along in all seasons without you, Red Wind can get along without you!"

Here Lost Wolf whistled and out of the woods bounded Red Wind, ten years old, but young-hearted as a horse of five, so little work had he done in all those years. He galloped full speed to the hand of his master and halted with his head and neck thrust over the shoulder of the youngster.

"I cannot go without Red Wind," said Lost Wolf.

"If you ride along with me on the bank," said Danny,

"you'll be scalped and your horse stolen by Indians. There's no doubt of that!"

"They may scalp me if I cannot swim out to the boat," said the boy, "but they will not catch Red Wind. Do you think that they are more wise than Standing Elk and his men? Or are their ponies faster than the ponies of Standing Elk and the other Pawnees?"

There was a sound argument in this, and Danny Croydon was willing to listen to arguments which were much worse in their sound and in their general tenor. For he wanted the boy with him. I must tell you in short that Danny Croydon loved that wild boy whom he had taught all that a white man needed to know—except law and the Bible. He loved the boy, but he dared not show his love, for to him Lost Wolf was a creature of iron.

"Very well," said Danny Croydon. "You may come with me!"

It was settled in that way. They had the boat finished and loaded within another ten days, and with a fair wind they whirled along down the river, Danny managing the sail and Red Wind flaunting and dancing along the shore.

I shall not speak of the trip down the river. I am too eager to tell you how I first met with Lost Wolf. However, I suppose that a whole book really should be devoted to the story of how they floated down the river to Zander City. Perhaps sometime I shall be able to write the narrative as Danny Croydon told it to me in part, and in part as I was able to learn afterwards from many other sources.

I remember, among other things, that the total pleasure on the trip down the river was not all for Danny. It was only about once every second day that he had a sight of Red Wind glancing toward the river.

The rest of the time, he and his rider were galloping away toward the southern horizon, dipping out of sight and then a day or two later dipping back again.

"Where have you been?" Danny would yell to him,

bringing the boat closer toward the shore. "That country is full of Indians! Damned dangerous, Lost Wolf."

"Good!" Lost Wolf would answer. "I shall not forget the next time."

So they came down the river in the dusk of an evening and they saw the lights of Zander City floating on the river far before them, looking like quite a great city indeed! And, far off, they heard the noise of guns. Danny Croydon squirmed. Then he looked at the statuesque horseman on the river bank. He felt that perhaps he had been a trifle in a hurry in bringing his wild man to town.

27

Everything was easy and smooth in the beginning. Danny brought his boat to the shore and left Lost Wolf to keep guard over it while he went to the town to procure conveyances to carry the stuff to a place of safe-keeping.

There was no disturbance. One or two loungers by the riverside came to peer at the boat and its heaped contents, but a single deep-throated grunt from Lost Wolf gave them warning and they retired in haste.

Two wagons came for the pelts. They were loaded and drawn up to the little warehouse and there a guard marched up and down all night long to watch them, together with a score of similar treasures.

Then Danny Croydon started for my house. He walked in the lead and Lost Wolf, on the red stallion, followed. What Danny wanted least to do was to pass through the noisy central portion of the town—that section where the light was glowing above the streets and where voices were shouting and singing—with the distinct rumbling of many feet stamping on the board floorings.

When I say that Zander City was a fur town I say a thing which most people of these days don't understand. But a "fur" city was a masterpiece which the devil would have admired and placed his own stamp of approval upon. And as Danny Croydon heard that hell roaring and singing and yelling and stamping and shooting, he felt that he had played the part of a jackass indeed in bringing this bit of oil and tinder close to such a fire!

However, he had proceeded so smoothly and easily so far in his journey that he hoped that he could bring Lost Wolf to me by back ways. He turned a corner, in this process, and suddenly found himself in the midst of the night life of Zander City!

The trouble was that the city had grown huge during the past year since Danny was last there. Where there had been, formerly, open lots and a few scattering shacks, leading up to my house on the edge of the town—and the quietest edge—there was now a wide extension of the miserable little hovels which were called residences or stores. There were wide, high boardwalks on either side of the streets; the center of those streets was sure to be knee-deep in mud or fetlock-deep in dust. Since there had been a few dry days and wind, the streets were now deep in the dust.

Finding himself in the midst of such a street, and knowing that to turn back would be simply to attract attention to himself, and to his strange-looking companion on the beautiful horse, Danny stepped to the side of Lost Wolf.

He said: "Down there you see that big house? That is where we are going. Now, Lost Wolf, I have told you that this town is filled with rough men—very wrong, bad men. If you go alone there will be less chance of getting into trouble. Go as straight and as quickly as you can to that house behind the big red fence. I'll go in the same direction. I'll walk on the sidewalk. You ride straight to the house. You understand?"

Lost Wolf nodded, keeping his back very straight and stiff and his face immobile, like any true Cheyenne in the midst of confusion and strangeness.

"Very well," said Danny. "Remember that there'll be trouble there if you give trouble a chance!"

He regretted that warning, afterwards.

Then he stepped back onto the sidewalk and mixed with the crowd. Faces and voices out of hell, as I said before. Gamblers, murderers fled from civilization and hanging on this farthest outpost, traders, trappers, wild men, Indians—and a mere sprinkling of decent men newly come in from the plains, or come up the river bound for the plains, and even these half-maddened by the poisonous stuff labeled as whisky which was sold in the saloons.

No one remained long on the street. All over the little town men were hurrying from saloon to saloon—from one gambler's hell to another—hurrying, hunting for pleasure, never finding it, but frightfully excited with the pursuit of it.

And, I suppose, pleasure is really just the pursuit of pleasure. It is not whisky we drink, but something beyond the whisky, a phantom of delight the doors to which will be opened by the demon in the bottle—

Well, one cannot help moralizing a little if one has lived in such a place as Zander City!

Meanwhile, we have left Danny on the sidewalk, and in the dusty street, a hundred yards from my house, was Lost Wolf, sitting on the back of the finest horse that ever trod the paths of that wicked town.

As for Lost Wolf, he looked like a rather pale Indian—that was all. From his braided hair to his moccasins and his short-stirruped seat in the saddle, he was exactly what any Cheyenne might have been expected to be. And so he might have passed unnoticed in the crowd had it not been for Red Wind.

You must understand that there was a good deal of light, of a very uncertain sort, cast by big lanterns with huge burners which smoked and flared on either side of every saloon door up and down the street—and from open doors and windows, since the night was warm, there were paler shafts to illumine those crowds on the sidewalks and that other crowd of wagons and horses in the street itself. And so there was plenty of light to show Red Wind.

That was enough. It caused a murmur and then a stir. Men stopped their wagons. Men stopped their horses. And they stared at the beautiful stallion.

And, in a trice, mischief was afoot. A big fellow turned his horse straight across the path of Lost Wolf. And he turned with a grin to the latter.

"How much that horse, son?" he asked.

Lost Wolf returned no answer, but he looked the ruffian in the eye and saw that here was a white man unlike the type of Danny Croydon, to say the least. He made a motion with his hand indicating that he wished to move on.

"I've asked you a question!" roared the big man, very angry.

"Hold on, Bill," called a companion. "Maybe he don't understand English."

"That's his fault, damn him," yelled Bill.

"I understand English very well," said Lost Wolf. "Do not damn me."

For that was the manner in which Lost Wolf had been taught to speak by Danny Croydon. Without violence. One does not learn to yell and shout in the silences of the mountain forests. This quiet voice and this excellent pronunciation and this use of words took Bill much aback, and it made a pause during which Danny Croydon spied the mischief and made a desperate effort to get to the spot where the trouble was.

But the interruption of traffic had now lasted long enough to make a jam of people on the sidewalks, and the street was packed with horses and vehicles at a stand.

As for Bill, though somewhat abashed by the answer of the "Indian," and though he saw that the skin of the boy was a good deal paler than that of any real redskin, his second glance angered him more than the first.

"It's a damned squaw man!" he yelled. "Squaw man, what's the price of that horse? It's got a price and I'm gunna have it!"

Lost Wolf did not pause to think of more than one thing at a time, and the thing which occupied his mind was that he had been called a squaw.

He switched his horse a little to one side and reached out with his long, muscular arm. The hard fist at the end of that arm hooked down on the point of the chin of Bill. And Bill dived headlong out of the saddle, followed by a yell of alarm and astonishment.

Indians are not supposed to strike like prizefighters!

And in the stir of confusion, in the rushing of his friends toward the fallen form of Bill, Lost Wolf put the stallion through a breach in the wall of people and vehicles.

He was stopped in the midst of his escape from the focal point of danger by a wild yell behind him.

"You damned pirate, you red-faced hydrophobia cat, turn around and fight, or I'll—"

Lost Wolf glanced back over his shoulder and saw three or four men in threatening attitudes and one settling a rifle at his shoulder.

Of course it sounds impossible—now! But I lived in Zander City in those days, and I understood when I heard the tale. There were not many questions asked before bullets began to fly in those good old days! Lost Wolf had, perhaps, a fifth part of a second to pitch up his hands, jump off his horse to try to shelter himself in the crowd, or else fight back.

He did not pause to think on this occasion, either. You must remember that for five years he had been practically the slave of another man—a man of infinite kindness of heart, infinite wisdom and good-nature—but with a dread-

159

fully firm will. For five years, with a rancorous heart, Lost Wolf had been accumulating the desire to fight. For five years he had been waiting for the moment when he thought himself able to free himself from the bondage of another man's will. So, on the whole, it is plain that he was in excellent temper and training for a fight. He was just as much an Indian as ever in impulse. For though Danny Croydon had taught him many lessons from books, and otherwise, Danny Croydon was not in himself an entire social setting, and it is only from a whole social setting that people learn *mental* habits. So Lost Wolf was simply an Indian with some of a white man's powers added.

And when he saw that threatening gun settling at the shoulder of another, he used the fifth part of a second which was left to him in drawing a revolver and spinning in the saddle and opening fire!

28

Danny Croydon was making his way toward the point of danger the best way he could, but it was a poor way that he made, at the best. People were in a frenzy of excitement as they saw what was about to happen, and with the ring of the first shot there was a wild yell that drowned out all thinking like a flash.

The first shot brought the man with the rifle out of his saddle with a shrill scream of agony.

The next shot was from the revolver of the tall man's right-hand companion. It plunked a hole in one of the boards of the tall fence which surrounded the house I lived in.

The third shot was from the rapid revolver of Lost Wolf and it took the left-hand mate of him of the rifle fairly in the middle of the forehead and spilled him backward out of his saddle. The fourth shot was for Lost Wolf's gun also, and it was just a shadow before the gun of him who punctured my fence. That slug tore through the right shoulder-joint of the unlucky fellow and tipped him out of his saddle also.

Very lucky for Lost Wolf that he had shot straight, because just as his gun exploded, the last bullet of the enemy whirred past his ear. If his own slug had not gone home first, it would have failed to put the other just the necessary fraction off balance.

Then Lost Wolf turned to make tracks for safety. He heard pandemonium mount to high C behind him. So he flattened himself over the pommel of the saddle and stirred up Red Wind with a yell that would have made the heart of any Cheyenne leap a pair of octaves. Red Wind hardly needed that urging. He got to top speed in half a dozen bounds, and those bounds brought him just under my tall fence—a full six feet I think that fence was in its lowest place, and six inches more in the highest. I presume it would only be possible to say that the red horse took the lowest spot, but certain it was that he flew that fence and left no heel mark on the top of it.

Some score of bullets left uneasy guns in the crowd as they saw the youngster make that prodigious leap with the stallion. The only harm their bullets did, however, was to smash one of my windows to flinders.

But I was accustomed to that.

When the excitement began—and it happened at least twice a week in the town—I merely made sure that my family was gathered in the front room of the first floor of the house. I knew that the logs around that room were

161

bullet proof! I had heard enough in the past few seconds to herd them in there. And accordingly, when I heard the tinkle of window glass dropping, I merely shrugged my shoulders.

When Lost Wolf topped that fence and dropped into my back yard as into a pool of blackness—for it was loftily fenced all around—he dipped out of the saddle and remembered that this was the house to which Danny Croydon had told him to report. However, it was not that consideration that stopped him. If it had been that only he would have been scattering for the open plains, and all the miseries of his life to come, and all the joys of it, would have been lifted from my shoulders.

Well, I hardly know whether to sigh or to smile when I write that the boy, as he shot down into my yard—and spattered my wife's rose-bed into a tangle of mud—slipped off his horse and whispered a word as he did so.

That word made Red Wind drop to the ground like a trained dog, close against the wall of the house. In the same instant, Lost Wolf was at the tall gate on the farther side of the yard and pushed it open. Then he himself settled down in a corner—and quietly proceeded to reload his half-emptied revolver.

Oh, a tolerably cool lad was Lost Wolf, for a boy of eighteen. About as easy a hand at a killing as anyone that ever wore guns in the West!

He had barely reached his place in the dark corner of the fence before half a dozen athletic youths swung over the top of the fence. What a frightful temptation it must have been to Lost Wolf to pick them off as they came flying up against the light of the crowded street beyond.

Those young men, however, were spared. They saw the open gate beyond the yard and they yelled back to the crowd: "The Indian has ridden through the yard. Cut around behind, boys, and we'll trap him in the soft sand!"

For there was a stretch of soft sand—regular blow

sand—beginning just behind my house. It was only spotted with half a dozen little squatters' shacks.

When the crowd of mounted men in the street heard what had happened they let out a yell of triumph. And then they came foaming around the front of my house— for not one of them could have jumped his horse over that high fence of mine—and swished around into the deep sand, while a full half of them stuck to the hard going to the right, planning to circle around the soft going and so hem the Indian in a trap.

They were yelling like devils as they rode. And they *were* devils. Half whisky and half desire to kill Indians used to turn the boys into devils. There's no doubt of that. And every one of those hard riders and straight shooters wanted the blood of Lost Wolf.

But they didn't find him, of course.

It was a most mysterious thing, and Zander City talked about the remarkable disappearance of Lost Wolf for the next month. Half a dozen of them came swarming back to the gate of my yard and there they found me in the act of closing it. I was fairly hot, because I had seen the crowd charge over my flower bed and I knew about what had happened to it.

I simply said: "Keep away from my house. If you are intending to do murders, do them away from my premises—and bad luck follow the lot of you!"

When they saw and heard me, they turned aside. No one else in the town could have talked to them like that, but Zander City had a peculiar pride in me. They declared that I was the only real preacher within several hundred miles—and they liked to talk of the church which I had started. Sunday mornings I usually had a score or two of them in my little church, and their guns were hung up in the little waiting room. By unwritten law, nothing more formidable than a bowie knife could be carried into my presence when I was to occupy the pulpit.

163

I may say that they had a patronizing air toward me. And they were glad to donate to the charities and the sick-fund which I maintained. They kept my hands filled with the good coin of the realm and tradeable commodities. If speculation had been my talent I could have been rich in five years, I know.

Well, when I nod my white head over this paper and think of those days and those people, I am forced to decide that they were simply children—violently bad and violently good—in spots. They needed hard spankings several times each day. But there were no giants to bestow the spankings!

"This was extra bad," one of them apologized to me in a mumbled voice. "An Indian shot down six men—"

"Killed?" I cried.

"Killed every one!" was the answer.

That was a moderate exaggeration. Only one had been killed. But ten at least is the unusual multiple of exaggeration and rumor.

I closed and barred my gate with a sigh, wondering if it had been justice—not to myself but to my poor family—when I started West to this end of civilization. Then, as I turned away from the gate, a shadow rose beside me out of the ground. I carried a gun in those days—foolish me! And when the shadow rose I snatched at it.

Five biting talons took the wrist of the hand that held the gun and squeezed until my fingers turned numb and the gun dropped from the tips of them.

"Croydon sent me here," said a soft voice in my ear.

There was something foreign in the pronunciation. The words were carefully clipped and divided.

"Danny Croydon!" breathed I.

"He sent me."

"Why are you waiting here in my back yard?" I could not help asking. "Why, Danny Croydon is an old and dear friend! And who are you?"

"I am the Indian who killed the six men!"

I stood paralyzed while he laughed softly in the darkness. Through that darkness, too, I made out the glimmer of the two braids that ran down his back and I knew, I thought, that he was certainly an Indian.

"You did that!"

"Ah," said he, "they lied to you. Do they all lie—all the white men? Only one is dead. One was shot through the shoulder. One was shot through the hip. And I knocked another man down with my fist. That is all. It was a small thing, but they are squalling like children over it. Yelling like squaws. Waugh!"

I gasped again. When one has killed a man and downed three others—well, even in Zander City it was not a small thing!

"Where is Danny Croydon?" was all I could say.

Because I saw that I should need the help of an interpreter and a controller in the handling of this man!

"Croydon will come."

"Are you alone?"

"No."

He whistled, hardly louder than a whisper, and the figure of a horse rose from the other side of the yard and trotted as stealthily as a cat to his side. There was nothing but scattered starlight and the glow of lanterns and lamps from across the street to show the horse to me, but I could see enough. I knew that this was one of those horses which come into a man's life once and no more.

I stretched out a hand toward him. Lost Wolf struck my arm down just as the teeth of the stallion snapped on the place where my hand had been.

"You see," he said, as softly as ever, "Red Wind eats meat, too."

And he began to laugh, laughter no louder than the murmur of a bee.

29

In the meantime, no Danny Croydon appeared to me. I was staggered and mute for a moment. Then I remembered that I was a host and suggested—hoping he would not accept—that he would put his horse into my barn.

He did not even thank me, but walked into my little barn with the stallion following like a dog at his heels. He tethered the red beauty in a stall and fed him with some good hay and a little measure of oats which I had for my best driving mare. He found all of these things for himself, without asking me, as though he were able to smell them out for himself.

"Now," said my odd guest, "I am ready to eat."

I went beside him to the house and opened the kitchen door. There I had my first chance to view him in detail as I turned up the flame of the lamp. He had divested himself of his leather jacket during the excitement of the fight and the chase, so as to be ready to give the best possible account of himself, and therefore I saw him stripped to the waist. I guessed him twenty or even two or three years beyond that. His color was not coppered in tinge, but thoroughly sun-soaked, so that I put him down for a half-breed. And it seemed as though his harsh features must surely bespeak an admixture of savage blood. His chest, shoulders and arms were simply magnificent, robed with closely compacted muscles, but each dimly distinct beneath the skin. It was such a body as one sees in an athlete trained to the very pink of condition.

But it was the face that fascinated me most. Those slant, wicked-looking eyes sent a shiver through me. I cannot tell you how he affected me except to say, first of all, that he impressed me as a creature of the night who could not have come into the lamplight of my house for any good purpose.

I asked him to come into the front of the house.

He said: "I smell food near. I shall stay here till I have eaten."

He did not look around him for a chair but sat down cross-legged on the floor.

I did not protest and offer him a better seat. I merely turned my back on him and staggered into the front room where my family was waiting for my return. When my wife saw me, she started up at once and came toward me with his lips tight.

"Steady, Charlie," she said.

I dragged her into the hall.

"You'll frighten the children to death!" said she. "What is wrong? Is the house on fire?"

It is a frightful habit of Marcia that she underestimates every report which I bring into the household. I could not help trimming up the facts a little bit. I said to her:

"Marcia, there is a half-naked Indian in the kitchen, armed to the teeth, and demanding food."

Marcia cast one of her glances at me.

"Well," said she, and folded her arms. "I don't believe it!"

"At least," said I, feeling the wind slip out of my sails, "the fellow is a half-breed!"

"Humph," said Marcia, "I suppose the rest of the story can be divided in two, also!"

I could not answer. What *could* one answer to such a thing?

"My dear," said I coldly at last, "this attitude of yours takes from me every vestige of dignity that becomingly should—"

"Stuff and nonsense," said Marcia, and strode past me

down the hall. But when she reached the kitchen door, I heard a gasp from her.

I reached her in a leap and peered over her shoulder. What I saw was the stranger seated in the middle of the kitchen floor almost where I had left him. But he was now occupied. That transcendent nose of his had located food and now he was armed with a great ham from which not a third of the meat had been carved. Lost Wolf was truly wolfing down what remained of it, and in the process he had distributed grease over his mouth, his lips, his cheeks, his very forehead—yes, there was grease on his broad chest, giving it a bright burnished look, and there was grease on hands and wrists and arms.

This was not the only provision which he had made against famine. A beautiful chicken, roasted to be served cold the next day, had been purloined by this villain and it rested upon the floor between his feet. He had not paid much attention to it, beyond sampling it by tearing off a mouthful from the breast. He was apparently leaving it as a dessert to be consumed after the huge ham was gone.

Ah, what an appetite. But no one can eat to rival an Indian. Nothing but a boa constrictor. But the boa takes five times as long to digest.

Lost Wolf favored us with a single glance above the torn and ragged edge of the devastated ham. My wife gasped again.

"Steady, dear," I whispered.

"Steady!" said Marcia in a terrible soft voice. "What scum have you allowed into the house?"

At this moment there was a distraction. Our best and biggest mouser, which we kept lean to make it keener on the hunt, was a huge maltese cat. Now I saw Tom emerge from the pantry, one of his favorite hunting grounds, and instantly he smelled both ham and chicken and glided across the room toward the bird which lay on the floor between the feet of Lost Wolf, apparently quite out of the reach of his hands.

As a thief, Lost Wolf himself was hardly more dexterous and more daring than Tom. The huge cat slipped up and sank a tentative paw into the chicken. I think that Tom could have dragged the whole bird away with him, such was his size and strength.

But here fate intervened.

It appeared in the form of two darting hands. They were free because the ham bone was now suspended from the massive jaws of Lost Wolf. One hand caught Tom by the tail and swung him above Lost Wolf's head. The other hand had drawn with the speed of a whip lash a murderous long hunting knife, of the bluest, brightest steel.

"Heavens!" screamed Marcia, "save Tom!"

She started forward at the same instant. For she was a bold woman, but in this case boldness was a folly. For as she started away, the knife slipped off Tom's tail and sent him screeching at Marcia's face. She had barely time to duck her head. He landed in the coiled masses of her hair, scratched it into a tangled mass, and then leaped on out the window and disappeared, leaving a blood-curdling trail of sound behind him.

Of course I was horrified. I detest cruelty, on principle. However, I confess that I have never loved cats, not even the efficient Tom. And besides all of this, when I saw the face of Marcia as she raised her head—a face partly frightened, partly sorrowful, partly enraged at the Indian for his crime and at me for not avenging the wrong—I cannot tell why it was—I regretted it terribly—but I burst into a foolish giggling.

Marcia settled me with a side glance and took an ominous step toward Lost Wolf. If she had had a weapon in her hand, he would have been lost indeed!

However, he suddenly removed the ham from his mouth with one hand, and with the other extended toward her the bleeding tail of Tom.

"This is to make you happy," said Lost Wolf.

I seized Marcia because I felt that a crisis had come and

169

that in another instant she might anger the ruffian into murdering the lot of us. But Marcia astonished me. She said to me, calmly: "Take your hands from my shoulders, Charles—unless you're trying to hide behind me!"

It was insulting, of course, and a villainous broad grin on the part of Lost Wolf assured me that he understood the imputation. He had finished tearing most of the meat off the ham bone by this time, and now he turned his attention to the roast of cold chicken.

"Very good," said Lost Wolf, pointing to his stomach, which was swelled already to an enormous size. "This is good, too!"

And with one sidelong, wolfish snap, he tore off the remaining flesh from the front of the chicken.

Marcia turned to me and I fixed my eyes on the floor. I was truly ashamed that I had not the courage to try to oust this rascal from the house. Because he wore a revolver at either hip, and there was that knife which he handled in such an efficient fashion that it made my innermost self feel exceedingly ill at ease. However, Marcia merely patted her hair into some semblance of a proper shape.

"Stir up the fire, Charlie," said she. "I must make some coffee for your friend."

There was no irony in the last word. But the man on the floor corrected her.

"*He* is not my friend," said this terrible youth. "Croydon is my friend."

It sent a flash of fire through the eyes of my dear wife. She loved Croydon. If she had been a man, she would have been a brother to Danny, I know.

"Ah" said she, "did he never tell you of me?"

"No," said Lost Wolf.

My wife's face fell.

"You haven't known him long," said she.

"Five years is long enough," said Lost Wolf with a certain grimness of expression.

I was to understand what he meant by that afterwards.

"Five years!" cried Marcia. "Do hurry with that wood in the stove, Charlie. The dampers now—"

The fire was roaring in a trice, and she shook a great portion of coffee into the pot. I swear to you that she was smiling upon this rough scoundrel out of the night—this bloodletter—this butcher of her best and favorite cat!

My dear Marcia, she is long dead, but her memory is a lamp beside me every day of my life. I never understood her; I never could. And when I attempted to learn her by study—I found the effort always too irritating. I am frank, at least. And yet we loved one another; I because she remained an undiscovered country to me, and she because she pitied me, I suppose.

She said: "I never find men who can eat—except you boys from the plains!"

And still smiling, she put the pot over the fire and stirred the coffee into the water. From that moment she understood and loved Lost Wolf.

30

I cannot tell, as I write this, whether the motive behind the writing of it was to show that Marcia was a remarkable woman in her day, or to demonstrate that I was a remarkable man because I had been able to live with her so long. Perhaps there was a share of both in the motive.

At any rate, there was my dear wife smiling in the most pleasant fashion on a wretched half-breed.

"Silly creature!" said I to myself. "You are admiring that scoundrel because he seems a natural man and because there is an air of romance about him—partly because he has broad shoulders and strong arms and shows them. Ah, but if you had been married to him; if you had galloped romantically across the plains and wound up at a lodge! If you had been forced to slave and drudge for the villain, then you would appreciate what it means to be a minister's wife!"

Such were the thoughts that were running through my head when there was a tapping at the door. I did not need to tell the Indian to hide. He was in a dark corner in an instant, with two most workable-looking Colts in his hands. Also, he had the last half of that unfortunate chicken tucked under one elbow. I may interject, here, that dirt did not in the slightest spoil the appetite of Lost Wolf.

I went slowly to the door, looking sadly at the great grease spots on the floor of the kitchen, for I was afraid that even the most casual eye would take note of them. And then the search would begin and God alone could tell how my poor house would be a-drip with blood before that savage youth was subdued!

However, when I opened the door I uttered a shout of joy—for it was Danny Croydon.

"God be praised!" said I.

"Is he here?" asked Croydon.

"Yes! Yes! Yes!"

"One 'yes' is enough," said Danny. "The other two frighten me. What have you done with him?"

"He's yonder in the corner. When we heard the rap—the town has been in such an uproar—"

"I know!" sighed Croydon.

He went to take my wife by the hand. Then he turned to the corner. Lost Wolf had not risen to greet his friend, if you can call Croydon his friend! He was now busy picking the last bones of the chicken. And he merely cast one eye, so to speak, up at Croydon.

"Well," said Croydon, "you've been having a happy little game, I see!"

"It was not a game," said Lost Wolf with the utmost

simplicity. "They started to fight me, and I fought back. That is all. Do you see?"

He showed a tiny bloody spot on his ear.

"They were shooting as close to me as that, Danny!"

"Stand up!" said Croydon, still snarling at the boy in a way that frightened me. Because I expected to see the claws of the tiger appear at any moment.

However, young Lost Wolf stood up.

His stomach had become a deformity—a balloon thrusting out and straining against the skin. No ordinary white man, I am sure, could have eaten as that boy had done.

"Did you steal that?" asked Croydon sternly, and he pointed to the enormous stomach.

The logic of Lost Wolf was a matter beautiful to listen to!

"Is this man your friend?" said he.

"He is my old and dear friend," said Danny Croydon, with a look at me that made me very happy.

"Then he would feed me," said Lost Wolf, "because I was sent to this house by you. However, I did not trouble him to get food for me. I let his squaw have rest."

Here he pointed to Marcia, who merely laughed at that term of "squaw."

"I went myself," concluded Lost Wolf, "and I got a little food. Is it well in the lodge of your friend?"

"A little food," groaned Danny Croydon, still staring in fascination at the enormously distended stomach of Lost Wolf. "Is there a thing in your pantry now, Marcia?"

"There is plenty," said Marcia. "Besides, I like it. The poor boy was hungry!"

"He was," said Croydon, "he is, and he always will be. He needs half a deer a day, a gallon of coffee, and a few pounds of flour done into biscuits. Then a dozen jars of jam—oh, his stomach is a pit, Marcia!"

Lost Wolf yawned.

"He is ready to sleep," said Croydon. "He eats and then he sleeps. Like a snake! Have you told them your name?"

"No."

173

"Then it's time for you to go to bed! Charlie, have you an extra rug?"

That was how we got rid of the "half-breed." Of course I had plenty of "robes," and we unfurled one in the empty attic room. Lost Wolf simply dived for it and was snoring before we could close the door.

Then I went downstairs with Danny. When we went into the front room we found that the children were already in bed. So we had the room to ourselves and I was glad of it.

"I'll tell you the name, first," said Danny Croydon. "He's a Cheyenne, but the Pawnees gave him a new name when they caught him. The Pawnees called him Lost Wolf! He was called White Badger by the Cheyennes. Does that mean anything to you?"

I need words to express astonishment adequately. But Marcia needs nothing but her mouth. She opens it and pops out her eyes in a ridiculous fashion and looks from one person to another and then gasps: "Of all things!"

I tried to drown her out. I said nervously: "Confound it, Danny, you don't mean that he was the great big medicine boy of the Cheyennes?"

"Of all things!" brought out Marcia, and I glared at her in vain.

"He was the medicine boy," said Danny complacently.

Like the lion-keeper after the circus!

"But the one who killed Clouded Sky and—" began Marcia.

"Good heavens," I cried, "it is Red Wind that I helped him put into the stable!"

"Charles," said my wife, "if you intend swearing, I wish that you would swear like a man, at least!"

"You didn't help much," said Danny with a wicked grin. "Or else part of you would be in Red Wind's stomach. He has a lot of playful habits."

We sat back to digest this wonderful news. For, like everyone on the plains, we had heard of the death of Clouded Sky, duly decorated by distance and time and rumor which had a chance to expand all the way to Zander City. And we had heard other things during the seven years of the captivity of the boy among the Cheyennes.

We had to stop wondering in order to hear and enjoy the tale of Danny Croydon which began with a point seven years before, when Danny Croydon, sitting on the plains and smoking, had the muzzle of a rifle thrust into the hollow of his back. It was an odd tale and took past midnight in the telling.

"But," I cried, when the story had ended, "what under heaven will become of you, poor Danny, when this human tiger turns on you at last?"

"Humph," said my wife, "I presume that Danny is able to take care of even a tiger!"

Danny thanked her with a foolish smile.

"I think I can manage him," said he. "I've taught him to fight fairly, for one thing. Beyond that, I presume that I can handle him. He's a husky boy, but after all, he's not a man—"

"You're thinking of something!" I exclaimed.

"Of the way the first man dropped," said Danny dreamily. "I don't know that I'm so sure, after all!"

It was one o'clock when we all went to bed and fell asleep lulled by the steady roar of the streets in Zander City, a roar which never died down until the broad light of the dawn.

It was not a pleasant night of sleep for me.

I wakened a dozen times, I presume, with the hands of the white Indian fixed, in imagination, in my throat. And all through the time of darkness, I could hear stealthily stirring, creaking sounds.

I was very glad when I wakened in the morning with an aching head and sat up dizzily to make sure that Marcia and I were both intact.

By the time I got downstairs, Marcia was busily cooking breakfast, and in a corner, sitting cross-legged on a child's high stool, was Lost Wolf. No white man except himself

175

could have endured the agony of that position for a moment, but he was contentedly smoking a pipe which he removed to greet me with a guttural "How!"

I answered with a feeble echo of the same grunt. Then I warmed my hands over the fire. Murder in the morning does not look half so thrillingly delightful as murder in the night. And when I looked at those long, big-boned hands, I could not help a shudder. All signs of grease were gone, however, and to my amazement, the stomach of that unusual eater was as lean as a greyhound's.

"He has had a bath already," said Marcia.

"Where?" I exclaimed.

"In the trough," said Marcia, pointing out the window to the watering trough in the back yard.

And she looked at him with those great, staring eyes which command one to understand but not to laugh.

"Yes," said Lost Wolf with a childish contentment. "Some Indians are like pigs. But I am a very clean man!"

31

I shall not tell you how I watched Lost Wolf breakfast on half-raw meat. I had to turn away from the sight while he bolted enough solid food to have lasted a normal man for three days. And this added to his supper of the night before! Then, according to the advice of Danny Croydon, our "half-breed" went up the stairs back to his attic room. For it was agreed that it would be best for him to keep strictly under cover until night came. In the meanwhile, Danny would do his best to dispose of his pelts, so that when the darkness came, he and Lost Wolf could get away quickly.

"But what will happen to us when your back is turned on the villain?" said I.

"Stuff!" said Marcia. "I am not in the least afraid of him. I understand him. After all, he *isn't* an Indian!"

"You're wrong, I'm afraid!" put in Danny Croydon. "I'm afraid that he *is* an Indian—"

"How you talk!" cried Marcia, while I was amazed to hear her talk back to Danny. "Hasn't he a white skin?"

"If you whitewash a rattler, it's still got its poison," said Danny rather sententiously.

"Don't talk at *me* like a book," said Marcia. "Because I won't stand it, Daniel Croydon!"

Danny tried to apologize.

"I only mean," said he, "that I've lived with him five years and that I've worked over him as if he were a brother. I've taught him what I could. And he went on where I had to stop. I know that he has the *powers* of a white brain. But I'm afraid that he has an Indian's heart! I've been with him five years. He has never so much as spoken one gentle word to me. That time when he had me stuck in the mud—well, you might count that one, but when I tried to talk to him in a brotherly way after that— why, his face was made out of stone. You would have thought that he didn't hear me!"

"You don't understand him," said Marcia.

Danny and I both stared at her. It was a *very* foolish thing to try to teach Danny what Indians or men were.

"I know," said Marcia, snapping her fingers at us, "that deep down under the skin he's simply a great big baby. Like the rest of you men! Don't tell me anything else, because I won't believe you!"

That day, Danny had no trouble in getting what he wanted for his pelts. I cannot tell how it was or why it was. I only know that during the five years in which Lost Wolf was with him, the very finest pelts always seemed to come out of Danny's traps. I shall not even mention the ridiculous superstition with which Danny Croydon re-

177

garded this fact. I shall only admit that, the very winter after Lost Wolf left him, all the luck fell away from Danny, his traps took the most ordinary stuff and not much of that, and in the middle of winter a carelessly left fire in some way ignited the dry flooring of his cabin, and he came back to find that the cabin, pelts and all, had been consumed. I, of course, attributed that bad luck to the natural turn of fortune, which after lifting a man for a time is almost sure to turn on him and dash him down again.

But again, I dare not let you know to what Danny attributed all of this very bad fortune! I shall only say that he never again trapped in those mountains or in any other place. He declared that a curse had been put upon his traps and from that moment forward, he became a trader, pure and simple.

However, he came back by noon having sold everything he possessed, and received a handsome profit for it. He told us he planned to take his money south with him down the river to the next and larger town. There he would buy what commodities he needed and take them with him in a trading trip among the Indians. We noted to Danny that his "half-breed" had not stirred out of the attic room.

"He may stay there all day and never open his eyes once. He can sleep the way a camel eats—not often, but long! Or again, he may slip out for only five minutes—and five minutes is just long enough to take a scalp—when he is doing the scalping."

"Danny, Danny," said I in sad reproach, "have you left these barbarous customs in his mind?"

Then said Danny rudely: "If you think that you can do better, try your hand!"

I did try that very evening. I sat Lost Wolf down in a chair—though he kept eyeing the floor as if he would have preferred that—and I took him thoroughly to task for his evil habits, in lifting the scalps of other folks. He listened to me with much gravity, sometimes cocking his head a little to one side as though he were pondering my points. Now and again, also, he nodded as if in agreement, and I felt that I was really impressing the young scoundrel. But when I ended he turned his back on me and spoke to Marcia.

"He talks very long. He has a great many words to say little things. But I remember Black Antelope. He used to talk very much. Also, he used to take money for his talk. Does this chief take money for *his* talk, too?"

It was quite enough, as anyone will admit. Besides, Marcia and Danny were rude enough to laugh uproariously.

Now that Lost Wolf was prepared for the trip that night, he looked much more civilized and like any other young frontiersman—aside from his braided locks of black hair. And I could see that Marcia was studying him with the most intense interest. You see, in her heart, Marcia was incurably romantic and inclined to think that the world was a queer compound—almost everyone in the world was a villain, except those whom she knew; and among those whom she knew, almost everyone was a hero or a saint!

I could see that she was heroizing the boy in her mind; at least, she could not very well saint him! Not while our poor cat Tom cowered in a warm corner, with an unforgettable look in his eyes and no beautiful fluffy tail curled around his feet.

"But," said I suddenly to Lost Wolf, "what did you do when you came down the river beside Danny? Where did you go when you disappeared south?"

"I was hunting," said Lost Wolf.

"Yes, and did you find much game?"

"Yes, a little."

"Did you kill?"

"Three," and he held up that many fingers.

"What was it?"

"These," said the boy.

179

He produced a small flat package, unrolled it, and suddenly held up in his hand three human scalps, all neatly cured and sun-dried.

Is it cruel to admit that I triumphed over Marcia? She was so dreadfully sickened that she had to leave the room, and indeed I could hardly maintain myself in front of that young tiger. But the knowledge that I was proving myself stronger than Marcia sustained me.

Danny Croydon stood up without a word and ordered the boy to put away his treasures. And Lost Wolf, with an indifferent air, began to fold them with much care and restore them to their first hiding place. Then he stood up, grunted a farewell at me, and marched out of the house behind Danny.

I started after them with a lantern, which went out, and I had to spend some time relighting it. By the time I reached the barn, I found that Danny had discovered and lighted a lantern which he found there on a peg. Also, he had discovered other things. Spread out on the top of the barley box I found two of our best carving knives, a big silver knife, my best watch, two of my wife's rings, about fifty dollars in gold, and a dozen other little items.

Danny Croydon said: "My friend, Lost Wolf, wanted to remember you, I think. So he took along a few little keepsakes. But he didn't tell you he was taking them, because he is so embarrassed at the thought that you might know how much he thinks of you. He was sure that you would not need any of these things, and so he took them along, because they would be a great comfort to him on the plains."

He turned, here, and glared balefully at Lost Wolf.

"Charlie!" called my wife from the house at this moment.

"Come on out!" I yelled in return. For I wanted her to see her hero shrunk to normal size.

She came singing. That was her way! And she popped into the open door of the stable. There she saw the loot spread on the top of the barley box, beside which stood Lost Wolf, with his face grandly oblivious of the loot Danny had taken from him, and grandly oblivious of the rest of us, also!

Danny made a speech to her, but with his eyes fastened on Lost Wolf. I could see that he was trying to shame the boy.

He said: "I brought Lost Wolf down to your house, my dear old friend, because I thought that he would be grateful for the kind treatment. I wanted him to come here, so that he would understand that while there are many bad white men, there are many *good* white men, also! And now I find that he has stolen through your house at night and taken things which—"

My wife broke in:

"You've said enough and a great deal more than enough, Daniel Croydon!"

She stepped past me and scooped up all the valuables on top of the barley box. Then, while I gasped, she actually poured that loot into the hands of the "half-breed." No, I was convinced by that time that his soul was wholly red and wholly lost!

Into those greedy palms went all the loot that the thief had taken in the first place. And then Marcia said:

"I'm not going to give you the knives, though, Lost Wolf! You'd be cutting yourself on them. Come along, dear!"

She caught me by the arm and hustled me away. Lost Wolf had merely bowed his head.

"Why in heaven's name did you take us away before we had at least a chance to thank you for your crazy—"

"Hush!" said she. "If we had stayed another minute—oh, I know boys!—he would have been blubbering!"

32

No doubt Marcia was absurdly wrong in thinking that actual tears could ever come to the eyes of such a man as Lost Wolf. But it *was* true that her magnanimity was a crushing blow to him. He had been reverting to the purely savage in his nature during the past day. Now the white man in him came to the surface and he was ready to act as a white man should.

First, he put all of the pilfering back on the grain box. But Danny Croydon was now furious. I may say that he and I were very old friends and very good friends, and he and Marcia were still more intimate. He felt that Lost Wolf had given us a mortal blow from which he, Danny, would long feel the effects.

Of course a plainsman is sure to be oversensitive. Danny absurdly overestimated what our anger would be. In fact, there was no anger at all, and Lost Wolf remained as an amusing experience.

"Now, Lost Wolf," said Danny through his teeth, with the long hitting muscles of his arms hardening in his fury, "you've done a fine piece of work for me. I've worked over you for five years—"

Lost Wolf held up his hand.

"You," said he, "have worked for *me?*"

"Who taught you your books?" snapped Croydon.

I suppose a memory of the crowded hours of toil on the

trap line, of skinning, huntings, and wood chopping rushed through the mind of Lost Wolf. Now he laughed softly. It is the most irritating sound that one man can hear from another—that soft laughter.

"Don't do it!" snarled Danny.

"What?" asked Lost Wolf.

"Don't laugh at me—because I won't stand it! And I don't have to. You've disgraced me!"

"I have disgraced myself," said Lost Wolf sadly. "I did not understand, at first, but—"

It is this moment which Danny Croydon regrets most of all the moments of his life. Here was Lost Wolf fairly launched on a humble apology, and yet Danny chose to interrupt him. Danny himself has told me a thousand times that there must have been madness in his brain, and I could only agree with him.

"You did not understand?" snarled Danny, "why, damn you, I—"

"Do not damn me," said Lost Wolf.

"I'll damn you all day long!"

Danny was beside himself now.

"You must not," said Lost Wolf, more sadly than ever.

"Why not? Why not?" yelled Danny.

"I must fight you, then."

"Stand up to me," cried Danny through his locked teeth. "Ain't I been longin' and prayin' for ye to stand up to me for these five years?"

And reaching out a flashing arm he spatted Lost Wolf across the mouth with his hand. The answer of the other was to leap back and begin to drag off his shirt. And at that moment, Danny began to doubt the wisdom of the thing which he had done. He followed suit, however, in the lantern light.

When he saw Lost Wolf stripped to the waist, he regretted very much what he had done. I have said before this that the torso of Lost Wolf was a beautiful picture, but it

183

was a terrible picture, also. Terrible to Danny Croydon, at the least.

Then he remembered that there was no great difference in his weight, that the strength of Hercules was in his long arms, that the craft of a hundred battles was in his brain, and that his body was compacted power. He was a little past his athletic prime. He might be a little brittle. But the boy was ten years from his manly prime; he would be too elastic—not set enough in power. Moreover, in their wrestling and their boxing for the past two years, they had never indulged in a slugging or straining match, but Danny was confident that, when they did, he would snap the other in two.

He raised his confidence in this fashion and found that Lost Wolf was standing waiting for him in the center of the barn floor—waiting, and looking him over with a calm eye. That calmness sent a chill through Danny. But he should have known that there was even more terror in the heart of Lost Wolf than in his own. But a course of seven years in Indian dissimulation had not been wasted on Lost Wolf. He eyed his master now with a smiling contempt though there was ice in his heart.

Danny took one deep breath to rouse his heart; then he rushed into action with driving arms—and lunged almost against the barn wall. Certainly Lost Wolf had not remained for his coming.

It must have been a mistake. For certainly no pupil of his ever could have shown such phantom cleverness. He whirled, therefore, and went dancing in, both hands ready to strike with a crushing power. A trained left hand flashed between his and flecked his nose. Then Lost Wolf slid out of the way of a smashing counter.

"You are fat," said Lost Wolf, "and you are very slow. Have you eaten too much, white man?"

"You red-skinned thief!" cried Danny, and smote again.

Lost Wolf stepped inside of that swinging punch and snapped a left hand like a leaping flame into the face of

Danny. It was a hard blow, and it put Danny back on his heels.

But the hurt was to his spirit, not to his body. It merely slightly dazed his head, not stunned his brain. But it was the sheer beauty of the boxing of Lost Wolf that startled him. He breathed out fiercely through teeth and nose and rushed once more. This time he got in a glancing blow to the body.

A glancing blow does not sound like much. Imagine a log, however, with a rough edge; imagine the log flung through the air with the speed of light, and imagine the rough edge of the log grazing your naked ribs. That was what a grazing blow to the body from the hand of my friend Croydon meant. I had seen him box too often for the pleasure of a crowd of trappers, selecting as an opponent some burly ruffian twice his size. I have seen one of those glancing blows of his double up a giant.

It stopped Lost Wolf and made him stand flat in his tracks badly stung, indeed.

"And now the finish!" said Danny to his fighting heart, and struck with all his might, straight at the jaw of Lost Wolf—and found his mark.

But oh, what a shock for Danny. It was like hitting a silken cushion, so easily and so lightly did Lost Wolf allow his head to fly back with the weight of that stroke. He was stepping back at the same moment, but he checked his backward movement at that instant, and as his head bobbed up on his shoulders again, he dug both fists into the stomach of Danny.

Ah, then Danny felt that he was no longer a boy. Those fists sank into him like edged knives and sent shooting pains and a dull sickness through his body—through his brain! He lunged forward and floundered heavily towards a clinch—

Floundered towards a clinch and fell, instead, into a volley of thunderbolts. They ripped and they tore him. Hammers began to beat at the back of his brain. And he

185

slipped when he tried to step in, fighting as he went. He slipped—his knees refused to straighten under his weight. He dropped to the floor.

He heard a cool voice saying: "Is that enough, Danny Croydon?"

He looked up out of a heavy sleep and there he saw before him the sleek, dapper, graceful form of Lost Wolf.

"Is that enough?"

"Damn you!" shouted Danny. "I haven't started in on you yet. I slipped—"

He rose and rushed.

It did not seem possible. The smooth stepping Lost Wolf vanished neatly from before that charge.

"It is time to give up," said Lost Wolf. "I have done enough harm since I came to this city. I do not wish to hurt you, Danny Croydon. But I am going back to the people where I belong. I am going back to the Cheyennes!"

Danny should have known that the time had come. But when a man has never been beaten—when he has often wrested victory from the jaws of defeat—well, it is a hard thing to surrender. Besides, he told himself, it was impossible that Lost Wolf could be like a dancer on his feet and yet be able to strike like a hammer. He refused to believe it.

"I'll break you in two!" groaned Danny, and spun about with a sweeping blow.

Through the circle of his arm the long, straight punch of Lost Wolf slid like a rapier and caught on the end of his chin, and sent him staggering.

"Will you stop?" asked Lost Wolf.

It *was* the impossible made real. And Danny Croydon realized, bitterly, that for many months this cunning fellow had been showing only half of his craft in their practice bouts. He lunged again. Half a dozen punches snapped against his head. His own arms flailed the thinnest air and he was borne back, groggy, his mind darkening.

186

"Will you stop—because you taught me?" asked Lost Wolf.

But Danny resolved on another style of battle. If he could not box with this phantom, he could at least crush him with sheer strength at wrestling. He made a flying leap, got his hold, and closed on Lost Wolf with all the strength in him.

But only for an instant. Then he felt his enemy shift and slide in that grip, and presently Danny was whirled from his feet and went down heavily, with the weight of Lost Wolf on top of him.

He struck on his head, and darkness rolled over the eyes of fighting Danny Croydon.

When he wakened, the lanterns were still burning, but as he sat up, he saw that Red Wind was gone from his stall—the trinkets remained on the feed box—but Lost Wolf was lost indeed.

So Danny came staggering back to the house.

When Marcia cried out at the bloody sight of him he merely groaned: "I've lost the one big game of my life. He's gone amuck again, and he'll never be tamed, now!"

We did not have to ask what he meant.

33

As for Lost Wolf, he scurried out of the town like a frightened rabbit, and when he reached the complete security of the plains beyond, by the verge of the broad-flowing river, he checked the stallion and turned to look back at Zander City. It seemed a very sad thing to Lost Wolf, as he sat on the back of the great horse and stared back at the little town. For you must remember that it did not seem little to him, but very grand and great indeed; and out of the heart of that city there came a stir of voices so soft that it went like a sad music through the heart of Lost Wolf.

He sat there for a long time. He was beginning to be aware of the starlight which was showering so softly around him, and behind him and halfway around him, he heard the noises of the plains with which he was so familiar. Yes, now his ear was drinking in those sounds which spoke from the far verge of the horizon, sounds half-heard, strange and wild and wonderful to Lost Wolf, no matter how long he had known them. And now he heard the voice of a buffalo wolf calling loudly and despairingly out of the nearest hollow. He felt that it was his namesake crying for his return.

"Well," said Lost Wolf, "I shall come back to you, have no fear!"

But ah, there was a sadness in his heart.

For it seemed to him that half of his life was left there behind him. And, no matter what habit had made of him, he knew that his blood was the blood of a white man. And a thousand matters rushed through his soul. He could see, now, a great many differences. Had it been an Indian with whom he had been a companion through those many years, would the Indian have schooled him in the use of his hands and his wits to defend himself, as Danny Croydon had done? No, he would not! There was no question as to that, and the moment that the Indian felt that he was becoming dangerous, he would have taken the scalp of this obstreperous youngster and then gone upon his way rejoicing.

But this was not the way with Danny Croydon. Now it probably was not the way with any of Danny's friends, and as a proof, had it not been demonstrated that even the squaw of the minister was not like any other women that Lost Wolf had ever known?

Lost Wolf looked hungrily back at that light and that

murmur, and he could see the long, thin arms of light that stretched across the river. This world, then, was closed behind him and he could never return to it again!

I wish that Lost Wolf could have known that when the body of Peg Hunter—who had fallen dead under the revolver-fire of Lost Wolf—was examined, it was found that he carried on his person the loot of two recent robberies, robberies which had been accompanied by murders also. And as for the two who had dropped with mere wounds, a great portion of the rest of the lost money was found on them; as for big "Bill," he had disappeared from the town and nothing was heard of him again.

So that the gentry who had been so hot for the capture and the immediate execution of the "Indian" were now rather downfaced. But, of course, that sad-hearted young barbarian could know nothing of this. Like a child who has been shut out from the party and looks at the others having a rare good time within, and hears their merry shouts and their laughter, in just such fashion Lost Wolf looked back to the lights and the noises of Zander City.

Finally, it was Danny Croydon's fault. There was no doubt of that. And he himself freely accepted the blame of all the evil that afterwards happened. Because, now that the boy had broken away from him with such immense ease, he could see that Lost Wolf must have known for many months that if he wanted liberty, all he had to do was to put out his hand and take it! But he had not wanted it. He would have been perfectly content if he could have gone on for many years, perhaps, as the friend and the pupil of Danny, working loyally for him in the meantime, and developing all the time a true attachment for him. Well, this chance was lost when the "half-breed" turned his back upon Zander City and rode off through the dusk of the starry night.

He came straightway to the river. He sent the stallion straight at it, and he himself stripped off his clothes and tied them on top of the pommel of the saddle, and then dived in and showed the way across with Red Wind snorting and struggling beside him.

Some of the joy of life came back to Lost Wolf as he struck across that river, breaking up the star images and casting little waves to the right and left from his broad shoulders. It was not in this guise that he had left the Cheyennes. What would they think of him when he returned to them, a man? Ay, and what a man! With what thousand of devices learned from the white man!

He whipped the water from his hard body with the edges of his hands, and he started forth across the plains, heading south and west, south and west.

He had two fine Colt revolvers. He had a beautiful double-barreled rifle. And with this armament and the speed of Red Wind at his disposal, he felt as safe as though he possessed the wings and talons of an eagle. He traveled half the remainder of the night. Then he made a dry camp and slept for a few hours. It was after dawn when he went on again. He shot a rabbit a little later. Then, with foolish boldness, he built a large fire and, regardless of the smoke that boiled up into the air, he roasted that rabbit and ate the last shred of it.

By the time he had finished, he knew that danger was hurrying fast towards him. He knew it by a sudden stir of birds which had been sailing high in the air, placidly, a few moments before. But now they were swirling about here and there, much disturbed by something which was passing on the earth so far below them.

Lost Wolf did not ask what the strange thing might be. He simply jogged his horse to the top of the nearest hillock, and there he waited with the double-rifle poised, its length pointing down along the shoulder of the horse.

And all that he saw was a brace of wolves which sneaked up over a rise of ground two hundred yards away, and then, starting with surprise at the sight of him, sat down and stared.

Wolves indeed! He had seen those cunning disguises,

however, before. A Pawnee inside the skin of the creature for which he is named can take all the parts of the savage brute. But this was a trifle close range; these must be two young and rash braves, trying to distinguish themselves as they had seen older and most expert warriors do on similar occasions.

So he jerked his rifle to his shoulder. The wolves did not wait to see what he would do. They whirled and sprang to their hind legs—which proved wonderfully long—and raced to find cover beyond the rise of ground. There was only time for one snapshot, but that shot gave Lost Wolf a sweet recompense, for he saw the figure on the right throw up its arms and then pitch with a shriek to the ground. A very badly hurt Indian, indeed!

He did not turn the stallion and run after that. He merely shoved a new load into the empty chamber and brought the gun to his shoulder. There followed exactly what he had expected—a brief roll of horses' hoofs and then two dozen Pawnees came over that hill like foam over the top of a breaking wave. One general yell of dismay followed the sight of him with the rifle at his shoulder. He fired at the leader—apparently the chief in command of this war party. Horse and man tumbled head over heels down the slope. He sped another ball after the first and watched some copper-skinned hero pitch out of his saddle.

That was enough for that Indian charge. They split away right and left and dashed back for cover, with a loose and badly aimed discharge of arrows and bullets towards him.

In the meantime, the frightened horse of the second warrior leaped wildly away straight to the front, and accordingly, straight towards Lost Wolf. He snared it with a dexterous cast of his lariat. And then, in another instant, with bullets whirling liberally after him, he was away across the plains with his prize horse running frantically ahead on the end of the lariat. He made sure of cutting across the path of the war-party, and with a side-wise streaking target, they proved themselves, as usual, notably poor marksmen. Away went Lost Wolf, and now, shrieking for revenge, the Pawnees rushed after him.

He had not a doubt of what the result would be. This long-striding horse he had captured, a beautiful limbed roan, was no mere Indian pony. This was a white man's horse, stolen on some raid, no doubt, and now he showed good blood by the way he stepped away from the pursuit.

In half an hour the Pawnees, furious as they were, had enough. They pulled up the heads of their mounts and slowed them down. They confessed defeat.

Yet until they were at the horizon, Lost Wolf kept on at a smart pace, and then he halted to examine his prize. What first caught his eye was a series of dark splotches on the fine leather saddle. Blood, of course. And then he saw bulging saddlebags. He examined them and found that they were filled with things of interest. But, first of all, on top of all the rest and bedabbling all the rest with blood, there was a scalp of red hair, torn from the head of some mature man, for the red was sprinkled with white. He looked further. There was money, there was a new Colt, there were other things of infinite value in that saddle bag—infinite in the eyes of an Indian. But Lost Wolf was not, at this moment, particularly delighted in being an Indian himself. He closed that saddle bag with a sudden shudder.

And he had the odd feeling that a friend of his had gone down, and the scalping knife had taken a cruel vengeance upon him! It was an odd thing. Lost Wolf could not make it out, but he felt that something had snapped and broken and changed forever within him.

34

When the dark came, he struck away for some low hills, covered with trees—rocky upthrusts through the level surface of the prairie. As he rode, he came upon a slight trickle of water, where a stream ran down from the base of one of those hills. That assured him of a good camp, and Red Wind was sadly in need of water, while the roan snorted with eagerness when it smelled the stream.

But Lost Wolf kept smoothly on his way, paying no heed to the thirst of his horses. For this was ingrained in his soul—that no matter what the comfort of the dumb beast might demand, the comfort of man himself was of the first consideration, and he had not yet examined the hills for a hunting ground.

He wound suddenly around a shoulder of the first hill when he saw before him a pale glint of a running form. He snatched at a revolver and fired. There was a yelp, and the streaking form ducked out of view in the face of the rocky slope.

But living, moving animals do not disappear in the face of solid rock. Lost Wolf pitched his camp at that very spot and built his campfire just at the mouth of the narrow tunnel which he found. And, when he stretched his head into the tunnel, he caught the rank odor of wolves.

Lost Wolf laughed with a cruel satisfaction. That cave faced east, and when the morning came, he would have plenty of light for the work and pleasure which lay ahead. So thought Lost Wolf. Besides, what is better than a wolf skin for a saddle blanket?

It was not a particularly easy night which he spent, for at every moment he had to open one eye, as it were, and cast it north and east towards the moonflooded plains. Out of that horizon the Pawnees might come, and if they found his traces—

However, when the morning came, there was no trace of Indians, and the shaft of light from the sun was streaming steadily into the throat of the cave.

He prepared a revolver in each hand, because when one enters a wolf cave, one never can tell, for it may be only one old veteran, living a solitary existence, or, again, it may be a mother and a number of helpless whelps, or, still again, it may be a mother surrounded by yearlings almost as big and savage as herself.

He crawled through the entrance, therefore, and then lay flat on his belly so that his body might not cast an inconvenient shadow before him to dim the work which he had to do. He saw all that he wanted, at once. The cave shelved back from a considerable height to a sandy-bottomed alcove not more than a foot and a half in clearance. And at the farther end, he saw a gray mother wolf, no doubt she whom he had hit with a bullet the night before. Yes, now as she turned and snarled at him he saw her limp. The other three were big cubs, and the biggest of the three was a great white one so huge that it would have made the dead White Hawk a puny thing beside it, and so white that White Hawk would have seemed yellow in comparison!

He settled the mother with his first shot, and then a very strange thing happened. For you must know that wolves, on the whole, do not rush on danger. But there are

194

exceptions, and the white giant was a notable one. For, with the crack of the gun, he bolted straight at the face of the danger. Lost Wolf had time to put a bullet through the monster. It bored through his neck and then traveled down his back, but he came in with great fangs prepared and Lost Wolf was lucky indeed to down him with a blow of the revolver which landed in a vital section of the big fellow's skull. But as their brother lay quivering and still in a stupor, twitching himself forward at the enemy, the two remaining wolves crouched merely lower than before. Lost Wolf, in contempt, shot them neatly through the head. Then he turned his attention to the fallen wolf.

Its heart beat; it was not dead. He took out his hunting knife, ready to cut its throat. Then he hesitated. For it was a magnificent pelt, for this season of the year. And, when he ran his hand through that pelt, he felt beneath the hair a hard-muscled, big-shouldered body. This was what White Hawk had been, except that this was far better than White Hawk. This was a king of his kind—a very emperor, whereas White Hawk had been a fighting prince, one might say! White Hawk, indeed, was half dog, and the hand of man had debased the breed from its pristine strength.

However, it is impossible to train a wild wolf. So say the books; but Lost Wolf had seen it done. And he was very willing to try it himself.

He regarded the monster with a keen glance. Then he tied his feet securely and dragged him outside of the cave. After that, he brought out the other three carcasses, and skinned them, while the big white fellow looked on snarling and trembling as though the knife and the strong hand were removing the pelt from his own living body.

But when the three pelts had been taken, Lost Wolf disposed of the carcasses by whirling them around him and casting them among the rocks of the hillside. Then he came back to pay closer attention to his captive. It cost him just half an hour of careful study and thought to make up his mind. A touch of his knife would convert this creature into a very fine bit of saddle blanket. On the other hand, a great investment of care might transform him into a servant like White Hawk. If he were even a tithe as useful as White Hawk had been, he would be worth any investment of effort. And then again, being big and white, might he not pass as a sort of reincarnation of the dead dog with which the Cheyennes had last seen him?

That suggestion decided Lost Wolf. It tickled his fancy immensely, and straightway he began to dress the wounds of the big animal. It was no easy task. A wolf can take off a man's hand at the wrist, you know, with about as much trouble as you clip a twig off a tree with a sharp knife. And the head of this white giant was free. Purposely, Lost Wolf left it free, because he knew that neither men nor beasts can learn very much when all their bodies are imprisoned in ropes.

It took him three hours of steady labor to wash and care for the raking wounds of the big fighter. When that time ended he was well exhausted, and so was the wolf. But they knew each other fairly well. And Lost Wolf had lost all impatience. For he found that he could sit and look at his captive for hours at a time, satisfied and smiling.

And there he sat, every day, all day, week after week, and month after month.

I am sorry that I have referred to Lost Wolf, somewhere, as an impatient fellow. I meant, that he was impatient compared with an Indian, or a hunting wild beast; but compared with his white cousins he was as patient as the deeply rooted hills! I say that he remained there on that rocky little hill, like an island in the midst of the immense plains, until the wolf cub—not much more than a yearling in the first place—grew very close to maturity, though a wolf does not reach a hardened maturity until it is two and a half years old. But in the meantime, this second White Hawk gained formidable dimensions and a weight of thirty pounds over the hundred. In fact, even a white man might have been tempted to spend dreary months waiting for the new White Hawk to reach more amiable manners and a better disposition all around.

How much danger Lost Wolf accepted in this task of training and taming, I dare not think upon. And what frightful beatings the second White Hawk absorbed, it would be impossible to narrate. What is true, however, is that tenderness would not convince this new White Hawk that he had met his master. But cruelty would, and the instant that Lost Wolf made that discovery, he spent cruelty upon the giant lavishly—with both hands, so to speak. He so awed the second White Hawk that the brute stopped cringing. Cringing is a form of begging. But White Hawk the Second came to understand that no sort of supplication was of the slightest use. If there was a whipping in the offing, that whipping he would get—every stroke of it— and it was vain to attempt to dissuade the master. He stopped cringing, then. And he would stand erect, with his lips snarling back from his terrible long fangs, his mane standing up and his jaw muscles, like points of hard rock, trembling with fury. Many a time, when the eyes of the wolf were green, his master stood by and flogged him until the green light died through the exhaustion which torture brings at last.

These floggings filled the first month, only. After that, it was a matter of time and much patience. Lost Wolf kept at his task until White Hawk the Second would run always ahead of his master, sliding along with an effortless trot, or striving in vain to rival the headlong gallop of Red Wind. But, on these occasions, there was no danger that White Hawk, lost beneath the horizon, would take this opportunity to get his liberty. No, the training which Lost Wolf had given him was much too thorough for that. He dared not stay away from the master long; but he had a deep longing, while he was close at the side of the master, to take the unguarded moment and sink his teeth in the soft gullet of the man.

However, it was extremely difficult to discover just when the master was really entirely off his guard. Three times, in the black of a moonless night, White Hawk had crept as stealthily as a flying owl towards the sleeping master. And three times, as he lowered his head above the sleeper, he had received across the tender snout the club-like weight of the leaded end of Lost Wolf's quirt. And that blow was always followed by a beating so frightful that for some days White Hawk could not tell whether it was better to live or to die!

He could not be sure, then, when the master was on the look-out even though all the signs were of utter sleep, say!

At any rate, Lost Wolf, at the end of the summer, was jogging across the plains oddly accompanied.

He jogged on foot, because five years with the trapper and trader had taught him to love a round lot of exercise— and that jog trot of the Lost Wolf would have seemed like very hard running to most white men. In front of him loped White Hawk. Behind him followed Red Wind, at a trot, and led by a lariat attached to the pommel of Red Wind's saddle followed the roan. Not until the morning was half worn away and the starting point many a mile behind them, would Lost Wolf swing into the saddle!

35

A week later, skimming across the plains, he came at noon in sight of a long line of dust against the horizon, and when he came closer, he knew that it was composed of mounted men. Straightway, Lost Wolf disappeared into the face of the prairie by dismounting and lying flat and making the horses follow his example. The white wolf ran fifty strides ahead and lay down in turn to keep a nearer lookout.

In the meantime, the riders approached at right angles, drawing nearer and nearer until he saw, by the speed with which they traveled and the regularity of the pace they held, as well as the even order of the men, that these were white soldiers. He had had mere glimpses of them, before, none closer than this. But now as they drew nearer to him, he remembered that it was by a Pawnee that the owner of the roan horse had been slain; and the chiefs who ruled the white men from the East would be interested in the story which he might be able to tell them. Yonder were the trained warriors of the white men. And a great yearning possessed Lost Wolf to speak to them face to face.

However, that was a dangerous business. One could never tell what the white men would do. At least, the Cheyennes had averred to him that this was the case. For sometimes they would act like cowardly village dogs. And sometimes they would fight like madmen. Sometimes they were the fairest of the fair in all of their dealings, and again, they were treacherous, cunning and wary as so many foxes. Lost Wolf hesitated as to what he should do. It was dangerous to come too close, because these men might have very long-range rifles, and in that case, they were apt to use him as a target for practice, so soon as they made out that he was only an Indian.

However, he could not resist the temptation which was stirring in him more every moment. He stood up and raised his trio of animals. On the reins of Red Wind, he tied the well cured scalps which he had collected on that happy trip from the mountain camp to Zander City.

In the meantime, a section of four troopers had swung out from the line of march and whirled towards him. He held up his hand and gave the signal to halt; but they rushed on at him, as though vying one with the other in getting to him. He could not take such a chance as this. He

199

whipped Red Wind around with a mere jerk of his knees and instantly he was flying across the plains and leaving the well-mounted troopers a yard behind him for every two he covered. When he saw them despair of the chase—and half a mile of running was enough to convince them that they were hopelessly outclassed—he turned his horse again. They had stopped, and now he advanced towards them slowly, waving a bit of white rag. Such was said to be the flag of truce among white men. They, in turn, produced a handkerchief and signaled back. And he came straight on until he was within twenty or thirty paces from them. Then he turned Red Wind sidewise and rested his hands on his hips, so that they would be near the two revolver holsters. In this position, he was turned sidewise to them and gave them a smaller target. They seemed to realize it, and one of them, who seemed superior to the others, waved back the three who rode with him and advanced still closer, holding up a hand in sign of amity.

With a sharply barked command in Cheyenne, Lost Wolf stopped him. To his astonishment, the white man replied instantly and very fluently in the same tongue. He declared that he was a friend to the Cheyennes and that his enemies were the enemies of the Cheyennes. In a word, he was hunting for the Pawnee band led by none other than Standing Elk.

What a thrust of joy went through the heart of Lost Wolf when he heard that! For he registered Standing Elk in his heart as his oldest and his greatest enemy, the man who, in return for the saving of his life, had sold him into five years of slavery!

"I am Lieutenant Macreary," said the white man.

"I am Lost Wolf," said the other.

The lieutenant tossed up his head and grinned broadly. He seemed a scant twenty or twenty-one to Lost Wolf.

"You're the lad who made the trouble in Zander City?" he asked.

"Have they sent you to hunt for me?" asked Lost Wolf.

"No," answered Macreary. "If you go back to Zander City, you'll find them ready to give you a vote of thanks for what you did there! And I'll give you a vote of thanks if you can teach my greenhorns how to shoot straight!"

"Give them a great deal of powder and lead, and a great deal of time, and teach them to pray to Tirawa!"

The lieutenant laughed.

"Only," said he, with a suddenly darkened face, "how do you come by that horse—and that saddle?"

"It was a white man's horse," said Lost Wolf.

"And he lost it?"

"He was killed."

"Lost Wolf," said the lieutenant gloomily, "this is bad news to me, and it may be bad news to you."

"I did not do it."

"Can you prove that?"

"I took it from a Pawnee. There is a white man's scalp in the right hand saddlebag. There is his blood on the saddle."

The lieutenant was only a moment in making sure of the truth of these assertions. Then he asked bluntly: "Lost Wolf, I believe you. And I can make the major believe you. But—tell me why you told me so much? Do you know that it is my duty to take the horse and the saddle and the guns in the saddle bags?"

He had his hand on his own revolver as he spoke, but Lost Wolf smiled.

"I shall tell you why," said he. "It is several moons since I got that horse. And I have not ridden him, because I cannot be happy in a saddle where a white man was murdered."

An exclamation came from the lieutenant.

"I have hunted for men to give them to. Tirawa has brought me to you."

They rode in to the column of troopers, White Hawk hanging in the rear, and there Lost Wolf was brought to a pleasant-faced man, very red, very sweaty, and damning the sun with what seemed to Lost Wolf a dangerous fluency. He was introduced as Major John Beals and then the lieutenant made a little speech to him—in English of which Lost Wolf, of course, understood every word! But it was easy to keep a straight face while he listened to the lieutenant.

"Major, I've hooked a prize for us! This is a Cheyenne, and I know that he's a red-hot one not only by those three scalps that he wears on the reins of that horse, but by the horse itself. No common Indian ever rode a stallion like that. Besides, I've heard of him and you have too. This is Lost Wolf, who shot up a dozen thugs in Zander City a few weeks ago. He hates the Pawnees so much that he wants to help us. One more thing—he can't ride in the saddle of that fine roan because a white man owned that roan and was murdered in the saddle! I call this a queer Indian, major!"

The major agreed, and then he thrust out a fat hand to Lost Wolf and tasted the grip of that young Hercules with a grunt.

"Tell Lost Wolf," said the major, "that I'm damned glad to have him with us, that he shall have the best of everything, and that if he can bring us to the camp of Standing Elk, I'll make him rich!"

The lieutenant translated with his broad, Irish grin, and so Lost Wolf was taken into the camp.

I don't mean that it came about as easily as all this. There had to be a process of initiation, of course. In the first place, Lost Wolf was only a boy, and in spite of his muscles, he did not look any too large to a number of the troopers in that command. Besides, the Indian seat in the saddle does not set off the figure of man or squaw. The short stirrups bring the knees to the withers of the horse and put the rider back on the small of his spine. There he sits hunched up, looking straight ahead of him—but not missing a stir of wind in the sky or of grass on the earth! And so it was that Lost Wolf rode hunched with the train.

They made their camp at a rivulet long before dark. And Lost Wolf smiled to himself. No wonder these punitive expeditions of the whites never reached their goals. For an Indian troop would have marched on and on and into the night, reckless of their horses, and taking a chance to find water, or else turning a pony loose at the end of the march, and following to see if it would not bring them to water.

And, while he journeyed with them, Lost Wolf wondered at the big, strong-stepping horses of the cavalry. They were well made, but heavy, heavy, heavy for such work as this. They could not forage for themselves as an Indian pony could. They would starve where ponies grew fat. And they lacked the verve and the nerve which the very wildness gave to the ponies.

He saw these things, and he saw, also, that the big soldiers were passing jokes freely back and forth and roaring with laughter and insults. He understood every word. He even understood that the scalps which dangled from his bridle reins were actually abhorrent to even such rough fellows as these!

"I'm going to have a fall out of him!" bellowed a huge corporal, "before it's dark—major or no major! I want to choke the murdering redskin!"

Therefore Lost Wolf, when the camp was made, was only a trifle more wary than a tiger in a cage with lions. And, after dusk had gathered, sure enough a hand fell on his naked shoulder.

He turned. There was the big man making challenge in dumb show and with savage faces; while a semicircle of grinning and expectant troopers stood behind him, waiting for the fight.

Lost Wolf merely whirled on his heel and slapped the big man lightly across the mouth. There was a snort, a growl, a hurried lunge forward. For what white man expects an Indian to understand the merest rudiments of fist-fighting?

Lost Wolf smote him at the base of the jaw and then stepped aside to let him fall.

36

After that feat, there was no more question of the ability of Lost Wolf to take care of himself as a man—even a white man; and when it was learned that he could speak English like any white, the respect for him increased a hundredfold. There were a hundred and twenty odd troopers in that little command, with Major John Beals at the head of them, with two captains, and three or four lieutenants; for in Indian warfare, where there was such an endless amount of detail work to be done, there was a great necessity of many officers. And as they journeyed across the plains, Lost Wolf, who was guiding them now, took note of those troopers with great care.

Two things astonished him. The first was the apparent self-respect of every man, as though he was a chief of note. The second was the willingness of these proud men to obey the orders of their officers and do work which even a squaw would have grumbled at. Lost Wolf tried to put these two things together and understand them—but he could not. And he knew that if an officer spoke to him as they did commonly even to corporals and sergeants, his knife or gun would be out on the instant. So he gave up trying to understand these men; he merely studied them as a race apart, always wondering that he himself could be of their very blood!

In the meantime, he was driving the column straight towards the old camping grounds of the Pawnees, but where they might actually be he could not guess. And, when he picked up a broad trail of travois five days later, he turned up the trail until they came to a fire, and near the signs of the fire a broken arrow was found.

Lost Wolf studied it with care, and there was a reward for his study. No two Indians make arrows in the same fashion. And by the chipping and the binding of this arrowhead, he felt sure that he had picked up a spent shaft of none other than that dashing young brave, Running Deer. If that were so, unless Running Deer had changed his allegiance to another band, this was the path made by the band which Red Eagle led.

They followed up that trail for two days at a round gait, and as they journeyed, he kept his council to himself. For it seemed to him that the white men were foolish in speaking their mind so much.

The major himself had expostulated with Lost Wolf on his silence and Lost Wolf answered, in all honesty: "A man who always talks, is always likely to make mistakes."

"Come, come!" said the major. "You Cheyennes are as talkative as women when you're camped for the winter, they say!"

"In the winter," said Lost Wolf, "a man tells a story. Do you believe the stories that you read in books?"

The major was stumped.

In the evening of the second day, Lost Wolf, scouting ahead, saw something like a buffalo wolf jump up ahead of him. White Hawk waited for one approving call and started in pursuit. He walked up on the other as though it were standing still; and by the time Lost Wolf came up, White Hawk was licking his chops and lying grinning with content near his kill. The mystery was explained easily enough. It was no wolf at all that White Hawk had killed but an Indian dog which had roved too far afield in search of game and had found it to his cost. His swollen belly was ample reason for the slowness of his running.

So Lost Wolf ran Red Wind back to the column which was halting to camp for the night, and told Major Beals that he was riding ahead to scout and might not be back until midnight. The major pulled down a fringe of his short mustache so that he could bite at it.

"Lost Wolf," said he at last, "I'm trusting that you don't find trouble and bring it back on us. And I'm trusting the lives of a hundred men to you, along with mine! You understand!"

The eyes of Lost Wolf glinted. There was indeed such a thing as trust among the whites that the Indians did not know of. Danny Croydon had taught him something of that, in the first place. And as he rode off into the night, there was a lump in his throat as he thought of Danny, and how with Danny's own tricks and Danny's own teachings, he had been able to beat the sturdy trapper down. Now he found trust again in the major, and it was a sweet-bitter taste in the mouth of Lost Wolf. For among the Cheyennes, where would he find it?

He sent Red Wind softly ahead, for he did not wish to use up too much of the strength of the stallion. If he had to make a retreat, it was apt to be a hurried one! There was no cause for a long trail, however. In four miles of riding, when the light had faded from the sky and the stars were out, he saw the fires of the village.

He left Red Wind and White Hawk a quarter of a mile away and sneaked up to the nearest lodge. When he peered under the loose edge of a buffalo hide, he found that he was looking into the tepee of Three-Tree-Standing-by-the-Water, a respectable warrior who had taken three wives to his bosom and had a flock of children. It was one of the largest families in the village. They had been of ages from infants to adolescence when he was with the band before. Now there were two young braves old enough to have lodges of their own. And the smallest of the lot was a little girl helping two of the squaws at cookery. He lay on his belly with his face on his folded hands and listened to the chatter.

It was like everything—and like nothing. It told nothing and yet it told everything. He learned in fifteen minutes that the great medicine man, Black Antelope, was still living. He learned that Red Eagle still lived and led the band. He learned a score of other things. But what pleased him most was not the information, it was just the chattering of the familiar dialect, for five years almost unheard. It was the smell of the buffalo hides, soaked with wood smoke. It was the odor of the boiled buffalo meat from the corner of the tent. Even now, the little girl ran to it and dipped in her hand and took out a handful. The mouth of Lost Wolf watered!

So he crept from tepee to tepee, forgetful of time, until he noticed that the lodge fires were waning, as though for the night. And here he found the thing he wanted—his old companion in war, Running Deer. But what a change was in Running Deer! He had been a boy when Lost Wolf left the camp. Now, he was a tall, magnificently made warrior of two and twenty. And a lodge all his own!

Ah, but the treasures of that lodge were not to be scanned from a distance. They must be looked at and examined openly.

"Close the flap!" he heard Running Deer say to one of the women, and a sprightly girl leaped up—and another sprang to rival her—and there was a musical chattering of voices as they reached for the flap.

At that instant, springing around the side of the lodge, Lost Wolf was before them. They gave him not a look but shrank back into the lodge. For those were Cheyenne manners in the old days. No Pawnee or Arapahoe freedom of ways and speech when a woman was near men, but even if he who approached was a known friend, so long as he was not of the family, a whole group of women and girls would rise at his approach and retreat into the tepee!

There was a whispered scurry of voices as they shrank into the lodge and then the tall form of Running Deer stepped into the space of the open flap.

Lost Wolf raised his hand: "How!" said he.

Running Deer made a step nearer. "What are you, brother?" said he.

"The fire will help you," said Lost Wolf.

Running Deer stood back and followed him into the lodge. They confronted each other on opposite sides of the fire.

"I have not seen you, but yet I have!" said Running Deer.

Lost Wolf stepped to the still-open flap and whistled between his fingers. That blast, if all went well, should reach the keen ear of White Hawk and bring him on the trail.

Ay, when he turned back to the fire and faced Running Deer for a moment, a heavy breathing sneaked to the opening of the tepee, and there stood the mighty head and shoulders of the new White Hawk. It brought a gasp from Running Deer. His dignity melted from his face and from his rigid body. He threw up both hands with a faint cry.

"White Badger! And the White Hawk!" cried Running Deer.

"The Pawnees gave me a new name."

He could not pronounce it. For there is no greater height of ill manners in an Indian than for him to utter his own name, except after a new coup when he chooses to rechristen himself.

"Lost Wolf!" exclaimed Running Deer, and as Lost Wolf smiled, Running Deer caught him in his arms.

Oh, for some believer in the stoicism of Indians to have looked in on that scene and beheld Running Deer weeping and laughing and crooning like a mother over a child at the return of this long vanished companion in arms. And around them the two young squaws hovered, laughing, wringing their hands in sympathetic joy, and embracing one another until a child set up a tremendous squalling in the corner of the tepee. One of the girl brides leaped for it and covered its nose and mouth, the good old way of producing silence in one's descendants!

But that noise was enough to furnish the necessary interruption.

The youths stood apart.

"You, Lost Wolf—grown so mighty—with a man-look in your face and more wisdom than ever—and White Hawk made never to die. Is he not eleven years old, now? How the tribe will shout for you when they know that you have brought yourself and your medicine back to us. Oh, brother, there is such happiness in my heart!"

"Show me what is yours. I see the feather in your hair. You have become a chief under Red Eagle. Not under him long! These robes are all yours—and the knives—and the beads—and the quill work—and the guns—ah, Running Deer, you have become a great warrior! And these wives— ah, and a child! A daughter, Running Deer?"

"Waugh!" said Running Deer in disgust. "Look!"

In a stride he was at a folded robe on the ground and from it he drew forth a naked boy and cradled it in his arms over the firelight. The mother came softly to his side and in anxiety held her arms under his, as though he might let that treasure fall. And then mother and father looked at Lost Wolf with a laughing joy in their eyes.

37

It was as happy a lodge as Lost Wolf had ever seen. They were comely girls which Running Deer had taken as his squaws. He took the hand of one and the hand of the other.

"For this one I paid six strong ponies. And for this, I paid eleven ponies, which her father came and selected from my herd."

"You are rich, Running Deer!"

"Yes, I am rich—and also—"

He pointed to a lodge pole and there were three scalps. Rich and a great, proved warrior was Running Deer in the twenty-second year of his life.

"But you, Lost Wolf! Where have you been? What have you done? You have been to a place where men grow older but wolves do not! For White Hawk looks younger than when I saw him last—but bigger and stronger, I think! And what has made you come sneaking into the city? Why have you not come shouting? Why has not Red Eagle heard that you have brought back your medicine among us? He would be a glad man, for the Pawnees have beaten our band three times."

"It is Standing Elk, is it not?"

"It is Standing Elk. He has become like a hundred buffalo bulls. Three times he has come—so!"

He pointed to his thigh, his breast, and his cheek. There were three scars, and the one on the cheek was new.

"Still," said Running Deer sadly, "you are the White Badger of old. You will not talk! You will only make us wonder!"

"Come into the darkness with me. I cannot talk before women!"

They stepped out into the cool of the night; the hand of each was on the broad shoulder of the other.

They said with one voice: "Oh, brother, it is happiness to have you beside me!"

Then: "Hear me, Running Deer. There are six scores of white braves a little ride into the night."

"Ah! There will be scalps for you and for me, Lost Wolf!"

"No, they are my friends. But they ride on the trail of Standing Elk. Can you find that trail for us?"

"Let me carry the tidings to Red Eagle. It will make his heart swell. All of us will ride with the white men."

"No, but you only, if you know the way."

"I know the way, Lost Wolf. But it is not an easy way to travel."

"Are there many warriors with Standing Elk?"

"There are twenty scores of warriors. The best of the braves of the Pawnees leave their chiefs and come to him. He will soon be a famous man. He is famous already. What other Pawnee has made the Cheyennes turn their backs?"

"You do not love him?" smiled Lost Wolf.

"I would have his heart!"

"You or I shall have it. Have you a fast horse?"

"It leaves the wind behind."

"Bring it, then."

"You do not go on foot?"

"Red Wind carries me."

"I have not forgotten! They cannot escape from you if you wish to take them. They cannot follow you if you wish to fly. What guns will you carry?"

"I have a rifle that speaks twice at one loading. I have two revolvers."

"You, too, are rich. But there is not a bead or a quill on your clothes! Will you go to the lodge of Rising Bull?"

"I shall not go. Tell me only that he is contented."

"He has lost many horses. But he still has a few. Little Grouse works very hard for him. They live!"

"But they are not happy?"

"They had a great treasure; it has been gone for five years. It would have filled their lodge with fine painted robes! Will you not go to your father and your mother?"

"Running Deer, I have come out to this village to find you only. I have come to get you as eyes for the soldiers. Then when we find the Pawnees, there will be a great killing. And this is what I know—that I shall find Standing Elk in the fight and that I shall take him. Then I shall bring him back to Red Eagle. I shall give him to the women. I shall watch him die slowly. I shall taste his death for many hours, like a sweet honey. After that, I shall give many things to Little Grouse and Rising Bull. And after that, I shall go back to my people."

The clutching hands of Running Deer were like points of iron in the flesh of Lost Wolf.

"Do you leave us?"

"Ah, brother, my people are men with white skins. I have come into this country to be an Indian for the last time! I have come to take you with me to fight our last fight side by side. Is it well?"

But Running Deer could not make an answer. He turned with bowed head into his lodge and came out again and closed the flap while he showed his friend revolver and rifle. Then he went out to his horses, of which the finest were tethered with lariats near to his lodge. He selected what looked to Lost Wolf like a shaggy, most commonplace beast, but he did not have to ask to know that a rare spirit and a rare turn of speed must be in this chosen pony.

So they left the village and went out onto the plains, Lost Wolf running beside his friend until they were well cleared from the village. Then he whistled, and out of the darkness before them the form of a galloping horse loomed suddenly and came to a pause near Lost Wolf.

"Is it Red Wind?" asked the young Cheyenne, filled with excitement.

"Kneel!" said Lost Wolf, and the horse kneeled.

"It is he!" cried Running Deer. "There will be a great happiness in our nation when they know that you have returned. There will be a great sadness when they know that you have come back only to leave again. Is it for some white-faced squaw? Come back to us, Lost Wolf. I shall find you six squaws! They will be happy to come to the tepee of such a famous warrior!"

"A squaw," said Lost Wolf scornfully, "is a good thing for

a man that wants many robes made in his lodge and many children crying and scolding. I, for one, do not wish for such things. No white squaw could ever take me half a day's ride out of my way!"

"Then why do you leave us? I shall be sad without you!"

"And I shall be sad without Running Deer. I have thought of you every day, for five long years. But I have heard it said that what a man is born, he is bound to be. I was born white and I must live as the white men do."

"I wish," said Running Deer savagely, "that all the white men on the plains were killed and their scalps burned, and all memory of them taken away from us!"

"But if you killed them on the plains, there would still be many more to come. You have heard, Running Deer, of the big cities of the white men along the great river?"

"I have heard many lies about them! I have heard that all the Cheyennes and the Pawnees and the Dakotans, even, could be gathered together into one village, and still it would be smaller than one of the white villages along the great river."

"Those lies are true lies. But if the great cities along the river were all wiped away and all the people in them dead—do you know what it would be?"

"Tell me, brother, for I shall believe you!"

"Believe me, then! If the great cities along the big river were blotted out, it would mean no more to the white men than the loss of two or three scouts to the Cheyennes!"

They rode along for a time in silence, and once or twice Lost Wolf heard the deep sighs of his companion as he struggled to believe this prodigious thing which he had heard—and as he struggled with an untrained mind to gather such conceptions of figures and muster them as matters of fact.

At last he merely said: "I cannot talk. I cannot think. I try to understand you. It only makes me sleepy. Let us talk no more tonight, Lost Wolf!"

They talked no more, then, but followed the ghostly

form of White Hawk the Second floating vaguely before them through the starlight as he ran straight as an arrow on the back trail towards the encampment of the soldiers.

They reached the camp; the challenge of the sentry was answered by Lost Wolf; and the sentryman's companion flashed a lantern in their faces.

"We know you, Lost Wolf, but who's your friend?"

"Running Deer will take you to find Standing Elk and all his men. Bring him to the major, now!"

"The major will sweat the freckles off my nose if I wake him up now."

"The major will be glad to listen to Running Deer."

So the sentry took that word and marched Lost Wolf to the tent of the major—marched Lost Wolf and his friend with the glimmering saber naked behind them and a revolver in the other hand.

"But are we safe?" whispered Running Deer.

"We are safe!" said Lost Wolf. "The white man does not strike from behind. And his word is a strong law!"

"Ah," sighed Running Deer, "they have stolen you away from us. For that I shall never forgive them!"

The first words of the wakened major were profane enough, but when he knew who waited for him, he fairly dragged the two into his tent and turned up the light of his lantern. There, for an hour, he sat whispering to Lost Wolf, who translated questions and answers softly, back and forth. And not a soldier's sleep was broken, while White Hawk kept guard at the flap of the tent; and the plan for the battle formed swiftly in the major's mind. The two slept in the major's own tent that night.

38

Of the plan of Major Beals for the battle, I shall content myself with giving the opinion of that hardy young warrior, Running Deer.

"If the battle is won by the white men, then their chief will be called very great. But if it is lost, he will be called a great fool."

For the plan of the major was simply to divide his force and so to attack the Pawnees upon two sides the moment that they should be found. The first thing, however, was to find them; but Running Deer took care of that. His hatred for Standing Elk made him doubly keen upon the trail. For eleven days they wandered across the plains, with Running Deer and Lost Wolf ever far ahead scouting. And on the eleventh day, when the soldiery began to question the skill of these young guides of theirs, the two scouts saw a pair of warriors on the dim distance of the plains. They started out in pursuit at once.

No doubt those other men were brave enough, but the Indian has no desire to rush into a hot encounter when he sees an equal force attacking him. These two trusted to the speed of their ponies until they found Red Wind and his rider fast overtaking them. Then they whirled about to charge before Running Deer could come up. It was the old story. They came shrieking on to frighten Lost Wolf—he who had a double-rifle and could strike a tree stump easily at three hundred yards in quick fire! One of them was waving a blanket above his head to frighten the stranger, and Running Deer was yelling wildly in the rear in his grief at being left out of the shock of battle, while White Hawk danced on the side eager for the strife. But it was over very quickly. For my part, I would as soon jump over a cliff as come running within three hundred yards of a rifle in the hands of Lost Wolf. And these two men had reason to follow my judgment. For when the rifle of Lost Wolf came into his hands, his shots followed in quick succession, and then there were simply two riderless horses rushing towards him.

He hurried on towards the men on the ground to count coup. Neither was dead, but White Hawk reached one and finished him with a single slash. Luckily, Lost Wolf got to the other before the wolf.

It was what he wanted—a living, breathing, talking Pawnee—and no hero who would die rather than speak. Lost Wolf tied up his wound and then showed a knife under his eyes. The poor brave found his tongue readily enough. He could tell where the Pawnee camp of Standing Elk was to be found half a day's journey away. He could lead them to the place, for the price of his life!

In the meantime, with true Indian thrift, Running Deer had ransacked the clothes of the other Pawnee and taken his scalp. After that they captured one of the runaway horses and mounted the Pawnee on its back with his horse tethered to the pommel of Red Wind's saddle.

He was only a youth. He had a young squaw and a young son. And Lost Wolf could almost understand why a man should be a coward under those circumstances. As for the other who had been counted coup by Lost Wolf and scalped by Running Deer—that was Big Cloud, a warrior of eminence in the Pawnee tribe.

As for Major Beals, he was so delighted when he saw the captive that he ordered a fifteen-pound present of powder and lead to each of the captors. Then he went into conference with the prisoner, with Lieutenant Macreary of the omniscient tongue to act as interpreter. The conference was short. Then the troopers started on in haste, and the wounded brave was carried in a horse-litter between two riders.

Lost Wolf went back to the major.

"He is your man," said Lost Wolf, "but when the battle is over, he is mine. Is that true?"

"What would you do with him?" asked the major, frowning.

"Running Deer has a scalp," said Lost Wolf. "But I have none. I have counted two coups, but I have no scalp."

The major brushed a hand across his face as though he would wipe out a most unpleasant impression.

"I have promised him—" he began.

"You have not made a promise of his life," said Lost Wolf, "because that is mine. I have loaned him to you. Is not that true?"

The major swallowed hard.

"Have it your own way, Lost Wolf," said he. "I'll—I'll be honest with you—after the battle!"

There was such a strange look in his eyes, and there was such a strange intonation in his voice, that Lost Wolf was stirred with strange fears and forebodings. And yet he vowed to himself that he must not take such thoughts into his mind. For he knew that the major was an honest man— a very honest man! He had seen his dealings among the troops every day. He could have laid down his life in a wager on the honesty of the major.

And with a sudden, rare outbreak of emotion, he laid his hand on the arm of Beals: "Yes," said Lost Wolf, "for I know that you are honest. I have trust in you. There is more to trust in you than in any Indian. Do you know what that is doing to me? It is drawing me away from my father and my mother—it is taking me from the Cheyennes—it is taking me back to life like a white man among white men."

"Lost Wolf," said the major, more troubled of face than ever before, "are you not part white?"

"All!" said Lost Wolf.

"All?" cried the major. "But there is a reddish tint in your skin—"

Of course there was, for the one thing that Lost Wolf had carried away from Zander City, outside of sorrow and a sense of loss, was a liberal leather bottle filled with a reddish stain. The trace of it rubbed into the skin lasted long. Only wear would take it out. And now Lost Wolf said: "Hold out your hand!"

The major took off his glove and obeyed; and presently Lost Wolf stretched out beside the major's a hand with a palm as white as his. And he looked with a grin into the eyes of Beals.

"My God!" whispered the major. "And yet you are living with—"

Luckily the wind had blown up at that moment, and that whisper was not heard by Lost Wolf. As for the major, he reined back his horse, and called up Macreary.

"Mack," said he, "the damnedest thing has happened that I ever ran across. Lost Wolf is going to claim that Pawnee prisoner from us after the battle!"

"What for?"

"He wants that scalp—because Running Deer got one out of the same mixup. Lost Wolf has only *loaned* us the life of that man, to squeeze all the information we can out of him, make whatever promises we want to him, and then turn the poor beggar over to the captor!"

The lieutenant spat.

"That is sweet!" said he. "These damned—"

"Wait! That boy is trusting in me to do what he wants because he says that he knows that I am honest. And our honesty is the thing that is going to bring him back to live with white men."

"I'd rather have a panther for a neighbor! These red-skins—"

"Man, man, that's the frightful part of it! He's as white as you or I!"

218

"Are you daft?"

"I saw the palm of his hand—it's as white as mine—or was! In another minute, he'll have it stained like the rest of his body. He's white, Macreary!"

"And living in a nest of murderers?"

"Ay, that's it! Mack, we've got to get him away! What's to be done?"

"We make a flying start with him by keeping the Pawnee from him?"

"Of course, I can't turn over that poor youngster to be murdered by the boy!"

Macreary threw up his hands so that his horse shied violently, but the lieutenant was a flawless horseman and sat unshaken.

In the meantime, they were drilling through the plains at a round pace; and the day wore old when Running Deer rushed back to them out of the horizon.

He bore word that the Pawnee had spoken the truth. The village had been located on a broad highland between two dry ravines. Which complicated matters a great deal— for the major's plan. But he stuck to it grimly, as a man of few ideas is sure to prize any one that comes to him!

He split up his party out of sight of the village. Running Deer was assigned as guide to one of them, and Lost Wolf to the other. They rode furiously almost at right angles to their trail and then circled around, through the dusk, until they were on opposite sides of the village. There they halted and there they made dry camp and slept as much as they could—which was not a great deal. For it was known through the ranks that they, with their little force divided, were to attack four hundred Pawnees under the great war chief of the tribe. No wonder that there were stirrings of the heart!

As for Lost Wolf, who accompanied the contingent over which the major had command, he regretted one thing above all, that he could not stay behind with the red stallion. As for the outcome of the fight, he had seen

219

Pawnees in battle before this, and he knew how they worked!

Long before daylight the ranks were up. A few troopers were left behind to keep and guard the horses. The rest, including officers and Lost Wolf, numbered exactly sixty men. And they started forward on foot, with muttered groans. For all cavalry disdain the torment of marches afoot! They struggled over three steep-sided ravines. And then Lost Wolf, scouting a little ahead, smelled the wood smoke from the lodges—the wood smoke of the dying fires—and came scurrying back to the head of the column. It was high time for the news to arrive, for the gray was just beginning around the rim of the horizon. The troops in mortal silence were deployed in a double line, and they began to climb up the side of the last ravine. They did not reach the top unnoticed, however, for suddenly out of the darkness above them, a man's voice chattered at them rapidly in Pawnee, and then a bowstring twanged loudly and an arrow whirred.

The next instant the yell of the scout echoed wildly through the air and was answered by a hundred distant shouts from the village.

39

In the first gray of the dawn, those wild yells out of the distance made the heart of Lost Wolf leap in his throat; and he himself would gladly have raced towards the rear— but here was the major himself at his side! He could not turn. And yet he wondered greatly that any sixty men could be found in the world able to hear the terrible war-yell of Pawnees who outnumbered them almost ten to one.

If he had wondered at the sixty troopers before, what was his astonishment, when he heard them answer the terrible, beastlike cries of the Pawnees with a cheerful shout. And then, with Macreary leading them, three regular and thundering cheers, even though his eyes were fixed upon them, magnified them in the sight of Lost Wolf. And he guessed at another strength in white men—a quality that sprang out of their trust in one another. They were marching into this battle exultantly, not in terror!

But when the two lines crawled over the upper lip of the ravine, they saw enough to daunt them even had each man been a hero.

An Indian can dress himself with a single gesture. His horse waits outside his lodge. His arms are ever at hand. And a village can be ready for battle thirty seconds after the first alarm. Ready for fighting but not in order! That requires time! But now, like wasps whirring up out of their nest in the ground the Pawnees flooded out from the lodges into the open spaces, shouting and shrieking and brandishing their arms, and looking larger than human against the light of the distant horizon. There should have been a solid volley thrown into that whirl of horsemen, but instead of that, some soldier fired and then a random fire ran down the line. It brushed the Indians from before them like a wave of the hand, but it left only a single brave on the ground. There may have been other casualties; but an Indian will cling dying to his horse so that he may be carried away to safety among his friends. Otherwise, if his body is left and his scalp is taken, his soul lingers in the dust forever!

Thrown back on the village, the Indians whirled in pools there for a moment, and then, in greater numbers than ever, shot away in two separate bands, one to the right and one to the left. The soldiers hurried forward onto the level and that was the greatest mistake of all that stupid Major Beals committed on that day, for had he remained at the ravine, even a fool could have seen that the gulch would have afforded shelter for his rear. His excuse afterwards was that he hardly recognized the overwhelming force of the Pawnees and that he had hoped to throw them into confusion by directly charging upon the village! As though it would have been anything better than insanity to confuse that little body of troops among the lodges where the Indians could butcher them in detail and the squaws with their terrible knives and clubs could take a share in the struggle!

However, when the major saw the Pawnees lurching at him like two thunderclouds, one from either side, he halted his men and made them scatter in a loosely formed circle. There they had barely time to kneel in place when the double torrent burst upon them. Lost Wolf cast one glance into the sky, which he was sure he would never see again; then he paid attention to what was happening around him. He saw Lieutenant Macreary walking back and forth with a revolver dangling idly from his hands, while he called out to the men: "Steady, lads! These fellows look like devils coming and like babies going!"

And there was the huge voice of Major Beals: "Wait for my word! Wait for my damned word!"

Lost Wolf could not have spoken. His throat clave together; he was mute. But there was a cheerful shout from the cavalrymen. And their guns were marvelously steady in their hands. Lost Wolf stuck the butt of his own rifle into the hollow of his shoulder and then the double wave of Pawnees loomed above them and was followed by a shrieking and a shouting that filled the ears of the boy with roaring. He sank to the ground. He was ready to fight with most, but Indian style had been his schooling! And to lie there on the ground waiting for the massacre—

"Fire!" thundered Major Beals, and half the rifles crackled.

"Fire!" and the other half were spitting fire and lead.

But the Pawnee charge? It vanished as a cloud of steam

vanishes when cold water is flung at it. Back went the warriors yelling, and not unaccompanied. When Lost Wolf saw the Indian charge stagger before these few whites, his heart became suddenly as cold and as stern as steel. A riderless Pawnee pony whirled just in front of his place in the line and scrambled to start back. But it started back only with the clinging body of the boy on his back. He was ten yards, and scantly that, behind the rearmost verge of the main body, and in his hands were two revolvers making play! A yell of delight and savage laughter rose from the white troops and Lost Wolf, whirling the pony about like a flash, shot back towards the cavalrymen with his body flattened in Indian style along the side of the pony. And, stooped over as he was, a swinging blow of a revolver barrel counted coup on two warriors whom he had shot out of their saddles. What a shower of arrows and bullets whirred after him, and what yells of sublime rage from hundreds of Pawnees. They brought their fleeing horses up on their hind legs and sent them plunging back after Lost Wolf.

And as he sprang from the pony, that poor little brute, shot through and through with half a dozen bullets intended for its last rider, dropped dead. There was no sentimentality in Lost Wolf. He used the fallen pony as a rifle pit and from behind its body leveled his rifle. Straight before him the Pawnee charge was sweeping, looming higher and higher as the soldiers looked up from the shallow shelters which they had scraped for themselves in the ground. But the blast of their first half-volley shot away the forefront of the charge, and before the second round was poured in, the well-known waver went through their whole body which precedes a flight. For Indians in the midst of the fiercest charge are always poised and ready for a swoop away from the foe.

Then, out of the shuddering mass of naked bodies, that commanding form of Standing Elk which Lost Wolf knew so well, shot through to the front and waved his followers on. There was no doubt that he wanted to send this charge crashing home in white-man's style. And, if the front ranks of the Pawnees could ever summon enough courage to close, it would be over in a twinkling for all of the three score men in the little circle. But the heart of Standing Elk was not in his men. They began to sit back on their horses, and already the foremost ranks were swerving to either side.

Then, his heart beating fast, Lost Wolf clutched his rifle to his shoulder and fired straight at the big target. Then he shouted in dismay. At thirty paces he had missed a target he could not fail to strike at two hundred! With a thrill of his very soul he told himself that a charm hung over the life of the chief. He took a lower aim with the other barrel of his gun. Just in front of the knee of the rider he took his bend and fired.

The war pony of Standing Elk dropped in the very instant that his master was swerving him to the side, despairing of sending that charge home like a driven nail. The horse dropped, and Standing Elk was flung head over heels and finally lay unconscious ten short strides from the line of the soldiers.

It was the most dangerous accident that could have happened, for the Indians were sure to make a vigorous effort to redeem the body of their senseless chief. Already they were swirling towards the spot where he lay, coming in the maddest confusion as the front ranks strove to change their direction, and veer from flight to a new charge. Ay, and there was Standing Elk beginning to rouse himself, and staggering on his knees.

At that instant the half-naked body of Lost Wolf leaped from the line and bounded to the side of the chief. A blow from the clubbed butt of a revolver dropped the chief, and from behind Standing Elk's own pony as a fortress, Lost Wolf opened fire with both guns.

The soldiers, half maddened by this crazy act of courage, poured in shot as fast as they could load. But nothing could have stopped the vengeful thrust of the Pawnees, now. Not the loss of half of their numbers—nothing could have stopped them and nothing could have saved Lost Wolf at that moment except the very thing which happened. From the village itself, from the face farthest from the battle there arose a wild clamoring, and then a universal scream. And, in another moment, a hoarse blast of rifles fired in unison.

The second division of the major's men was coming into action, even thus belated. But never more welcome. Half of the men around the major himself were wounded or dead from the pitching fire of the Pawnees. But this second half of his attack ended the battle instantly. The Pawnees in the very act of thrusting home the charge which would have saved Standing Elk and would have swamped the soldiers, heard the rear attack on the village, and the whole force turned with frantic yells, each man to save what he could: wives, children, mother, father, horses. Only living things were worth saving at such a time as this!

So they went rushing into the village and they found sixty soldiers lying in the center of the circling lodges, each comfortably at rest, with leveled rifles—ay, and revolvers at their sides if any foolish group of Pawnees wished to drive home a charge!

Before the withering blasts of those rifles, the Pawnees turned to flee, or to scatter to the sides, and as they did so, Major Beals' frantically cheering men came swiftly in upon them, too panting, too exultant to shoot straight, but sending a dreadful panic through the Pawnee host—and in five minutes the only Pawnee warriors who remained in the camp were the dead and those who were too wounded to ride.

The major's plan had won! It was so completely successful that the oldest Indian fighter in that command was staggered. None had seen such a victory before. There was a colonelcy in it for the major. But he was not thinking of that. He was at work now with three times the energy he

had ever shown in the battle, though he had been headlong enough in that. He was using his efforts now, however, to bring swift relief to the wounded.

And the only soldier in the lot who thought of Standing
Elk was Lieutenant Macreary, who ran back to the spot and
found the chief tied of hand, with feet hobbled, and a
rawhide lariat around his neck—a bruised, dusty, dirty
figure, his whole side raked raw by the fall from the pony,
and now led along by Lost Wolf!

40

It meant tragedy for Lost Wolf, of course, but he could not
tell that, and when he met Running Deer with two scalps in
his belt and the red devil in his eyes, Lost Wolf merely
laughed and pointed to his captive!

And then, when all the swirl of victory was ended, and
the lodges ransacked for plunder and for captives, and
while the wounded lay thanking God for their first drink
of water and for the coolness of the shade, Lost Wolf was
brought by grave-faced Lieutenant Macreary before Major
Beals.

"I'm bringing in Lost Wolf," said Macreary gloomily. "He
wants his other captive and a pair of Pawnee horses to
mount them on."

The major lost at least three shades of color.

"Not two horses—but a hundred, Lost Wolf," said he.
"You shall have a hundred horses, my son, but what are
these two captives to you, compared with a hundred good
ponies! Yes, you shall have the first pick of the entire
camp!"

Lost Wolf stared as one who cannot comprehend a simple thing.

"And you shall have guns, Lost Wolf," said the major, sweating most profusely. "You shall have beads and quill work. Look—there is the loot—wade in it as deep as your armpits. Pick out what you will. For it is yours."

Lost Wolf drew himself rigid and folded his arms. At that sign of certain Indian obstinacy, the major altered still another shade.

Lost Wolf said: "I have not asked you for pay. I have had no gifts from the soldiers or their chiefs. I have guided them. First I returned to them the scalp of a dead companion. They can find his body and put the scalp on it, and his soul will be free! I gave back a good horse, too, and a saddle and other things of great value, and yet I had won these things in open fight from many Pawnees. I did all of these things because I wished to make the white men my brothers. After that, I joined you and lived like a brother with you. But you can tell if I lived from your food or did I not kill game for myself and for fifty others, also. I guided you to a Cheyenne camp. I, who stand here, am a Cheyenne. If I had not been your friend, I could have brought many Cheyennes and they are great warriors. You see Running Deer? There are hundreds like him, terrible and silent fighters in the night. They could have made a harvest of your scalps, but I, your friend, would not bring them back. I took only one man to guide you. I brought you to the Pawnees. I carried you softly to their camp. They were beaten. And in the fight I counted coup on two Pawnees, and others fell before my rifle—but two I killed and counted coup upon them. Ask your warriors if it is not true. I did not do this thing in secret or behind a bush but out where many men could be witness. Then the great chief, Standing Elk, rode on our lines. I shot him down! I stood up; there were many scores of his friends riding hard to bring him a new horse and to save him. I ran out from the line and I knocked him down. I fought over him,

227

and the Pawnees did not take him again. He is a great war chief. He is worth many scores of men. And he has had me in his hands. And I, also, have had his life under my knife when I was a boy. In those days I was called White Badger, but afterwards I gained a better name which Standing Elk gave to me when he found me sick and weak. And he carried me away to his camp where he wished to give me to the women—but a white man was there and saved me from that death and took me away. For his sake I have loved the white men, because they are just.

"Then I bought my freedom from this man in the coin which he wished for. I became free. I found you and joined you and served you. In the battle, I was not the worst fighter. But I do not ask for any reward except two ponies, where there are so many. I do not ask for victims and scalps. I ask only for this man I took with my hands. Also there is another man I took with my hands. They are my own work. I do not take anything from your pocket."

"I only ask you this, Lost Wolf, and that is: What will you do with them?"

"I shall take them to the Cheyennes and show them that Lost Wolf is not a child any longer but that he works like a man with a man's hands."

"And then?"

"Then I go to the cities of the white men to make them my brothers."

"Good," said the major, biting his mustache with frowning industry. "But what becomes of the two captives?"

"How can I tell? I make them my gift to the Cheyennes. They are mine. They are not yours. You cannot ask what I shall do with them, and when I give them to the Cheyennes, I cannot ask what they will do with them!"

The major turned his back with a groan.

"You, Macreary. You talk their damned lingo better than I do. For God's sake, talk to him."

But Macreary merely mopped his brow, as one very glad to escape from such a position as this.

"Do your best, old man," he said in a soft voice. "No man can do more."

"But he's logical, clear, exact—not a lie in anything that he said. Only—he's wrong! But how am I to tell him that he shouldn't have these two men? How can I explain to him that humans aren't property to be traded back and forth like knives?"

"You can't do it, man. Simply state the facts and then let him do what he wants to do!"

The major found a better way. He picked out from the great herds of the Pawnee village a hundred ponies. And he heaped a load of some kind upon the back of each: robes, guns, powder and lead, and all manner of Indian finery which was, to be sure, of little use to the whites. He marshaled this array of great Indian wealth. Then he had the two prisoners put beside it.

"I give you your choice, Lost Wolf. Take the prisoners, or else take the ponies."

Now Lost Wolf stood for a long time staring into the face of the poor major. But at length he threw his blanket over his head and turned and walked slowly away.

Running Deer followed him soon, but paused only to say: "White chief, you will wish that Tirawa had made you more honest. Lost Wolf is gone to make a great medicine. He shall take white scalps like blades of grass in the mouth of a buffalo!"

Macreary understood the words. The rest understood the fierce gesture. And a chill of silence passed over the camp.

From that riding there remained to Running Deer three scalps and two coups, and to Lost Wolf no fewer than five coups—but no scalps at all. He had only the three which hung from his bridle reins.

More in riches of reputation had fallen to that pair in this adventure than in whole lives of many a noble warrior. They rode side by side towards the Cheyenne camp and

Running Deer was silent, because the face of his companion was like a thunder cloud.

And, after their days of travel, they came to the village. They entered under the blanketing dusk. And before the third lodge, Lost Wolf saw his foster-father, Rising Bull. He dropped from the back of the stallion and greeted the older man with a raised hand.

And then a storm of excitement.

It was only a storm of leaves to Lost Wolf, however. He did not see the face of Little Grouse. He did not hear her exclaiming over her dear son who had returned to her. He did not see the neighbors thronging in about them.

For all was known. Rumor, like a prairie fire, had swept across the plains to the Cheyennes. Ay, and there was the voice of Red Eagle himself as he came running to greet the most famous warrior of his tribe—Lost Wolf!

But the face of Lost Wolf was a face of wood.

He retreated to a corner of the lodge. He wrapped himself in a blanket and bowed his head. After that all of the lodge was filled with silence except for the whisper of the feet of Little Grouse as she went about some cookery for the returned.

That food was placed before him, but Lost Wolf did not stir to taste it. So he remained until Little Grouse and Rising Bull went to sleep whispering to one another: "He speaks with Tirawa!"

The fire dwindled and grew small. The utter blackness of midnight fell over the village. But still Lost Wolf did not move. But all that silent time he was turning back to the ways of his childhood. He was growing Indian indeed, and all Cheyenne to the depths of his heart.